Homunculus

Homunculus

Jerry Stubblefield

Black Heron Press
Post Office Box 13396
Mill Creek, Washington 98082
www.blackheronpress.com

Jacket art and cover design by Bryan Sears.
Author photograph by William Lawrence.

The author gratefully acknowledges the editorial help generously provided by Alan Anderson.

Black Heron Press
Post Office Box 13396
Mill Creek, Washington 98082
www.blackheronpress.com

to Penny

Homunculus

CRS37725 BUNCOMBE COUNTY

State of North Carolina vs. Hector Owen

EXHIBIT 14

ASHEVILLE POLICE DEPARTMENT INCIDENT REPORT
DATE: February 27, 1998
OFFICER(S): Bullock; Ferebee
LOCATION: 10 ½ Boxelder Street, Asheville
NARRATIVE: Officers knocked on door of garage apt. at location. Occupant Hector Owen answered. Officer Ferebee advised Owen that his estranged wife had complained about his observing her through the bedroom window at her residence. Owen agreed to cease doing so.

CRS37725 BUNCOMBE COUNTY

State of North Carolina vs. Hector Owen

EXHIBIT 15

ASHEVILLE POLICE DEPARTMENT INCIDENT REPORT
DATE: March 28, 1998
OFFICER(S): Marlette; Salazar
LOCATION: Pack Square, West end of Vance Memorial
NARRATIVE: Officers observed middle-aged man sitting on curb at foot of Vance Memorial, Broadway near corner of College Avenue, apparently disoriented, speaking in conversational tones, no one else present. Officers approached, man identified himself as Hector Owen. Owen appeared slightly intoxicated. He gave address as 10 ½ Boxelder Street and said he was on foot. Officers determined he was able to walk safely, issued warning against loitering, and sent him home.

CRS37725 BUNCOMBE COUNTY

State of North Carolina vs. Hector Owen

EXHIBIT 8

DESCRIPTION: Handwritten letter on notebook paper. Discovered tucked into journal surrendered voluntarily to Detective James Horne by defendant upon his arrest. TRANSCRIPTION ATTACHED.

Dear Hec,

Now listen, don't worry about me. I know you're worrying and don't. I'm just hanging with some friends I made downtown and we drink coffee and talk. They are so phat!! (That's good!) It's nothing against you, you are so kind and everything and I've enjoyed my time with you so much. This is not goodbye. I just mean to tell you I have changed (ha ha) as you know and I find you so transparent now, but that's not a bad thing, that's good.

I might know something about that guy Faye's seeing. He's dangerous. I wouldn't say he intends to kill her, but I wouldn't rule it out, either. Just thought you ought to know, and I don't have any proof or anything, but believe me I think I'm right even though I'm not free to tell you how I found out. His name is Michael something foreign-sounding and he once applied for a job from Faye and she hired him to tail you instead of selling underwear!!! Now they are involved and I'm not saying you should do anything about it but I thought you should be alerted.

Now I bet I've made you worry about that. Please don't. I don't think you should even care about her. You are too good a person. Weren't we wonderful together? I think you were so generous to get me the apartment and by the way you can change things (like the curtains) if you want to. Thank you for all the nice things you bought me. Now that I don't have to steal my clothes, I feel real (ha ha).

So I'll see ya maybe. Ha ha.

[signed] Robin [superimposed on lipstick 'kiss"]

CRS37725 BUNCOMBE COUNTY

State of North Carolina vs. Hector Owen

EXHIBIT 7

DESCRIPTION: Handwritten journal, surrendered voluntarily to Detective James Horne by defendant upon his arrest, containing his personal writings dating from June 20, 1997 through February 27, 1998. TRANSCRIPTION ATTACHED.

June 20

I've ached for intimacy ever since Faye aborted our pregnancy back when we lived in New York City. Our marriage was left mangled, and has never recovered. The homunculus is, I'm sure, a result of that long aching. When a man can't achieve intimacy with someone else, such as a wife, he ends up achieving it with himself, which is no good. Also, let's face it, I maintained an unstable mind for many years in order to do my playwriting work — teetering on the edge of reality, frequently getting lost in worlds created in my brain. It may help to try and analyze all that, but I'm concerned first with chronicling what's happening now. Haven't written in this journal for years, but it may help me understand.

I've produced an offspring, a little man. He was inside me and came out through my navel three days ago. There were some scary moments when I thought he wouldn't make it; I'll recount those. But he's going to be fine, and he's going to be a good friend — more than a good friend, something very special. With his coming, I'm free of his hurting me, wanting to get out from inside me. In fact, the world suddenly seems full of good. I'm in a good mood for the first time in many, many years. The brightest mood I've felt in my entire life!

In retrospect, I can see that something like this had been brewing, but as usual, I couldn't or wouldn't focus beforehand on a growing inevitability. Faye has told me countless times, "You're completely cut off." True, I've holed up here in the holler for the last few years, in the pretty town in the pretty mountains, and haven't been at all sociable. But I had no idea I was brewing up some kind of Angst devil, or whatever he is. Certainly didn't know the devil would be such a cute, personable little thing.

Three days ago I thought I just had a bad stomachache—gas, maybe, or constipation. It was Sunday so Faye was home. I was on the front porch when the pain hit. I hobbled through the living room, doubled over, holding my gut. Faye looked up from her magazine and asked what was the matter.

"Don't know," I said, and I sounded so weak and pained that she followed me into the bedroom.

"You look awful," she said, really concerned. I was curled on the bed, saw her from the waist down, basically, the magazine in her hand, her place kept with a finger thrust deep between the pages. *Vogue*. "What can I get you?" she asked. "Some Pepto?"

"Might just be gas," I managed. "Let me see if it goes away."

She lingered a moment. "You look horrible," she said. I saw the magazine rise up, heard the pages rustle. She was actually standing there beside the bed expressing concern for me and reading a magazine at the same time. It was laughable, but I didn't laugh. My stomach hurt worse than ever in my life.

"I'll be all right," I said.

"Well, you look horrible," she said again. "I can't stand looking at you. Sure you don't want anything?"

"No, I think it's working it's way down," I said, but the words were choked with pain.

"God, I can't stand it," she said. "I'm in the living room." She walked out.

Just a few minutes later it started. His coming out of me was messy. Gut hurting, I felt something wet and warm spreading on my belly. I pulled up my shirt—the palm-trees kind that you don't tuck in; there was a transparent pink viscous substance oozing out of my navel; the navel itself looked widened and deepened. My first thought was to keep the goo off the bedspread. I lay still—it hurt to move—and some of the ooze trickled down the side of my belly until it was absorbed in the folds of my shirt.

Fear exploded in me. I thought, Ebola virus? Some rampaging cancer? Something new, a mutant cousin of AIDS, maybe inadvertently unleashed by AIDS researchers or genetic engineers? Am I going to be in medical texts?

Light hurt my eyes. Lying supine on my bed, I had to look away from the narrow strips of Appalachian sky glaring powder blue through the mini-blinds Faye had installed in our bedroom.

I could hear Faye turning pages and clinking a coffee cup in the living room. I didn't want her with me. I wanted to retreat, like an animal about to whelp. If I'd been able to move, I would have crawled into the closet.

Just around the navel there was an odd, lumpy swelling, and more of the goo. Something was poking up from under my skin.

Another stabbing pain rolled back my eyes, lasted a minute or so, then subsided into a growing pleasure, like a drug, an endorphin coursing up each side of my body into my brain and then back down again into my sex. I may have had an erection; I don't know. The sexual arousal was powerful, spiritual even, but sensations were coming and going. The pleasure would subside, the pain would build to an excruciating climax, and then cycle back to pleasure.

I was afraid and in pain, but there was also an orgasmic wonder, I might say *love*, which was focused on the lumpy wet clod of flesh and hair. I saw fingers, a tiny hand, a stringy arm emerging beside the head (which I saw from the back). That hand, once the limb was free up to the shoulder, slapped down on the hair of my belly and helped push its body up out of mine.

It took about a minute more for the homunculus to squeeze his way completely out of my belly, leaving my navel reddened, stretched and sore.

I lay still, listening to my breathing slowly returning to normal, feeling my body begin to form itself back to its known shape. I heard the tiny hum and clicks inside the old electric alarm clock on the night stand next to the bed. I opened my eyes and stared at the vulvate floral images on the papered ceiling.

Ah! I thought. This is just the playwright making some arcane, if visceral comment on childbirth, gender roles imposed by society and the like, and it's all hogwash. It would turn out to be a dream, right? No. But maybe a hallucination? Which category of hallucination? Was it the kind you get from sleep deprivation? I know those. They look real, but subtle. A sweater on a wire hanger, carelessly left hooked over a doorknob...you look at it and you'd swear it was moving its arms. Or bugs crawling up the walls, but seen only out of the corner of your eye. No, this was not like that at all. How about LSD, my travel agent back in the sixties? Those visions were bright and colorful and funny or horrifying, but they didn't look real, they were cartoons or claymation. I never lost sight of the fact that they were drug-induced. I never thought I could fly, and I never saw truly solid-looking things that weren't there.

No, this was, after all, the playwright inventing a character. We do invent them, and they do take on lives of their own. Colleagues, isn't that true? Haven't we talked about it endlessly in our support groups? This is a step beyond talk, yes, a step beyond those writing sessions with periods of deep immersion in the reality of the play. I've gone insane, but I understand this thing. What honest person wouldn't say the same about some aspect of his life?

He was panting, lying beside my thigh. When I felt strong enough, I raised my head to get a good look at him.

He was about a foot long and was wearing sky blue Bermuda shorts and a white T-shirt. No shoes. Very knobby knees. Needed a haircut. He saw me looking at him and moved away from me with an unmistakable air of distaste (for me, I wondered, or for the slime that still adhered to him?) As soon as he gained his land legs he shinnied down a fold in the sheet, walked across the room as though the floor were covered with sharp stones. He stood in the corner, looking at me.

"You speako de English?" I said. He didn't look amused.

"You..." he said in a thin, nasal voice, but phlegm caught in his throat and he went into a fit of throat-clearing, had to put his hands on his knees and hang his head.

"Me man," I said, "me host, me Hector, me..." but he coughed and waved his hand to shush me.

Still leaning with his hands on his knees, he said, "You lousy womb, is what you are."

Womb, me. Fine, true enough, I guess. I suspected he would have considered *any* womb lousy, and I checked my thinking again to see if I was dreaming. Sometimes it's hard to tell. But I wasn't. I was hallucinating, I could tell. It was most like the sleep deprivation kind, but with all the power of my playwright's imagination somehow harnessed and in force. He was as solid-looking as anything in the room. And if the pain and sexual excitement I'd felt were hallucinations too, they were as real as any pain or arousal I'd ever felt before.

He took several breaths, seemed to calm down, and stood upright. He looked around the small room appraisingly, sniffingly. I saw him take in the dusty light fixture on the ceiling and smirk, it seemed to me, at the dark blobs of insect corpses visible through the frosted glass. He surveyed the walls, pausing and glancing at me when he saw cracks in the wallpaper. His eyes rolled when he saw the cheap print—*framed decently*, I thought defensively—of Maxfield Parrish's *Tranquility*. He sighed, put on a poker face.

"This is it?" he said.

We heard Faye's footsteps approaching, and he hid quickly behind a small wicker hamper. The slime that had besmirched the bedclothes had already dried and left stains so subtle that only I, knowing where the wet spots had been, could detect them.

I felt odd and weak for a while, but by the next day my strength had returned along with a feeling of lightness. (I imagined myself lifting off the porch and flying, as in dreams, up into the treetops to explore the habitat of birds and squirrels.) Relishing the thought of another day of this feeling of wellness, I stayed in bed yesterday morning, watching Faye dress for work.

"What's on for you today?" she asked me. No real curiosity. She knows I'm not going to do anything much. She does this and that; I do nothing. Superficially we go on as man and wife while time does what it does.

"Guess I'll do some reading," I said.

She turned to look at me, very deliberately. She executed this turn on one foot, as she was busy inserting the other foot into her high heel pump. She was hunched over in order to reach her up-lifted foot, and when she hopped around to look at me, I saw the flesh of her breasts bounce luxuriously. "I might do some reading myself tonight," she said. "What are you reading?"

I was distracted and didn't answer her. This was my first inkling that I was radically changed from the man I'd been two days earlier, before the strange birth. For the first time in many years, Faye's physical being attracted me sexually. Those wonderful breasts!

She went about her business of dressing. When she left the
room, her body stirred the air and left me with nostrils full of her
scent, something new with an emotional name she'd been wearing
for a few days.

And her hair was new, too. Not the style, necessarily, but its
buoyancy, way up there atop her five feet and six inches. I wondered if my own buoyancy made me see it in her hair. I tried to
retreat into mental wordsmithing: *what can we do with buoyancy?*
But I felt uneasy. I was paranoid about something; it was Faye; I
was suspicious. Of what? An affair, a friendship, various situa-
tions I could imagine, such as a man she might have met, or even
something *she* might have imagined, such as a plan to leave me
for someone who would hold up his end of things. All brand new
thoughts and feelings! She was attractive—*very* attractive. What
regular guy wouldn't go for her? Tall and slim, nice tits, beautifully sculpted rear, pretty face, soft gray eyes, *buoyant* damn hair,
and a breadwinner to boot. A Southerner, too. Isn't that drawl attractive in a woman? A Southerner from an unbroken home, parents still alive, still exerting influence on her.

Though it had been a long time since I'd felt it, I did recognize
the mixture of confused emotions that make up jealousy. Faye is a
faithful wife; I know that.

Midmorning I finally sat up to peruse the reading matter on
the night stand—three Travis Magees and a Doc Adams, the kind
of sensitive yet macho men into whose personas I love to escape
these days, regular dudes on the surface, but too good to be true—
when I heard a squeaky groaning and a thumping under the bed.

At first I didn't look, tried to squelch a feeling of dread. I
swung my legs down, went into the kitchen and found coffee in
the pot, had a cup, returned to the bedroom and dressed in jeans

and a cowboy shirt I'd bought years before at Macy's. I put on clean white socks and sat on the floor to tie my sneakers. Finally then, I lifted the drooping bedspread, flipped it up onto the bed, and looked underneath to the land of dust balls.

I knew he would be there, but I was shocked by what I saw. He was lying on his stomach, the side of his face flattened into the dusty floorboards. Brown drool had pooled where the corner of his mouth met the floor. He opened one eye, the one not jammed down to the floor, and it bulged out at me, bloodshot and yellow. I saw his jaw move slightly, as though he were trying to talk. He lifted his arm weakly and let it fall with a thump.

Pity rose in me, as strong as sudden nausea. I reached under the bed and gently pulled him out, leaving a clean track through the dust, which gathered in a grey festoon on his shirt and shorts. I lifted his almost weightless mass onto the bed, tried to pick away the dust. He still had one eye bulging and the other closed, glued shut with yellow matter glopped in his dark ragged lashes. His T-shirt had ridden up to his chest, and the shorts, too big for him— one of the legs twisted tightly around his thigh—slipped down far enough to reveal a paltry patch of pubic hair. On his groin there were terrible buboes, red and purple, as big as beans. I counted six of them, pulled the shorts down a little more and saw that there were more buboes, ripe to bursting, on his upper and inner thighs. On his tiny penis there were pimples, smaller versions of the buboes, and now I saw a lesion on his chest, greenish and purply— the way I envision Kaposi's Sarcoma in its early stages.

I saw his jaw working again. "Don't try to talk," I said. I hurried to the kitchen and filled a plastic butter tub with warm water, grabbed a roll of paper towels and hurried back to the bedroom.

For some time I worked on him, cleaning, straightening his ridiculous clothes so they didn't bind. I took my comb and tried to

fix his matted hair. But as I worked, I could feel the heat in him,
especially on his head. By the time I had his eyes looking like a
pair, it was clear that he was delirious with fever. He would say
"Calm down, shit, Hector..." and then a minute later he'd accuse
me of trying to kill him, telling me I'd abandoned him when he
needed care the most. I didn't say a word, but I felt guilty about his
condition. *Let him die!* something told me. It was common sense
whispering to me, but I was determined to bring him around.

I'd poured out the warm water and replaced it with cold, and
was dabbing it all over him to try and cool him down. I moistened
his lips.

"I'm losing it," he said hoarsely.

"No you're not," I whispered.

"...fk d'you know..." he said, closing his eyes. "...m dyin'."

"You'll be fine. We'll set you up a nice little place..."

"Why'd you leave me under there so long?"

"I didn't know where you were," I said, but the guilt was obvious in my voice. The truth was, I'd been trying to convince myself
for the last day and a half that he wasn't really there, that I'd imagined the whole thing. But I knew that not only was he in the house
somewhere, he was there for a reason. Little men don't just come
out of your body without a pretty good reason. I suspected he was
here to help me somehow. Yes, I know he's a hallucination, but in
an equally important sense, he's quite real, too.

"Gimme some milk or something," he said. He was so cute,
the way he made demands yet betrayed a fear that he was being
too demanding. He was, in fact, full of the subtleties real people
are made of—the very contradictions I could never communicate
to actors with my written words. I felt a thrill of expectancy as I
imagined a future of friendship and conversation with my own
charming little smart aleck.

Then he closed his eyes and stopped breathing.

For a moment I thought I must be mistaken. *Milk.* Absurdly, I jerked my shirt up to expose my chest. I lifted his face to my breast, cuddled his mouth against the nest of hair around my nipple. There was of course nothing there for him, and he was not conscious anyway. He was not breathing, but as I held him in my arms, I could feel very slight spasms in his back. I was beginning to panic.

Though I was by nature revulsed at the prospect of mouth-to-mouth resuscitation, didn't know the proper way, I did it anyway. Hysterically calculating, I tried to gauge how much air to blow in without bursting the tiny lungs. He would not breathe. I tried and tried. I began crying, begging him to breathe. He lay there, quite still. Suddenly it seemed as though he was more important to me than life itself. Nothing had ever been that important before. If he died, I would miss the chance to know him, and I might as well die myself.

I lunged into the living room and grabbed the phone, crashing my shin into the low woodwork on the arm of the Queen Anne couch. I fell, must have lost consciousness for a moment. But then I found myself with the phone to my ear, hearing a voice asking me what the emergency was, or where.

I was crying, sobbing loudly into the phone. I gave my old New York City address, and the voice, a woman, told me to try to calm down, to think about the address. Then, as if by magic—her computer had had time by then to generate information from my phone number—she gave me the address, my correct Asheville address. "Isn't that where you are?" she said, very nicely. "Yes," I said. "That's right." Then I begged her to hurry. "I'm Hector Owen," I said, though I think I'd told her already. I remember very little of what I said after that, but the thrust of it all was that she must hurry because he had stopped breathing and was lying very still.

An ambulance did arrive at the house, but by that time I had pushed through some of my panic. There was no ambivalence in me about the existence of the homunculus: he was lying there, apparently dead, on my bed. But I began to realize that an ambulance would do him no good, that however real he was for me, he would not exist for the paramedics. So by the time they arrived, I'd very deliberately taken care of my own reality by hiding the little body in the linen closet outside the bathroom, and had calmed down enough to tell the paramedics that I'd been hallucinating.

There were two paramedics. One was Josh, a sandy haired man in his thirties, slim but strong-looking. Though he was first inside the house, he hung back a little, I noticed, as the other, a pretty girl with lush chestnut hair and an extra twenty or thirty pounds on her, had me sit down on the Queen Anne and answer questions. This girl's breast was labeled "Marianne." Here, again, I've forgotten exactly what was said. Some of Marianne's questions made me anxious. I was trying to tell her honestly what had happened, but I didn't want her to know I was insane. I wanted to convince her that I was aware the homunculus had been a hallucination, but I'm sure I sounded like I was lying. I knew his body was within a few feet of where we sat. Once, I almost panicked when I heard a soft thump from the direction of the linen closet.

The two of them skillfully engaged me in a discussion of whether I should accept a ride to the hospital to see a doctor. I could see that they'd already decided I should go with them, and I was inclined to agree. So I did go.

I felt weak, and on the way to the hospital I was suddenly seized with thirst. Josh, who sat in the back with me while Marianne drove, gave me water, but it was not enough, and when we arrived at the hospital, I had several glasses more. Somehow I'd become seriously dehydrated.

I spent all day in the hospital, though I was not admitted. After I was interviewed by a doctor, I called Faye and had her come down. By the time we left, I'd been examined by three doctors and I pretty much had my wits about me again. There's some question about whether our insurance will cover the expense of my little outing.

Now I'm back home, here in bed under doctor's orders, supposedly being cared for by Faye, whom I convinced to go to work, that she had to, since there was no one else to open the shop, that I would be fine.

I have the name of the third doctor who saw me. I expect him to refer me to someone else, but I really don't want any more medical attention. These experiences felt traumatic and weird when they happened—like the jittery malaise of a high fever—but I'm left feeling well and whole, healthier than I've felt in my entire adult life. Why would I want to see a psychiatrist? To cure me of my happiness?

A few minutes ago the homunculus limped into the room from somewhere else in the house where, I surmise, he'd been holed up, not dead after all. He may have stayed in the linen closet the whole time. Without a word, he sank to the floor. He's curled up and sweating on my dirty undershirt where I tossed it on the braided rug, putting his own stink there, cursing quietly and spitting up brown phlegm and looking at me, when he does open his eyes at all, with recriminating disgust. The beads of perspiration on his forehead tell me that his fever has broken. His hoarsely whispered invectives demonstrate his spunk. Looks like he's grown two or three inches, too. I have the feeling he's on the mend, and this,

more than anything, has put me in a hopeful, energetic, adventurous mood. He's ugly, but consider the fact that he's a newborn, in a
sense, and give him the same break all babies get. Maybe it's only
because he's mine, but I can't help feeling he's sort of adorable.

June 24

He tried to kill Faye. She's fine; she never knew. But I have to think about this and decide whether I need to do something, and if so, what.

Early yesterday I got a phone call from the doctor who'd treated me at the hospital. "You haven't seen or felt any more of the fluid around your navel?" he asked me. I'd told him the whole thing, including describing the homunculus.

I chuckled as best I could. "I guess you'd classify all that as a hallucination, right?"

"Would you call it a hallucination?" he asked.

"Yes. Yep, I would. As far as I'm concerned, I need some rest, get rid of stress, do more piddling around in the yard. That's what I came to the mountains for." I was spouting back to him his own suggestions.

"Good," he said. "And look at the alcohol consumption, give it some careful consideration?"

"Definitely going to do that," I said. "No question."

"Would you give me a call in a few days, let me know how you're feeling? How's Friday, better make it morning, say ten o'clock, just a phone call."

"Sounds good to me," I said.

I felt I'd already convinced the doctor that the episode had been an isolated event and was over. By exaggerating the amount of gin I'd been drinking every week, I made it look to him like I'd kicked myself over the edge with alcohol.

The truth is, I drink very little anymore. Faye knows this, so I've worked my story a little differently with her. While denying that I was asleep at the time of the birth, I've given her every reason to believe that I actually was asleep, and the whole thing was nothing more than a dream.

Faye accepted my explanation. Her main concern was the medical expense. Neither of us started out being the practical spouse, but she's taken on the role by default. The clothing boutique she opened with a bank loan has turned out to be profitable. She has demonstrated a side of her I didn't know when I married her—a side that, up until now, has made me sad. My attitude, I now see, isolated me not only from her but from everything. Originally I thought we were both helpless, and in that I found at least some camaraderie. By becoming practical, Faye rescued our marriage from the disaster it should have been. Financially, she's kept us afloat, and look at the result. I've blamed her for my isolation, branded her a bad spouse, a defective component in my life. I convinced myself I no longer loved her, and wondered if I ever really did.

But now that's all out of me. I don't want her killed. Come on. This was horrible, this attempt on her life. I know I must come to understand this little guy who came out of me. He is not harmless.

"I'm referring you to Dr. Nelson Todaro," the doctor told me on the phone. "I'd like you to call his office and set up a consultation. I'll send over your file. Okay?"

I agreed and he gave me a phone number for the psychiatrist.

I hung up the phone, tossed the pencil onto the pad of paper where I'd written the number.

"I think it's working," the homunculus said.

"What, you mean snowing the doctor?"

"You're good at just feeding him what he fed you," he said, passing gas immodestly. During the day, he's taken to sitting on the floor in the corner of the room off to the right side of the bed so I can see him. He hides somewhere—on the back porch, I think—when Faye comes home from her shop. For the last three days his health has improved steadily. The buboes have flattened and faded to pink dots. He's stopped spitting up.

We've grown more accustomed to each other. He eats five or six times a day that I know about, very small amounts; he favors highly processed foods, delicacies, expensive items he doesn't mind wasting if they don't suit him. Yesterday he ate mostly mixed nuts; he also opened a can of smoked oysters but ate only half of them.

"How about with Faye? You think the ruse is working with her?" I asked him.

"I don't think she really cares that much, Hector," he said. "I wouldn't worry about her."

"I never do," I said, and picked up the Travis Magee I was reading.

"Yeah," said the homunculus, "you remain oblivious, all right. Obliviosity, that's your middle name. Yes sir."

I put down the book, sensing his intention to provoke me. "I'm tired," I said. "I want to read. I can't deal with you now."

"Nothing wrong with a little obliviosity. A little obliviosification is good in a lot of circumstances. Handwriting on some walls ain't worth reading. To an artiste in particular."

"Fine," I said. "Facetiosificationism suits you."

"Uh huh," he said. "So, what's the difference between artifice and fakery, when you really think about it?"

"I'm not a faker," I said. "And my work in particular was

never faked."

"I guess you believe that's true," he said, segueing into a yawn that incorporated a loud belch.

"I think I detect a little fakery in you, little pup," I said.

"Me? Not me! I admit everything. Voyeur, that's me."

"Me too," I said with all the disinterest I could convey.

"I want it up my bottom, too. Dead people." He yawned, smacked his lips. "Up a dead man's bottom, up a—"

"Oh shut up!" I put down my book and glared at him.

"—sheep. Young heifers. Play in my own urine. I crave golden showers from young maidens. And men. Blow dogs. Blow horses—"

As he spoke, I watched him pick his nose and wipe the product into a thin crack between two floorboards.

"—torture cats. Be tortured, wear rubber clothes while a mother figure, wearing leather, takes the butt end of her whip and—"

"What an imagination," I said, downplaying it, trying to shut him up. I picked up my book, determined not to laugh or cry, though I did think he was funny and sad.

No, let's get to the bottom of this. I didn't think he was funny. He was reeling off this line of images because he knew, from being inside me, or at least felt or suspected, that I've mentally explored every genesis of sexual sensation I could imagine. He probably wanted to see my reaction, which is why I gave him none. He doesn't deserve any explanation, not even the one I've given myself: that I needed, when I was working on a play, to understand perversions. It was a tool for building characters, a way of creating nuances even though the perversion itself may not have been part of the character. More honestly, I could say it was fun. Yes, bathroom fun sometimes. Also safe, since I kept it to myself.

"I'll be the psychiatrist," he was saying now. "You be you.

I'm Dr.—what's my name?"

"Todaro."

"I'm Dr. Todaro. You're you."

"No thanks," I said. He shrugged his shoulders and jammed a fist down inside his pants, scratching vigorously. With healing comes itching, I thought. He then busied himself with a finger in the ear, extracting copious earwax, which he examined closely. I tried to read.

"Und fere do you tink zis little man comes flom?" he said.

"I said, not interested," I told him. I made another attempt to read, but he had me thinking now. I realized he reminded me of a character in a play I wrote back in the eighties, *The Animal Fair*. In the play a Pygmy materializes out of thin air from time to time to confront the main character on issues that are supposedly very primal, very ancient, at the instinctual level.

I blurted, "You're just a character from a play I wrote years ago."

He cocked his head, looked at me with a psychiatrist's droopy eyelids, and said "I zee! Und zis play, vass it ever poot on?"

It had been—several times in New York. Once at the Norwich Off Broadway, a success that resulted in a published version. The play is still done regionally a couple or three times a year. The best thing in it, the real selling point, I think, is a long diatribe by the Pygmy at the end of Act I in which he describes flying over the world in a jumbo jet and seeing its cities as festering, glowing sores oozing toxins, and its deforestation as a skin disease, and so on. It's an indictment of Western Civilization, of course.

But I said none of this. Instead I sank into the spirals of irrationality that have worn deep grooves in my brain—grooves lined with resentment for artists with the privilege of money. The grey matter is pocked with envy, stained with a suspicion that I've been looked down on by friends and family because my plays never made me rich or famous.

The homunculus gave exaggerated voice to the strain as he stood up. He shuffled across the room and out the door to the screened back porch.

"Where are you going?"

"Exploring," he said, and he disappeared around the corner, pulling his shorts out of his crack.

There were boxes on the porch that hadn't been unpacked since the move. I heard him rip the packing tape off one of them. Annoyed, I got out of bed and padded to the porch.

"Leave that stuff alone," I said. He'd climbed onto one box in order to reach one higher up next to it. I could see brown stains on the seat of his shorts. "Why don't you clean yourself up some," I said. "Take a shower before Faye gets back."

He ignored me and pulled wads of newspaper out of the box. I saw that there were dishes in the box, a set we never use.

"Boring," he said, and climbed back to the floor. He started opening the box he'd been standing on.

"Oh for crying out loud," I said, and returned to the bedroom.

It was impossible to read even the fast moving Travis Magee. I was listening to the homunculus breaking into boxes. I heard him take out the cuckoo clock my brother Roger sent me from the Black Forest. He pulled the chains down and carelessly let the weights bang into the fragile wooden housing, evidently holding the thing up and trying to get it to cuckoo. He failed and put it down on the floor with a clatter. It was almost more than I could bear, but I kept quiet.

He came back into the room and exclaimed, "Ah! Now here's something!"

When I grudgingly looked at him I saw he was holding a disposable syringe. I rolled my eyes at him. "How about tossing that in the trash in the kitchen," I said.

"What's it for?" he said, fascinated.

"It's a hypodermic needle."

"I *know* it's a hypodermic needle," he said, fingering the plastic sheath protecting the needle.

"Don't take that off. You could prick yourself and get AIDS," I said.

"From a sterile needle? I don't think so. Where'd you get it?"

"I don't know. Somehow it ended up in my suitcase when I was at Mother's. She has diabetes."

"You stole it? Why?"

"I didn't steal it. It just got tossed in my suitcase.Would you stop playing with it and throw it away, please."

"But you must have wanted to keep it or you would have already thrown it away," he said, climbing up onto the foot of my bed.

"I thought I might return it to Mother. Then I forgot about it."

"You thought it was kind of neat to have a hypodermic needle," he said. He was right, but I wouldn't admit that in my childhood, at least, needles seemed to embody an evil power. The homunculus, I was beginning to realize, could make guesses about my fears, yearnings, emotions in general. And they were guesses very well educated by his having dwelt inside me for, apparently, my whole life, or close to it.

"I'll just toss it in the trash in the kitchen," he said, his eyes still wide, fascinated by the needle. He climbed back off the bed and left the room.

He was in an odd mood the rest of the day. He left me alone mostly, but when he came through the room, he would hum a tune—something light and gay, a little like "Here We Come a-Wassailing" or "Whistle While You Work"—marching music to work by. A couple of times he plopped down on the floor for a minute and then jumped up and hurried away. I tried to ignore him. As usual, he stayed out of sight when Faye came home.

She complained about the mess on the back porch. The homunculus had strewn the wadded newspapers, the packing, all over the place. Thinking fast, I told her I'd been looking for a coffee mug I wanted to start using, but couldn't find.

We had a dinner of pasta salad. I wondered if she would ask me how I was feeling. She didn't. I was both comforted and chagrined—safe, but only because I was so isolated.

The summer light faded between eight and nine o'clock, and we settled in the living room. I gave *Vanity Fair* one more shot. Would there be a photo, even *one* photo of a model with enough flesh on her bones that I would find her sexy? Nothing there for me. What a silly pastime. I must be an old man.

After a while, I started stealing glances at Faye. Very amusing. Lighter by one homunculus, I saw her completely differently. I hadn't forgotten that she had aborted our baby, that she had done it without consulting me, done it before I even knew she was pregnant, and that her reason for doing it was that the baby would have been cumbersome to me as I struggled in New York to make my mark as a playwright. I hadn't forgotten, either, that I never made my mark, that I ended up feeling the loss of our child was the result of my efforts at self-aggrandizement (for what else is an artist trying to do?) and eventually I equated my failure with the very loss of the child. Logic be damned, that's the way I felt until now. But now, I looked at Faye and saw her physical beauty remaining—still glowing. I saw a woman willing to work to keep a dysfunctional marriage together. I realized that Faye must, somewhere inside her, harbor some kind of hope for life, some kind of hope for me, for the two of us.

So last night I flipped through the pages of a *Vogue* and kept stealing glances at Faye, and wondering at the loss, and at the gain that seemed possible. Faye and I were to have visited our next door neighbors, the Stones, but Faye had that afternoon called them and begged off, citing my 'illness.'

Faye sat reading until about ten o'clock on the Queen Anne, then disappeared into the bedroom. I could see the heat on the couch where she'd been sitting—watched it slowly fade. She always leaves her own ghost behind when she leaves a room. I used to complain about that when I was working on a play, trying to get this scene or that to work, trying to concentrate; she'd leave our cramped apartment so I would have some space, some privacy in which to concentrate, but she'd leave her damned ghost behind, and I couldn't work because of it. Not really a ghost, of course, but the reverberation of a comment, an expression on her face, a punctuation of a general attitude she'd been projecting before she walked out the door. In fairness, maybe all I really saw was my guilt for not having done more with my career. But that was long ago. Now, I was aroused by the mindless heat she left on the couch, and was tempted to go to it and breathe it in.

Stared into space some more. Later I slipped out of my clothes, left them in a fireman's pile on the floor at the ready.

I went into the bedroom, found my pajamas in the dark, crawled into bed next to Faye, who stirred, gave me room, complained mildly. I lay there for a while, sleepy but sleepless, happy to be awake and relishing the lightness I felt, free of the homunculus. Faye was lying on her side, facing away from me. I brushed my hand against the satin stretched across her butt. I smiled ironically in the dark as I caught myself picturing her as a model in one of her magazines: I would have found her sexy! Faye's is the 1945 body ideal, the one I like, not the skeletal look of today.

I purposely summoned the monster that lived between us, which I call the Big Excision. It hung there in the darkness over the bed; its power came from me and Faye, not from itself. Could it be banished? Was there not some positive change possible, now that I had been lightened?

"That's nothing," I said, "Marty wanted a *menage a trois*." To begin a conversation in the middle like this was a suggestion of intimacy, a silly little act we invented when we were first married, something only we understood. I knew she would remember, but didn't know if she would respond, and was glad when she picked it up.

"When was this?" she said a moment later.

"Before any of us were married. Long time ago."

"I'd guess you were not interested," Faye said comfortably, and flipped onto her back.

"Not in what he wanted. I might like me and two women, but not me and another man and a woman. He wanted me and him and one woman."

"Gross," she said, and turned away from me, onto her side.

"It never happened," I said. "Marty was dating this stout, Teutonic woman. She looked like she should be wearing a Viking helmet. Once, she actually did wear her hair in long, heavy, braided pigtails. Bright yellow hair. The three of us in bed. It wasn't going to happen. Who was I seeing at the time? I can't remember. It must have been Sara Gore, the girl from Indiana. I remember taking her with Marty and the Viking to the Ocean Club, dancing until the place closed, getting stuck on the Eighth Avenue local, trying to get home, too tired to stand up, legs full of booze. Hate that."

I shifted, pulled the sheet up around my chin, let my hand slide up Faye's leg and along the crevice between her buttocks.

She shifted away.

My friend Marty, my Best Man, later married a singer named Brenda, gave up his acting career, disappeared for a while into New York Law School and then moved to California.

"I wonder if Marty's doing the same to me, telling on me to Brenda."

Faye sighed, muttered "You're completely out of touch with him. He's probably not even married to her any more."

"One time I spent fifty dollars for a girl," I said. "Not a classy hooker but an ugly, dirty whore. Fifty dollars, and Marty in the room with us drinking straight from a quart bottle of Jim Beam, reading a *Penthouse*. You awake?" I was brimming with some kind of hope, inexplicably.

"Yes. Why are you a blabbermouth all of a sudden?" She was quiet for a moment, then turned onto her back. "You never told me about going with a hooker."

"I wonder if he's there in San Mateo right now, in bed next to Brenda, telling her about it. Betraying me, like I'm betraying him. Who cares? It's all gone now anyway."

I thought she would ask 'What's gone?' or at least point out, in her practical manner, that in California it was still daytime. But all I heard from her was slow, deep breathing. I could tell she was falling asleep, but I talked on and on for a long time, maybe half an hour or more, Faye lulled by my mumbled, ever more disjointed words. Bachelorhood. Old stuff. Betrayal. A drama for the stage, *Betrayal*, then a movie. Or just a movie? A perfume. Print ads. TV ads. Temp work, the humiliation. Subliminal seduction. Whores. Fifty dollars, and I never had sex with her. I never did, Faye, and I want us to come back to life, but you are too resigned to our death, and you're dreaming by now, and I'm tired.

I fell asleep humiliated, amidst lingering feelings of hope and pangs of fear—it was frightening to know the homunculus was somewhere in the house, and he knew me very well, and he was mine and only mine, and outside me.

In the middle of the night I was awakened by a noise in the room. There's a thin old table next to the bed on Faye's side which serves as a night stand. Once awake, I realized what I had heard was the scraping of the legs of that little table on the floor—a quick scraping as though someone had shoved it, or bumped it lightly. My eyes opened wide, staring at the dim horizontal strips of light filtering through the blinds. I listened. Nothing. But then there was a rustling of the blankets. Faye moving? I heard her steady breathing. She hadn't moved, I was sure. Then quiet, stillness, and then slight movement, like a cat had stepped onto the bed. I turned over and looked, but it was too dark to see anything except the vague form of Faye's body, the hill of her hip—she was lying on her side facing me.

The silhouette of something rose up behind her. For a second or two I was paralyzed with fear and couldn't move or speak.

"What!" I whispered. The shadowy form was still and quiet. "What!" I whispered again.

"Shhh." I heard. Then I could see more small movements in the dark figure looming just over Faye's shoulder.

I reached for my reading lamp.

"Don't!" he said. Definitely the homunculus. I turned on the lamp. "Turn that off, you idiot!" he hissed, shielding his eyes from the sudden light. He was holding the hypodermic needle in his hand, the protective sheath removed from the needle, the plunger pulled back.

Faye has always been a sound sleeper. She didn't stir. I stared at the homunculus as he peeked at me through his fingers when he could stand the light. "What are you doing?" I said.

"Nothing!" he whispered. "Turn off the light and go to sleep."

"What the hell are you doing?" I said, using my voice fully now. He tried to shush me again, and Faye moaned and shifted onto her back. The homunculus leapt to avoid her. It must have been then that he dropped the hypodermic needle onto the bedspread. "Get the hell out of here," I said to him. Faye moaned again and opened her eyes, squinted in the light.

The homunculus snarled at me, shook an angry fist, then slipped out of the room.

"What's going on?" Faye slurred.

"Had to unwind the covers," I said, and switched off the lamp quickly.

"Mmm," she said, and turned onto her side, facing away from me. Then she was quiet. I checked the dimly glowing face of the clock on the dresser. It was a few minutes past four o'clock. I slept fitfully until dawn.

This morning I looked for him as soon as Faye drove away, but he was hiding. I drank extra coffee, returned to the bedroom to make up the bed.

When I grabbed the end of the bedspread, the hypodermic needle dislodged from a fold and dropped onto the sheet. I muttered a curse. The needle was bare, the plunger pulled back, but there was no fluid in it. Aside from whatever evil intentions the homunculus had had, Faye or I could have accidentally rolled onto it at any time this morning.

I carried it to the kitchen, wrapped it in a paper towel and placed it under the discarded coffee grounds in the garbage can. In a daze, I wandered back to the bedroom and made up the bed, then sat on the edge of it and stared into the infinity where the wall meets the floor next to the wicker hamper. I heard the homunculus tapping on the door frame (the door was open) between the bedroom and the living room.

"Where you been, little fellow?" I said without looking at him. I was feigning indifference, thought I'd see what I could see without letting on how upset I was. He shuffled into the room.

"Front porch," he said. "I can get behind that planter and see people walking by through the crack under the balustrade."

"No kidding," I said, sour as the morning taste in my mouth. I looked at him sitting meekly on the floor near the doorway. "What was all that about last night?"

"You don't want to know," he said.

"Then why did I just ask you?"

He stood up and made his way to the wicker basket, leaned against it and looked at me squarely. "Fine. I'll tell you." But he hesitated.

"So tell me."

"I will," he said, picking at his tiny thumbnail, then biting it. "You inject just the tiniest bubble of air into the carotid artery. You get a fatal embolism." He leaned there, examining his thumb, biting at it surgically with his sharp yellow teeth, *stupp stupp stupping* the bit of cuticle from the tip of his tongue onto the floor.

I looked away from him, feeling a mixture of fear and disgust that dried my mouth. "Yikes," I said hoarsely. "What's going on?"

"Nothing, just forget it," he said.

I looked at him, couldn't believe he was so nonchalant. I climbed onto the bed, propped myself on the pillows, turned my face toward the windows. I reached for the control rod on the blinds and twisted it to let in the light of day. The Appalachian sky was yellow with ozone. Trying to cover the trembling in my hands, I picked up the Travis Magee on the night stand and nestled it against my knees. Couldn't really read, of course; I was dizzy with panic and paranoia, but trying not to show this to the murderous homunculus. He pushed himself away from the wicker basket and, still looking at his thumb, ambled out to the back porch.

"Where does this go?" he shouted.

With an exaggerated sigh, I answered, "Where does what go?"

"This trap door."

"To the basement."

"Come open it."

"Forget it."

"You want me to play with your cuckoo clock?"

"Open it yourself, then."

"Open it yourself, then," he mimicked me. "I'm a foot and half tall. How the hell can I lift this thing?" He sounded angry now. I slid off the bed and went to the porch, annoyed but a little afraid not to appease him. He was standing on some of the packing paper he'd pulled from the boxes, staring down at the trapdoor, which was set flush into the floor. It was as large as a normal door, and was quite heavy, intended for only the most occasional use. I unlatched it and pulled it up.

The dank smell assaulted my nostrils. There were some cobwebs on the steps and the underside of the door. Without hesitating, the homunculus turned backward and descended the stairs like climbing down a ladder. I watched him disappear into the darkness.

Murder Faye? Innocent Faye?

I followed him down. I'd been in the basement only once, when we were considering buying the house, but I remembered the pull cord at the base of the stairs. When I found it, I switched on the bare light bulb. I had to look around for the homunculus, who had already made it to the little storage room, a converted coal bin, in the far corner. Access to the room was through a narrow door hung with large, exposed, gate-type hinges. Instead of a doorknob there was a sturdy hasp with a rusty lag bolt stuck through the staple.

The homunculus crept into the room. I made my way toward him, stooping to avoid the ancient, asbestos-encrusted heating pipes. Light from the distant bulb barely illuminated the interior of the room, but I could see the homunculus squatting just inside, picking through a crumpled magazine on the floor.

"*Gallery*," he said, bouncing his eyebrows up and down. He flipped back to the cover. "Nineteen eighty-seven. Wow. Antique. Might be worth a fortune."

I was still terrified of him, but simultaneously fascinated. He was so small. Weak, really, but able enough to wield a hypodermic needle against a sleeping woman.

At that moment my terror suddenly shifted, turned to anger, and I felt I had power over him and the inclination to use it. I said, "What's your name?"

He looked up at me, his eyelids drooping with snide indifference. He saw, too late, the change in me, the power, the energy and authority.

"My name's Robin," he said, and for just a second I saw flickering across his face a nervous expectation that this answer, this name, would cut me down to size again. But he was wrong; I looked him squarely in the face, the faint light in the room caught there on the wet surfaces of his eyes; I gauged our positions. He was on the floor, I was blocking his exit, my hand on the door.

"Have fun with the magazine, Robin," I said, and I shut the door on him before he could scurry out. He hit it with a thump, but his meager strength was nothing against me.

I removed the rusty lag bolt. The hasp gave a slight squeak against its unaccustomed movement as I swung it over the staple.

"You blind yellow-bellied son of a bitch!" Robin said, his voice strained to the point of breaking.

"I am what I do," I said, trying to sound gleeful, sadistically relishing my power over him.

"You are what you think," he said. "And you've thought plenty, you dick." I thought I heard him spit.

"That's funny," I said, "I don't remember thinking plenty." Maybe that was a lie, but at the moment I really couldn't remember ever thinking anything—no mental history at all!

Working the lag bolt into the loop—it was a nice, tight fit—I said to him, "I've maintained a moral stance," angrily quoting some unknown source. Oddly (and to our credit, I suppose) we both burst out laughing at the inane sentiment. But then I sobered, and I heard him quieten and then utter some obscenities. I said "Whatever pleasures I've imagined, I've been harmless to others."

"Hec, I don't know what you're thinking of," he said quietly.

"What should I be thinking of?" I asked, and really wanted to know.

"Think of me," he said.

That piqued my anger again. I refused to try and fathom what he meant. "I don't need you," I said.

I didn't intend to leave him locked in the little room for long—maybe an hour or so—but, intentions aside, I felt that the longer I left him there, the better he would understand that I would be the boss, that he would not plan events on his own. "I don't need you at all."

"I'll starve in here," he whined. "I'll die."

"For god's sake, if I wanted to be rid of her I'd just divorce her," I said.

"No you wouldn't, Hec,' he sang softly, and I caught myself straining to hear anything else he might add. "You can't, Mr. Morality, Mr. Under The Parental Thumb."

He was right, but I didn't want to hear it.

"The bitch is guilty," he said.

"Of what?" I said, and tried for a scoffing laugh.

"Something horrible," he said. "I don't know what she did, but I been in there, bud. Remember? I been in there feeling it all come down. It nearly killed you. Don't tell me she didn't do it. Whatever it was."

"It didn't nearly kill me," I said to the door, so close to it that my own breath bounced back onto my lips.

"Killed your soul, Hec," I heard him say. "Lemme the hell outa here, tell me about this thing she did, and we'll take appropriate action together."

I walked swiftly back toward the stair, forgetting to stoop, crashing my forehead into a crumbling cascade of asbestos. Brushing the clinging debris from my face, I shouted back at the little room across the basement, "I'm not going to tell you anything, and I don't need you."

I thought I ought to let him rot. I almost told him I was still in love with Faye, just to crush him, but I wasn't sure that made any sense. He was laughing as I climbed the stairs.

Faye phoned me this afternoon just before five to let me know she wasn't coming straight home, but was going to the mall. This wasn't unusual; she liked to keep an eye on the fashions on display there, and she's mentioned wanting to open a shop at the mall someday.

"Swing by for me," I said. "I feel like getting out a little."

"Okay," she said, sounding pleased. "Want to eat out there?"

"Sure," I said. I didn't, really, because locking the homunculus in the basement this morning left me with an unpleasant sensation in my mouth all day long, and no appetite. I was annoyed that his escapade last night was based on the correct assumption that I was trapped in my marriage and unable to make it right by myself. But that might change now, might it not?

His plan was absurd, but undeniably the motive had been to help me. I thought about it off and on all day. I knew I would never divorce Faye, and it was, as he'd said, because of some morality that I couldn't even contemplate. And Faye, from her straight-laced family, was even worse about it than I. As a couple, we're an anachronism: who, these days, stays married only because they're supposed to?

I sound old-fashioned even to myself. Why not just leave Faye? There are no children to consider. But I can't, and she can't leave me either. I don't quite understand why, but the homunculus was dead on target when he said she was guilty, and that her act killed my soul. Our loyalty must really be a protective device. If we divorced (or even discussed it), then the abortion, the Big Excision, nominally her existential act, *her* irrevocable choice, not mine, would need to come out of abeyance. And we're both afraid to face our respective culpabilities.

I did try to imagine a scenario of divorce, but it led to the horrifying prospect of my being left alone with Robin. Yikes! I had to force it all out of my head. I sat on the porch and watched no cars passing.

And then, after all that circular thinking—such a habit with me—once again it occurred to me that Faye is a good person, or was, at least, before things iced over between us. And she's gorgeous. And, most importantly, things have changed now: the homunculus is out of me. My body, at least, is free of him, and I'm sure I could get rid of him altogether. I can have my wife, and I want her.

"You hate women," Faye said to me, driving us to the mall by way of the tunnel through Beaucatcher mountain.

"Why?" I said.

"Every time I talk about women or things woman, you tune me out."

"Not at all," I said. "I love roll necks and skorts and low riders and leggings." I said this to prove I'd been listening to her, though actually I'd lost track and wasn't sure how long it had been since she'd mentioned those items.

"I was thinking today," I said, "You were the woman in every play I wrote after I met you."

"You mean the ingenue?" she said, interested.

"Yes, but always the antagonist. Always to blame. You were never capable of comforting the... you know..."

"The good guy," she said. "You."

"To whatever degree, yes. I created the Faye character early in our marriage, and now Faye imitates my art, at least to the extent that she never comes closer to me than a fictional character would."

"Are you working on something?" Faye asked me, looking away from the road, daring me not to answer truthfully.

"No."

"Sounds like you're working on something."

"No," I said. "Watch the road."

"Well then, that's a very shallow assessment of me, don't you think?"

"I know it is. I've been thinking about how superficially I've viewed everything for a long time." I almost said even more, but we were pulling off the interstate and Faye was occupied with getting into the lane for the mall exit.

"You *are* working on something," she said.

"If I am, I don't know it," I said.

"Doesn't matter to me," she said. "It was always a thing that stood in the way of us communicating, if you know what I mean. But we don't communicate now anyway, so..." she trailed off.

"Well, let's start back, want to?" I looked at her and she was giving me what she must have thought was a poker face. But I could see the flush coming up her neck and onto her cheek.

In scripting my own life, at least in my stage plays, I've carefully untwisted my apparent misogyny, laid it out plainly, and found that it evaporates in the open air. What looks like hatred is merely disappointment in everything about a woman that isn't heroic: when Faye left me alone with my stomachache just before the homunculus emerged, she was avoiding connecting with my pain. I can't blame her, but she would have been heroic had she stayed with me as midwife.

She appeared, in profile, to be smirking. "Okay," I said. "I do hate women. Doesn't affect the way I feel about them, though." I looked at her and she gave me a little smile. I placed my hand on her upper thigh for a few seconds, a small sexual gesture she chose to ignore.

Faye parked her sporty red Toyota far out in the lot. Mallward past rows of bumpers, the building grew in perspective, rising from the asphalt like a volcanic extrusion. Faye was hurrying ahead of me, a pulp villainess in her black suit and patent leather pumps. We passed through the sphincter of glass and aluminum into the netherworld of neon, fluorescence, incandescence, plastic and metal. Everywhere, the hand of man. I felt safely tucked away from the natural world, in an envelope where my humanity had power for a change. At last I escaped from my thoughts, which had been wandering again to the little room in the basement.

I struggled to get in step with Faye's businesslike stride. "Look," I said, nodding toward a boutique featuring black clothing. "You'll be right at home there."

She frowned heavily. "Too much," she said. "That shop's for women in their forties."

"So? You're in your forties."

I followed Faye into the boutique, and we split up.

I stalked a customer who was not wearing black, finding my way through the racks until, maneuvering behind a carousel of tops, I had a clear view of her from a distance of twenty feet or so. As I pretended to look at a sequined black elastic tube top, the woman knelt, ostensibly to examine the hem of a skirt. Her blue jeans contained her hips, and the stiff upper line of the corset top bit into her bosom. She had something black in her hand, wadded into a ball she could almost enclose in her fist. She caught me looking, continued to examine the skirt for a moment, stood back up, then wandered away. She may have had one of the scanty black bras in her hand and had been planning to steal it.

Someone tapped me on the back. Startled, I turned around.

"I'm ready," Faye said.

As I followed her out of the shop, she said "What were you doing, spying on that shoplifter?"

"Was she one?"

"Yeah." Faye, professional shopkeeper, would know a shoplifter when she saw one, though I don't think she'd recognize a lingerie fetishist if she lived with one. "Let's eat," she commanded.

Nearing the Piccadilly cafeteria I straggled, watched Faye's shapely buttocks rise and fall like two pistons in an engine, the black skirt of her suit catching the light, enhancing the taut muscular curves of her rear. Pretty, I thought. About as nearly perfect as a rear end gets.

As she clicked along the narrow corral toward the trays and the food, I thought how like a pretty stranger she seemed to me at the moment, and what a strange result my fragmented emotions brought: that I sometimes found real strangers concurrently frightening and appealing, but Faye I could not both love and desire. Hogwash. Hogwash. Hogwash.

Once again I was thinking in the old way; there was no reason I could not both love and desire her. In fact, I did! *I want her to be happy, at least,* I thought.

I watched her nose wrinkle as she decided between orange and red gelatin salad. Without looking at me, she murmured, "What're you getting? Cod?"

"Country fried steak, I think. I've cracked, you know," I said.

"What do you mean? I'm getting the cod."

"Like the time in New York."

She let the comment ripen for a moment. "Well, I thought you were acting a little like that. Cold, except it's summer. And then a hand on my thigh? Really."

I waited for her to say more. She ordered okra.

"You know, in New York, I thought I was going to die," I said. "It was like being in a nightmare all day long."

"Well, New York is a nightmare, what do you expect? I was ready to get out of there years before you would even talk about it."

"I know. New York was sandpapering my eyeballs. Have I ever pointed out the connection between my freaking out and a meeting I'd had with Denman Thacker. I'd thought he was going to produce my play. Instead, he said the play was like an eight cylinder engine running on five cylinders. Two days later I saw dead bodies floating in the Hudson river."

"You did? Really?"

"I thought I did."

"I remember you telling me about that meeting. The eight cylinders thing. You said you felt like you'd been kicked in the stomach."

"Lousy simile on top of everything. Five cylinders. Gimme a break."

Faye cleared her throat. "Now I remember you told me you called the police about the bodies," she said, staring toward little dishes of broccoli. "But they didn't find anything."

"Well, they didn't call me back and let me know one way or the other, let's put it that way. After that meeting, I wonder now if they were really there. One of them looked too much like me."

"Maybe they were the characters in your play," Faye said to me. We were considering breads, now.

Denman Thacker set himself up as the head of a theatre group and then refused to be a father figure to the artists who came to him looking for validation. I think that's what I really resented about him. Still do.

"What did you think you were going to die of?"

"Oh god, Faye, you'll either laugh or cry if I tell you. It was crazy, let it go at that."

"No, tell me. I care. I think I might understand you better if I know what you're afraid of."

I sighed. What the hell. "It was the blossoming of the AIDS epidemic. The media was full of it."

"No! Don't tell me you thought you had AIDS."

"There was no conceivable way I could have had it. I didn't fit into any of the risk groups, and hadn't done anything that could have exposed me. But I heard one night on the radio that a doctor in San Francisco had noted that some AIDS patients had complained of a sore on the tongue long before any other symptoms appeared. Okay, I happened to have a sore on my tongue, and that connection was enough to set off my panic. Forget that I've had sores on my tongue since the mid-60s when I discovered the joys of caffeine. Forget all logic. I panicked and the nightmare began."

"You thought you had AIDS?"

"Not really. I was *afraid* I had it."

"Because if you thought you had it, or even might have it..."

Now a man was waiting for us to move on. Faye was standing away from the rail, her tray apparently forgotten. She was staring at me, her hands on her hips.

"AIDS had been lurking in my mind, AIDS hysteria," I said, "straight from the media. Come on, let's get our ticket and find a table."

Faye stood her ground. I saw the man trying to decide whether to go around us.

"What I want to know is why, if you thought you had AIDS, did you have so much sex with me during that time. Were you trying to infect me?"

I started inching away from her, toward the cashier, and fortunately she took the cue and followed me with her tray.

"This is why you have to understand the difference between fear and thinking," I said. "Am I the only person on the planet who can know there's no monster under the bed but still be afraid of it?"

"And it was good sex," Faye said, too loudly, I thought. "The best we ever had. You thought you were killing me with it? That's why it was so great?"

I managed to take the checks for our food and get away from the cashier.

"Faye, for god's sake, I knew I didn't have AIDS. The nightmare was completely separate from what I knew. Knowing I wasn't really infected didn't mean diddly, except it allowed me to have sex with you in good conscience. I don't know why the sex was so good. I do remember it was. Maybe sex was a haven, a distraction."

We found a booth far from the smoking section. Wordlessly we unloaded our trays. I imagined that Faye was contemplating my admission that I'd cracked. Her brow was knitted and she seemed intent on arranging her little dishes symmetrically before her. I sipped my lemonade, placed my napkin in my lap, tried to detect any steam that might still be rising from the steak.

"Black underwear, yes," Faye said, suddenly looking up at me, "but that all-black wardrobe thing is for kids. It really is. I just don't believe it, but do you think I ought to put in a line anyway? I don't have that much space, you know, and my customers are all forty. Every one of them."

She took a perfect bite of cod and looked off sideways into the distance that was the cafeteria's flocked wallpaper.

I laughed, jarred away now from my self-absorption.

"What?" she said.

"I don't know. You're sitting there, in your forties, wearing all black."

"That's just a coincidence, Hec," she said, waving her fork in dismissal. She glanced around the room contemplatively. "Of course, this is a mall. You know what I mean? I'm a neighborhood boutique. Different."

Our eyes met, smiling, just for an instant. When she looked

back down at her plate, suddenly the spell of the mall was broken. I thought of the homunculus, pictured him in the basement. *Murder innocent Faye?* I hated him all over again, but remembered his accusations against Faye, and knew he was right about that. She had murdered — not that I call removing some jism from your own gut murder. It was our love — *my* love, that she murdered. She murdered normalcy, murdered our arguments and our growth.

I forced those thoughts out of my head.

"The mall has secret places," I said.

"What secret places?" She chewed and looked at me.

"Service entrances, stock rooms, janitors' closets, refrigerated vaults, places we don't know about, passageways that connect the mall back to the outside world. We're aware only of seeing each other in the perfect yellow glow of the air, and how beautiful it makes the girl from the town or the country, how it frees her from her poverty."

"You're talking like that," she said, and looked back across the expanse to the wallpaper. Over the years, Faye has become less impressed with my ability to talk, as she puts it, as though I'm reading the words. Many years ago, I seduced her with such talk.

I began eating my country fried steak and talked while I chewed. "Christmas, okay? The mall's aglow. The toy store has a huge display, hundreds of copies of *The Person Doll*. Completely androgynous. I'm with my girlfriend."

"You have a girlfriend?"

"A country girl. This is before I ever met you."

"Or in another universe?"

"Whatever. My girlfriend likes the dolls, breaks away from me and begins picking them up. Suddenly I realize that she looks exactly like the dolls, except she's clearly female, of course."

"Your girlfriend's cute, I guess."

"Oh yeah. I'm amused by the similarity between the dolls and her until she looks at me, smiling, and I see that her eyes have become the hollow, expressionless eyes of the dolls."

"Oh Hector, yuck. Sounds like a scary dream. I don't want to hear this."

"In a panic, I take her by the hand and pull her away, into a lingerie store, where I spot a door in a paneled wall, hurry us through it and down several flights of stairs to a basement. There, we meet a parade of my personal demons. There's a macho man who cowers and breaks like glass the instant I challenge him. There's a hopelessly fey man who tries to seduce my girlfriend. There are several women who threaten me both sexually and physically, but then reveal friendliness or benign indifference. Looking for more of these neato demons, we come across another stairwell leading farther down. A sign, in large red block letters, states *MONSTER BELOW/ TRULY BAD/ GUARANTEED/ DOUBLE YOUR MONEY BACK.* We take the stairs down."

"Now we're getting somewhere."

"Right. The other demons were merely diversions. Down we go to an earthen chamber. Against one wall sits a rotund, smelly animal with a head like a giraffe (no neck, though) and the body of a hog, but twice as large. This monster is glowing from within, a pinkish light emanating from its skin."

"This represents your mother?"

"Hmm. Interesting insight, Faye. Ho ho. Anyway, it suddenly charges at us, growling and baring shark's teeth, but it's chained to the wall and can't quite reach us. 'Look,' my girlfriend says. She points to a small tunnel the monster's been covering with its body. While the monster growls and snaps at us, I read the handwritten sign that hangs over the tunnel entrance. It reads *The REAL monster is below. This one merely guards the entranceway.*"

"And so on and so forth, right?" Faye said. "It's getting ridiculous. And we never get to the *real* monster."

Faye was stirring a tiny fish bone round and round where she'd pushed it with her fork, right at the edge of her plate. Without even knowing it until a few moments later, I took pity on her and didn't pursue the truly bad monster. Instead, I continued, "I'm beginning to realize that all the demons and monsters are there only to guard other demons and monsters. The farther down we go, the more ephemeral and meaningless are the monsters. The ultimate monster is life itself—figuring how to pay the heating bill in winter, wondering if we love enough, and watching our cholesterol."

Faye was staring darkly at her cod. She was quite still. It seemed as though my little story had affected her. I hadn't given a thought as to what my words meant—typical for me when I'm running my mouth—so I thought back and tried to fathom it myself. Oh, yes, of course. It was clear, now that I thought about it, and would certainly have been clear to Faye. I was leaving out the real monster, the Big Excision, pretending it wasn't there at all, and asking her if she might like to try giving our life together another shot. Silliest damn thing, I guess.

"Anyway," Faye said, "you want to talk about it? You know, you've been really cut off from the outside world for a long time. Not just since we came to Asheville. You were closing yourself off in New York. Closing everybody off. Everybody."

"I know," I said.

"You can always talk to Dr. Todaro, too, you know."

"Oh, you know about Dr. Todaro."

"Mmmm," she said, and took a bite of fish.

"Maybe I'll just come live in the mall," I said, smiling over to her. "Ever notice how it's another whole universe?"

She took a large forkful of cod and levered it into her mouth.

"Mmmm," she said. "You should have gotten the cod. After this, I want to hit Victoria's Secret." Chewing, she gave me a smile so bright it hurt my eyes. "I can't believe you wanted to come out here. I like having some company."

"Yes, I love brassieres and panties," I said. I bit into a stick of cornbread, smiled back at Faye, and realized in that instant how close we had come, there at the mall, to talking about the baby Faye and I never had, the Big Excision.

Then tonight, at home, I sat down beside Faye on the Queen Anne, where she was studying a magazine. There were plenty of other places in the room to sit. She glanced at me and I stared straight ahead into the brickwork around the fireplace. My mind was racing, trying to read Faye's thoughts, wondering how she perceived my sitting next to her. And my heart was pounding, which amazed me. We sat for some minutes before Faye placed the magazine on her lap and looked at me.

"What are you doing?" she said.

"Nothing. Just sitting here."

"Why don't you read something or something? You're making me nervous."

In a minor gesture of acquiescence, I let my gaze fall on the bookshelf, as though I might be searching for a title of interest. Faye went back to her reading. She had not sent me away, but allowed me to stay sitting beside her, even though it was clear (wasn't it?) that I was approaching her sexually. After all these years.

In our early years of marriage we were very comfortable around each other. Complacent. I think it was detrimental to our sex life. There has to be some uncertainty in the initial stages of foreplay. And it was that very uncertainty that excited me now.

Would she respond?

Faye kept glancing at me, frowning, and after a little while she put down the magazine and stood up. Watching her walk out of the room, I sized up her body like a stranger, and sprung a hard on. "Holy mackerel!" I announced in a firm tone of voice, ready to expound on it if Faye had heard and questioned. "Yikes," I said, and stood up, headed for the bedroom where she stood, undressing, the woman I'd saved from death the night before.

I quickly took off my clothes, timing it so that Faye and I were both down to our underwear at the same time. I stood at the foot of the bed and looked down at my shorts. "Hunh!" I said, "Well I'll be!"

When Faye looked at me, I dropped the shorts to reveal my erection.

"Uh huh," she said. "Very nice. What are you going to do with that?" She went into the bathroom. I pulled up my shorts, put on the pajama pants I wear to bed. At first, I imagined her preparing for sex, the way a woman prepares, in the bathroom. Then I remembered the birth control measures Faye used to take—those would be unavailable now, of course. I imagine she is fertile, though I don't know. At any rate, I lost my erection.

I was sitting on the edge of the bed when she came back, vigorously pulled her side of the covers back and arranged her pillows. "I don't want to assume anything," she said, "but if you're thinking of... touching, well, I'm not going to."

I answered her, "If I had that in mind, would you be saying not tonight, or not ever?"

"Kind of like we've been," she said. She couldn't have been clearer: she meant not ever.

She slipped into bed and I crawled in next to her. There was, I figured, the comfort of simply having her in the bed with me, a person other than myself, a warm body. Even that had some appeal at that moment. I let my leg drift up against hers under the covers.

Faye exhaled violently, sat up. "Look, Hector, we're about, oh, ten years of therapy away from what you have in mind. Maybe less. Maybe only seven or eight years, if we tried real hard. If I laid back and spread my legs, you still wouldn't get in, okay? It's not going to happen. One lunch conversation that didn't go anywhere anyway is not going to change anything. I have no idea where you're coming from."

I didn't touch her again, nor she me, but before we drifted off, she did say a few words to me.

"Maybe you really should see that Dr. Todaro."

"Oh, I don't know," I said. "Maybe." But I wasn't even thinking about Faye any more. I was thinking about Robin.

June 26 afternoon

He's still locked in the basement. I can't think about that.
Maybe it's wrong, but I feel good now. The lightness—I'm lighter
by one homunculus—is allowing me to touch the world around
me. For such a long time I've been somehow encapsulated, insu-
lated against everything but my thoughts. The capsule burst at my
navel and has ripped away completely now. I've actually had a
conversation, and not just the one with Faye, which of course led
to nothing, but with a city councilwoman!

I spent most of the day lounging in the wicker settee on the
front porch, reading one and a half Travis Magees, getting up now
and then to putter around in the yard and rehash my accidental
meeting this morning with Lainie Wishnick. I'd begun my outing as usual, walking to the convenience store for the newspaper,
which I perused while drinking a cup of coffee, tolerating as usual
the discomfort of one of the store's molded plastic booths. But
when I left there, on impulse I took a different direction, heading
across the public tennis courts in the park and into a neighborhood
of meticulously maintained old homes, many of them designated as
historical landmarks. One row of particularly comfortable-looking
homes overlooks a landscaped crescent covering a couple or three
acres of public land. I was strolling along the walkway in this little
park when I noticed Lainie Wishnick, a city councilwoman, sitting
on a bench facing the flowerbeds. I recognized her for a couple
of reasons: I'd seen her picture in the paper several times (she's

memorably attractive and has great puffed-out hair that reminds me of Carole King's on the cover of the Tapestry album), and I knew that her house was the first in the row overlooking this park. It was out of character for me, but I walked directly over to her and spoke. "You're Lainie Wishnick, aren't you?"

"Yes," she said, smiling with the lower half of her face, none too happy to have had her reverie interrupted, I'm sure.

"Hector Owen," I said, nodding, not bothering her with a handshake, "a neighbor from down the road, a constituent."

She smiled, squinted toward me — the sun was at my back–and proffered her hand, which I then shook. I struggled to find something else to say to her. She let go of my hand and looked at me squarely, leaving me free to move along, go away.

"I don't mean to stand here and take your moment away from you," I stammered, "but let me say I've admired your conduct on the city council."

"Thank you," she said with a pleasing smile.

"I like to take note that as the only woman on the council, you're also the only member who's at peace with every other member. I'm just going by what I read in the paper."

"Well, that's about right," she said, still smiling, nodding at me, glancing away toward the row of trees over which the sun was hovering.

I was seized with an impulse to tell her how downright attractive I'd always found her — from her pictures, of course — and that she was even more so in person, sitting on a park bench near her lovely home, but of course I didn't. Instead I said, "Keep up the good work. Keep up the *excellent* work."

"Thank you," she said, "I'll do my best." And then she held out her hand again, in case I had any doubt that the conversation was over. I shook her hand, smiled and walked away.

Then I wanted Lainie Wishnick to run the town. But even if she were mayor of Asheville, the good ole boys would still be running things. Everybody knows that. I let the sad thought go and thought about Lainie Wishnick herself and my encounter with her. I hadn't been too pushy, I reassured myself. My outward behavior never reveals how crazy I am. (If it did, Faye would find out all kinds of things about me.) A simple, short exchange in the park, this intrusion would not have ruined her day, not even her moment. Guiltless, I allowed myself to embellish the memory of it with what I might have said in addition.

Owen: I've admired your home, by the way. [tosses his head toward her house] I frequently walk this way, taking a morning constitutional, you know.

Lainie: Thanks. What do you do, Mr. Owen?

Owen: Do? Nothing. Putter around in the yard some. Drink coffee. Sit on the front porch and see if a car ever goes by.

Lainie: Well, that sounds pleasant.

Owen: I'm doing my bit for lowering the standard of living in this country.

Lainie: [smiles slyly] I see.

Owen: No, I'm serious. I'm anti-growth, pro-ZPG, although I'm all for babies. All for those, but only enough to replace yourself or slightly less, to let the population dwindle through attrition until it reaches a more reasonable level. Within that boundary, I'm certainly all for babies. Wah wah. Yes. Burp. I'm all for that, all for those little things. I once was going to... well, oh well. We're ruining the earth, we humans, with our growth philosophy, don't you think?

Lainie: It's a little sad, yes, because this town is the jewel of Appalachia, and we're surrounded on all sides by a hundred miles of backwoods populated by men who like to kill bears. The whole show is run by men, and it still would be, even if the entire city council were made up of women, would be if all of the public offices were held by women.

Owen: Just exactly what I was thinking!

Lainie: Good ole boys run the show, and make no mistake. I know what you're saying about growth, and I hate it every time another tract of forest is pushed down for more growth, but people want jobs, and without them, it's pretty hard to live.

Owen: Not really. Only if you think you have to have everything and a lot of it.

Lainie: So your solution is to not work?

Owen: Sounds radical when you put it that way. Lainie. You mind if I call you Lainie? [she smiles in acquiescence] But yes. Yeah. I realize *somebody* has to work. Somebody, let's say, in each family unit. But we all ought to make do with just one person working per family.

Lainie: Sort of like it used to be, you mean?

Owen: Sort of.

Lainie: Wife stays home and cooks the meals, and so forth.

Owen: No. Husband can do that in some cases, wife in others. Who wants to work is up to the individuals.

Lainie: Sure, but the wife is the one who has to take care of the babies, so pretty soon we're right back to the 1950's.

Owen: Wives don't need to feel they must have babies. Back to my earlier point. Too many people anyway. Americans in particular are using too many resources.

Lainie: Oh, yes. I know that.

Owen: The points I'm making are easy to see individually, but I suspect you balk at the conclusion.

Lainie: Which is?

Owen: Stop working so hard. Relax, do without the TVs and cellular phones and cars and houses too big for you and packaged dinners — take the time to make your own dinner. Sit down and relax. Lower your needs to something human, stop feeding the greed machine.

Lainie: I think you're right about that.

Owen: Stay in bed later. I'm serious, Lainie. Did you know that the alarm clock is a terribly destructive invention? Every time your body's own mechanism for waking up is stymied, it wreaks havoc on the rest of your body's biological checks and balances. If you're awakened artificially day after day, year after year, you lose touch with your inner clock, which is a vital connection with this world we live in.

Lainie: Very interesting.

Owen: I don't like the look on your face, Lainie. [He laughs good-naturedly.]

Lainie: This philosophy of yours—would you say it represents a school of thought, or just your personal thoughts?

Owen: Well, it's my personal credo, though of course there's *Principles of a Non-Exploitive Economy* by what's-his-name, the Princeton guy. Came out about ten years ago.

Lainie: I'm not familiar with it.

Owen: It starts with the old idea that all wealth is derived from exploitation, and goes on to set forth principles for an economy that allows for wealth without exploitation. Of course, he redefines 'wealth' pretty extensively. Daniel Chrane, Ph.D., with an odd little symbol after his moniker. I knew the name would come to me. Corcoran/Hill put it out. I have a copy if you'd like to see it.

Lainie: Maybe I'll scare up a copy for myself. You hang onto yours.

Owen: You wouldn't have real estate agents, for example. It's very interesting and down to earth.

Lainie: I'm sure it is.

Owen: I hope you don't mind my saying I find you very beautiful.

Lainie: Thank you, Hec, but I'm a happily married woman.

Owen: That's okay. It makes no difference in the world as to how I feel about you.

End of Scene 1

I began to meld pieces of Lainie Wishnick's dialogue with some lyrics off the *Tapestry* album, and Lainie Wishnick herself with Carole King—they did resemble each other. I was doing some jolly mental play-writing on Scene 2 by the time I ran into Mrs. Stone in front of her house; I was in love with Lainie Wishnick and I was wishing women instead of men ran the whole world.

Mrs. Stone was working at the white picket fence separating her front yard from the sidewalk, carefully untwining the morning glory tendrils and redirecting the vine. It was still early, and yellow light frolicked on the deep green of the lawn.

Directed by.............................The Sun
Choreography........................Drunken Zephyrs

With the unusually crisp air, I found the effect exhilarating.
"Good morning, Mrs. Stone," I sang.
"So beautiful," she said, "I like this air you can bring in." Even her clattering German accent pleased me. She probably expected me to walk on by, but I stopped, elated and full of the energy needed for small interpersonal exchanges. I was taken with

old Mrs. Stone's storybook appearance, her funny great flowered pedal pushers, white socks, blue canvas deck shoes, her wonderfully smooth, white hair and skin. All my previous perceptions of her suddenly shifted. She was stout, not fat, as I'd thought before. Her sleeveless orange blouse revealed strong arms that were smooth, porcelain, creamy. I had an impulse to apologize for having thought of her as pasty.

"How are you and Mr. Stone doing?" I asked.

"As well as we can," she said, turning to me with a smile as bright as the day, her cheeks red with exertion. "And you. You're all through with your grippe?

"It wasn't the grippe," I said. "I think it was just psychosomatic. Terrible tummy ache that hit hard but then disappeared by itself. I don't think I needed the doctor or the trip to the hospital at all." I was so full of energy and myself. "Although now they think I'm crazy."

"Who thinks you're crazy!" she demanded.

"The doctor. Faye. Asheville in general, I guess. The city council, at the very least. I've just spoken with Lainie Wishnick, you know."

"Pooh!" she said, and stooped to pick extraneous blades of grass from the fencerow, the vast expanse of her derriere testing the seams of her pedal pushers.

"They're right," I said. "It's the stress that built up in New York. I thought I was done with it, but it's not so easy."

Mrs. Stone stood back up and faced me. "You have to take it real easy," she said. "And I have a recipe for something to help."

I smiled. "Old German remedy?"

"It is, and you don't smile. You'll sleep with sweet dreams." Turning to remove a darkened petal from one of the morning's crop of glories, she said, "You and Mrs. Owen come over soon.

We'll work out a time. Mr. Stone and I had to play Scrabble when you didn't come last week. He gets so many i's he throws them through the door into the bedroom. I have to go in there later and find them, and one i I never find. We are still mad at each other." She looked up at me, her face ruddy with mirth.

"We'll do that," I said, and stepped zip-a-dee-doo-dah along the sidewalk. "You just let us know when it's convenient."

June 26 late night

He's out now. What the hell.

Faye arrived home from her boutique at about seven o'clock. She walked in the door, tossed her bag onto the floor, and plopped down into the recliner. "I didn't sleep last night," she said. "Did you hear all that noise in the basement?"

My eyes opened wide before I caught myself. "No," I said. "What noise?"

"Something is down there. Sounded like it was trying to get out. Or maybe it was looking for food. Scratching, bumping. And it makes a sound like a cat."

"You think there's a cat down there?"

"No, it sounds sort of like a cat, but a cat wouldn't be making a sound like that unless it wanted another cat to come and, you know, get it."

She was taking off her high heels, rubbing her feet. "It's probably a 'possum or something. You see them all over the place in this neighborhood. Would you go down there and look? I've got to get some sleep tonight."

I sighed heavily, as though bored and unbelieving. "Okay," I said. "But I haven't heard anything."

After dinner, I made a show of going to the trap door, opening it with grunts of exertion. Just in case Faye wasn't getting the message, I shouted through the house to her, "Here I go, into the darkness!" I barely heard her short acknowledgment.

I intended to just go down and stand at the bottom of the stairs for a few minutes, and come back. Once I was down there, I switched on the light. The emptiness emphasized and framed the door to the little room where I'd imprisoned the homunculus, and I felt drawn to it.

Carefully lowering my head to dodge the toxic insulation, I made my way over to the door, stood at it, listened to the silence. Guiltily I calculated that I'd left him there for two and a half days.

"Robin?" I said softly. Nothing. It felt odd, saying his name. I leaned close to the rough wooden door, my lips almost touching it. "Robin?" I said as loudly as I could risk, fearing Faye might hear me.

From inside the room, I heard his voice, strained and sickly. "Open the door, you prick."

Full of remorse, I pulled the lag bolt out of the hasp and opened the door. In the dim shaft of light that fell across the cold, damp cell, I saw him in a heap on the floor. His mouth hung open, drool suspended from its corner. His eyes were closed, but in a moment, they opened to watery, glistening slits. His tiny body seemed even more wasted than it had been when he was born, and the dark stubble on his face accentuated the awful hollowness of his cheeks. He lay in a fetal position. As I stared in horror and shame at what I'd done, he began to unfold his body, partially straightening first one leg, then the other, then his arms. Finally he struggled up onto his hands and knees, his head hanging limply toward the dirty concrete floor. In this position, he said "Thought I'd be dead by now? Sorry to disappoint..." and he broke into a spasm of coughing and fell back to the floor, rolling into the fetal position again.

I stood staring until his coughing finally subsided. My voice cracked when I said "I didn't intend to leave you in here. I..." But

I myself didn't know why I'd done it.

"You wanted me dead," he muttered. "You were mad because I tried to off that bitch you're married to."

"Not really," I said. "But I wanted to teach you a lesson about that."

"Fine, asshole," he said, and coughed some more.

"What is it you...?"

His eyes bulged from the strain of his coughing. "Want? I want some water and some food, you sadist." His coughing fit threatened to recur, but he brought it under control.

"All right," I said.

"All right? *All right?*" He snarled at me, "I want out of here, you moron. Get me out."

"And if I do, what do you want then?"

He sensed my strength, my resolve, I'm sure, because he eyeballed me then, and thought long about his answer. He pushed himself up to a sitting position, pulled his knees up to his chest, held them there with his arms, and rested his chin on his knees. "You surprised me the other night," he said.

"I did?"

"Yeah. I thought you would've let me do it. Off her, I mean."

"No," I said.

"Yeah, no, I know," he said. He was really scrutinizing me now. "You figure you saved her life, don't you? I guess that's true. 'Mah hero!'" he said like a southern belle.

He was making me nervous, the way he was staring at me, so I turned away, pretending to examine the framing around the door.

Then I heard him snickering, and looked at him again. "I bet I know what happened," he said.

"Who cares what you know?" I said.

"You felt like her big hero, saved her life from the horrible homunculus, and you got all hot and bothered. And now you're back here to let me out. Only one possible reason for that: she wasn't interested. Was she?"

"If I let you out, what would you want?"

He looked right into my eyes and answered. "I just want to be treated decently like any other human being."

The irony here didn't escape me. I didn't know what to say.

"She's coming," Robin said glumly.

I turned to look back across the basement and saw Faye's slender, shapely legs coming into view down the stairs. I quickly pushed the door to and walked back toward the stairway.

"Find anything?" she said, shielding her eyes from the bare light bulb's glare.

"No," I said. "Whatever it was, if it was down here, it must be gone now."

She looked around. "This is creepy. What's all that crud hanging off the pipes?"

"Decayed asbestos," I said. "Breathe it and you die. I wouldn't come down here if I were you."

"You get out, too," she said, turning to go back up. "But if I hear that noise again tonight, you've got to do something. I think it might be raccoons. Don't they make a noise sort of in between a cat and a human? That's what it sounded like."

She kept on talking about it but I didn't hear the rest as she was up the stairs and back into the house. I lingered at the base of the stairs, then went back to the little room and opened the door. Robin was sitting cross-legged, slumped over.

"Look," I said. "Can you... do you mind, I mean, you've been in here for two days anyway..."

"*Three* days, chump."

"How about I leave you here until she's asleep and I'll come get you. I won't lock you in."

"Thanks," he said without looking up at me. "I haven't had a bowel movement since you put me in here, you know. I'm going to have some recovering to do."

"Okay," I said, wondering where, if anywhere, he had urinated, and suddenly I thought I could smell it.

"Get her drunk," he said.

"I will," I said. "That's a good idea. She'll be out cold inside an hour. She's dead tired anyway because you kept her up last night with your banging and bumping."

I thought this would provoke him. Since I really had not heard anything the previous night, I wanted some confirmation that it really had been he who made the noises Faye heard. He cleared his throat, said nothing, and appeared to settle in to wait for my return.

Back upstairs, I went straight to the kitchen and made Faye a strong gin and tonic. I found her in the living room.

"Here," I said, presenting it to her. "Old German remedy. You'll sleep with sweet dreams."

"More like wake up with a sweet hangover," she said, taking the drink gratefully anyway.

I was antsy, kept darting in and out of the living room, kitchen, once to the bathroom for no reason. Faye was taking her time with the drink; understandable, as strong as it was.

"What is with you?" she said, her glass half empty.

I was standing near the fireplace, checking the crown molding in the room, halfway looking for cobwebs.

"How you doing?" I said.

She expelled a blast of breath which propelled her suddenly deeper into the cushion of the couch. She was eyeing me, now amused, smirking. "You act like we're married," she said.

"We married at The Little Church Around the Corner and caught a flight out of JFK to Nassau," I said. "The second day there, something was settled in a cool little conversation we had by the hotel swimming pool."

The room went hot, as though the fireplace were ablaze. I had absolutely not intended to say what I said, and had no idea where the words came from.

Owen: We are married, you cold, cruel bitch!

Faye: Hark! I think I hear someone talking from one of his parallel universes!

[Lights fade out on scene and up on downstage area]

I hurried out of the room, but hung near the door in the kitchen. I heard Faye just a minute later.

"Something was settled?" she said.

I spoke from the kitchen, out of sight, but she could hear me. "There was my career to pursue, fun to be had, youth to invest, and there was New York City itself. But the real gist of the conversation grated against an assumption, I later learned, that you'd made all your life. Remember?" She didn't answer. I poked my head around the doorframe and looked at her. "Offspring."

She looked back at me. "Oh. I can't believe you're bringing this up. Is that why you made me this drink? You think I'm going to talk about it? Ho ho ho ho ho ho ho ho ho. If you've got a problem with that, it's your problem, Hec. I'm fine with it."

"The thing that came out in that honeymoon conversation was that married, you would not just automatically start your family,"

I said, sauntering to the front door and looking out through the little window at eye level. "I made sure I married you first, and then I dispelled your illusions of having a nice little family. I was a writer, by god, a struggling artist. Incredible as it seems to me now, I thought I should be your *boss*. I was the *man*."

Faye leaned forward and placed her drink on the coffee table. She suddenly looked very sober.

I turned my back to the door, felt its cool surface with the palms of my hands. "Could I really have needed you to sacrifice your own dreams to prove mine were legit? I admit I did."

"That swimming pool in Nassau," Faye said. "There were dead crickets floating in it." For a long moment she sat hunched toward the coffee table. Finally she picked up her drink and, holding it protectively with both hands, leaned back, sank deeper than before into the cushions. "I took a turn in my thinking, all right. Eventually led me to fashion, you know. Lucky thing, I guess."

"Were we ever sure about our feelings for each other, Faye?" I asked.

Faye drank, looked away from me with some disdain. "I think you just wanted to see if you could get my attention away from Karl."

Owen: Let's put that caustic little remark in context, Dr. Todaro. It's been bothering me since she said it. We met at a dinner party. Faye was actually supposed to have been interested in my friend Karl Furst, a handsome, upwardly mobile suit. I asked her for a date. She went out with me — a movie in the Village, dinner at an intimate Italian restaurant on Minetta Lane. We spent the night at my apartment. No sex, she was on the rag, also didn't feel good. I comforted her, took her home the next day, was kind and warm. She was impressed that I didn't appear to feel shorted by the lack of sex.

Todaro: Did you feel shorted, in fact?

Owen: No. But Faye was impressed, and I wonder if that's why things seemed to work out that she was always having her period and wouldn't have sex on important events. The night I proposed, she was on the rag. On our wedding night, on the rag. Sex, when we had it, was fine, but Faye liked the way I was tender to her when she had her period. She liked that better than sex, I think.

Todaro: That all sounds pretty normal. After you were married, did the two of you become more comfortable with each other?

Owen: "Married" by Hector Owen.
Too comfortable with each other from the start/ you loose flappy wet farts in my face/ and think it's funny/ I stalk excuses just outside the telling/ relentlessly beyond our common ground

Ground which is too considerable/ we agree on politics/religion and lifestyle

I, I don't like your farts/ You, you want to know me

If not for the children...

So we stand by each other/ comfortable/ afraid/ desperation equal to that failure to court

Todaro: But I get the impression there was a courtship, and a pretty normal, typical one.

Hector: But there wasn't.

Todaro: Why do you say that? Explain.

Hector: I just know what a courtship is. A courtship is what trans-
pired between me and Ginger, the girl I was in love with at college.
I refused to let her come with me to New York, insisted she stay
and finish her degree first, which was going to take two more years.
When she finally broke up with me, I was devastated. I broke down
and cried in front of my friend don, little 'd' don, who had taken me
under his wing and was teaching me the rudiments of life in New
York City.

Todaro: I knew a woman once who refused to capitalize the first
letter of her name. phyllis. Never heard of anyone else doing that
until now.

Owen: For god's sake, Todaro, who gives a damn? This is about
me.

Todaro: Of course.

"Boy, you do go off into another universe, don't you?" Faye
said. I noticed now that her tongue had thickened. I glanced at her
glass. It was on the coffee table, empty but for some ice.

"That's funny," I said. "A minute ago I had you saying something very like that in a little scene I was writing. In my head."

"Eugene took all his clothes off right in front of me one time,"
she said.

"Eugene who?"

"Eugene Pugh. He just started taking off his clothes. But I

mean he took them all off, even his underwear." She let this hang for a moment before going on. "Gail was right there, too. I can't believe I didn't get the message: 'Time to go home, Faye.' To me, their apartment on East 83rd was just an extension of the dorm room at college. You know, you didn't worry about overstaying your welcome."

"Oh, I see." I nodded, trying to gaze back those twenty years. Eugene and Gail had been Faye's friends and I never knew them very well. "He was dropping you a subtle hint that it was time to go home."

"I think he did it to make Gail mad."

"What? Oh, Eugene? Yeah, probably."

Was she drunk enough? Should I make her another drink, or would she pass out soon?

"And he probably... well, he might have been trying to offer himself sexually to me, offering then and there, in front of his wife, for consideration at a later date."

Faye turned her eyes to me without moving her head, increasing their size and brightness momentarily, creating a coy, sexy countenance for the briefest moment before she put her hands on her knees and pushed herself up to an unsteady standing position.

She staggered toward the bedroom, passing me as though I didn't exist. I sat wondering if she was flirting, then castigated myself for such audacity. Finally I decided she must have loved me somewhere near the beginning, and probably still did in some small way. Certainly she was kind enough to provide me with my only connection to the world in practical, day-to-day matters.

But as for the two of us staying married, that was because of our damnable moral scruples, instilled guilt, and cowardice. Amazing, I thought, how alike we are in those respects.

It couldn't have been five minutes later that I went to the bedroom to check on her. She was sprawled, unconscious, diagonally across the bed. She'd managed to get her dress off but still had on everything else, including a half slip.

I resisted an urge to hurry back to the basement to liberate Robin. Instead I sat on the edge of the bed.

At 41, she still has her slender figure. Even her tummy is flat, never having been stretched through pregnancy. Her breasts, on the rare occasions they're freed from her bras, are full, round, and so firm they hardly lap over even when she's standing up. Asleep like this, Faye looked to be a sexy, even seductive woman, which she was when I married her. Yet her most noticeable aspect now is the rigidity in her posture emanating from a gelid center that also sets her jaw, knits her brow even in sleep. I removed her pantyhose. She seemed to awaken momentarily, but her stupor was deep—I'd put over half a cup of gin in her drink—and she was still again as I slipped the last confines of nylon off her toes, the cotton crotch now exposed and cooling in my hands. I considered unfettering her breasts, but I felt sure she was just as comfortable with the brassiere on as with it off.

Though it occurred to me, I didn't want to press the crotch of the pantyhose into my face and breathe in the smell of my wife's sex. It was too frustrating to desire her, so instead, for a moment I loved Lainie Wishnick whom I would probably never see again.

I stared at Faye in the dim light, and she became her sarcophagus, a stone carving sealing out the stench of death just underneath. Neither her beauty nor the memory of her love for me accounted for the longing I felt. It had nothing to do with Faye now. All I wanted was to go back down to the basement and take the homunculus gently with me, up to some food and fresh air.

June 29

Rinso
Wheatsworths
t.p.
pasta—shells or ?
baguette or decent rolls
sour cream
Endust
foil

He's sitting there watching me, and has asked several times to read what I'm writing, but I refuse. My journal is my business and no one else's, not even the homunculus.

Especially not him. We're on good terms now, but after I let him up from the basement, I began to regret it. I understood his anger, which he demonstrated by refusing to speak to me for the rest of the evening. The one exception was when he said, "Took you long enough. What'd you do, screw her after she passed out?"

"I did not," I said, following him up the basement stairs, ready to catch him if he fell; he was climbing on all fours. He said no more, and I wanted to talk, so I prompted him: "Not that it wouldn't have been nice."

I'd like to have seen his expression, but he reached the top of the stairs at that moment and hurried across the back porch to the bedroom, where he stood, holding the door frame and standing on tiptoes to look at Faye's sleeping form. Quietly he crossed through the bedroom and disappeared into the living room.

I tried not to seem in a hurry, but I did follow him shortly and found him curled up on the Queen Anne.

"Are you feeling okay?" I said, trying not to sound too concilatory. Ignoring me, he crawled off the couch and headed for the bathroom. He closed the door loudly—not exactly slamming it, but sending me a message. I listened carefully. There was running water—in the tub, I thought, but couldn't be sure. I heard the commode flush, then nothing for a while. More running water. Tidying himself up, getting back together—this is good, I thought.

The bathroom door opened and I waited for him to come into the living room, but he didn't. I didn't see him for the rest of the evening. I heard him, though. He was back on the basement stairs, banging around. It reminded me we'd left the trapdoor open. I admit it crossed my mind to sneak in there and close it on him—just as a joke, just for a moment. Dismissed that idea. Shouldn't try to force a relaxation between us that wasn't yet established.

It was late when I went to bed. And then I heard the homunculus puttering around in the house, opening drawers in the kitchen, returning to the basement stairway, making bumping and squeaking noises as though he were up to something.

The next day he stayed out of sight most of the day. I ran into him in the kitchen about noon. He was waiting for me to make him some lunch, which I did—a pimiento sandwich made with a single slice of bread folded over. I wanted to talk, but felt he should make the overture. He ate the sandwich, drank milk from a small juice glass, wiped his mouth on his forearm, and walked out of the room. But then he reappeared at the doorway.

"'Anks," he said.

"No problem," I replied.

"I'm busy, okay?" he said.

"What's going on?"

"Can't tell you right now." And he padded away toward the front of the house.

I suppose he's making a nest for himself somewhere, though I don't see why he needed my little crowbar.

Sir Richard: If a Man liveth inside his imagining/ And findeth happiness there,/ Yet is lost to all the world surrounding him,/ Is he more wretched than thee in thy Wise and Cognizant misery?

Dr. Morley: Never able to see into his imagining,/ I can nought say on that, and would not/ Vouchsafe that happy such a man/ May truly be.

Yet, heigh ho! From here he looketh so!

The Comedie of Surgeons
W. J. Smythe, c. 1694

July 4

Now I'm reminded why I keep this journal. Writing in it places me, for the time being, in a cocoon against the insane world. Well, *my* insane world. I'm the insane one, not the world, of course. At any rate, I called Mother this morning. I'm left reeling, and that's why I have to write it down.

I think I intended, though not consciously, to tell her about the homunculus. I did tell her about something I saw once, back in 1984 at a summer theatre conference in upstate New York. It was a swirling aquamarine glow out beyond the yard and the road, across the meadow in the glen where the hills began to rise steeply toward the Adirondaks on the horizon. It was a starry night, I was sitting on the back porch of the annex with Tinker and Cait, who were puffing reefer and engaged to be married. I was drinking gin and tonic, already married for some years, away from Faye for the weekend.

"People see things all the time, Hec," Mother said. "I saw puffs of smoke coming up out of the carpet. Here, there, over there. Puff, puff. It was my cold medicine keeping me awake for three days."

"That'll do it for you," I said.

"Did Tinkle and Cait see this blue light too?"

"Tinker, Mother."

"Well, I mean, maybe it was there. If they saw it..."

"That was the funny thing," I said. "I don't know if they saw it or not. I didn't feel I could ask them. We'd already exhausted con-

versation, which was mainly a rehash of the tragic death of Buford
Elslager, who'd been a very talented new member of AETNY."

"Oh, AETNY," Mother said with a note of disdain. "You've
told me about that place."

Artists Exchange Theatre of New York. I lost count of the
times I'd use the acronym and someone would say it sounded like
a financial institution. The place did have an abiding concern for
money, even though it was housed in a shabby walkup in Spanish
Harlem. The founder, Denman Thacker, came from a background
of poverty, which may account for his viewing art in terms of its
pecuniary potential.

"You know, Hec, whenever you talk about that place, you
sound a little disgusted," Mother was telling me.

"Being a member probably wasn't a good thing for me in the
long run. I did get produced there a few times, but you know what
I'll always remember, even if I forget the lousy productions I got?
Buford Elslager, discovered dead, suicide note in his shirt pocket,
the morning after he got a terrible review in the *Village Voice* for
his directorial debut at AETNY. He killed himself not on the set
of the play he'd directed, but dramatically sprawled across the top
of the photocopier in the office. Poisoned himself with arsenic.
Where do people get arsenic, anyway?"

"I remember you telling me somebody had committed suicide.
I thought it was an actor."

"No. Director."

"When I was Ophelia, the director said my artistic spirit kept
him alive. I'll never forget that. 'Your artistic spirit is keeping me
alive.' He said it in front of the whole cast."

This was one of those places in a conversation when both par-
ties go silent and diverge into their own little daydreams. I was
remembering my infatuation with Cait, and a drunken attempt to

steal her affection away from Tinker. Tinker, a good professional actor used to the foibles of artistic temperaments, was good-natured about the whole thing.

Where Mother's mind took her, I'm not quite sure, but after some moments, I heard her say: "Hec, now don't take this wrong. You know how much I love you, don't you?"

"Of course," I said.

"So this is only to be taken for what it's worth, and I only say it in case it helps. If it helps, that's good. If it doesn't help, you just discard it. If it doesn't help, it just goes in one ear and out the other."

"Okay, I'm ready any time you are."

"It's no big deal, and you know it anyway, but sometimes if your mother tells you something, it's good to hear it even though you may know it already."

"Shoot."

"Now I forgot what it was." There was a moment of silence, and she laughed. "Just kidding. I know I never get around to saying what I want to say."

"So just say it, Mother. Don't build it up so big."

"Well, it's just that you're a grown man. You make your own decisions, and there's nobody telling you what to do."

"Is that it?"

"Something to think about, Hec. That's all. Nobody's going to blame you or throw you in jail or beat you up for doing whatever you have to do. If you decide to make changes, then that's your decision."

"Okay. You're right, I did already know that."

"But have you thought about it?"

"I don't know. Maybe not."

"I mean this girl you're telling me about, this Cait. Maybe I would have thought it was wrong if you really went after her."

I'm sure my mouth dropped open. I had barely mentioned Cait. Was Mother reading my mind? "What are you talking about, Mother? What makes you think I would go after her?"

"You've told me about her before, Hec. You just forgot. You told me all about getting drunk and going for a walk with her in the woods."

"So you would have thought it was wrong, if I stayed sober and took action."

"Well, whatever. But that's me thinking. That's not you. I just want you to know I don't sit in judgment."

"Are you sure?"

She laughed a little. "I do sit in judgment. So let me put it another way. A lot of people sit in judgment, but you are a grown-up and you make your own decisions."

"I guess that's right, in a sense," I told her, though I really think that free will is an illusion. In fact I know it is, in the deepest sense, as shown by Descarte. I find that comforting sometimes, and depressing at other times.

"You were having your play done," Mother said. "I remember all this like it was yesterday. You came to see me, you and Faye, right after that. The next week."

"It was a reading, just a sit-down reading," I said, and again I sank into a recollection. During the so-called "critical discussion" after the reading, one actor, a man in his thirties who had no particular talent but was otherwise reasonably intelligent, prefaced his comments with a thoughtful, sort of doleful, "This play is a piece of shit."

Todaro: He didn't!

Owen: I swear it. I'll tell you his name. Geoffrey Weppner. It was an actory thing he was doing, grabbing my attention. Something he learned in a two-bit acting class, no doubt, doing two-bit improvs in front of some two-bit acting teacher. It was a thoughtless, cruel way to soften me up for a criticism that was so unimportant I've forgotten even what it was about. But for every one of the destructive, virulent comments that came out of that discussion, Cait jumped into the fray with a strong defense of the play or me, whichever was being attacked at the moment. Tinker made one or two innocuous comments, then settled back to observe, while Cait protected my honor, well, chivalrously.

After the reading, I began to feel that peculiar confusion I would get right after my ego was thoroughly masticated by a hungry group. 'I am in love with Cait,' my inner child babbled, 'but I am up against the daunting obstacles of her love for Tinker, her engagement to him, her relative indifference to me in spite of her admiration for my work. If I am to win her, it will take *action*.'

"Life becomes a play for me when I'm overwrought, Mother," I finally said. "It didn't matter that I knew Cait was just a friend and colleague. Her romantic indifference, however real, was on a different—if you'll excuse the play-writing terminology—a different *level*. I was operating on a dramatic level, and could think only in terms of my dramatic action."

"I think a lot of people are like that, Hec."

"Maybe. Later, sitting at a small table in the cafeteria, I decided that loving Cait, like anything good in life, would require action."

"But you loved Faye, Hec."

"That was real life, though, Mother. Don't you see? Cait was a drama. Drama requires dramatic action. I, Hector, needed to take action."

"And this 'action,' what did that turn out to be?"

"I spent the rest of the afternoon holed up at the annex, drinking gin and tonic. All afternoon, all evening, to the depletion of all three trays of ice at the annex."

Yet another silence fell between us. My drinking has always worried Mother. I didn't try to downplay it in the context of this reminiscence. It was an important part of it.

"Now, Hec," she said after a moment, "let me ask you how much you drink these days."

"Not much," I said. "Not much at all. I'll have wine with dinner when Faye brings it home, and maybe..."

"How often is that?" she interrupted.

"Not even once a week."

"What else?"

"Oh, I'll drink a few beers once in a while. Not even once a month. Very rare, in fact."

"I don't mean to be nosy..."

"No, I appreciate your concern. I really do. This is something I'll always be honest with you about, Mother. I did have quite a problem and it caused me some considerable pain, or at least contributed to it."

I was enjoying this conversation. It was nice that I had made the call, and I could relax about the time, since Mother is always worried about the cost of long distance. She's been a comfort to me, and still is. This call was a comfort.

"So this blue swirling light, Hec. Maybe you were a little too drunk. Maybe this was your body telling you to ease off."

"Yeah. You know what phosphenes are, Mother?"

"No. What are phosphenes?"

"They're the colors you see in the dark."

"What colors? You see colors in the dark?"

"Yes, and so do you."

"No I don't."

"Just close your eyes and tell me what you see."

"I see nothing. Black."

"Are you really closing your eyes? Really? Mother?"

"Okay. They're closed."

"Just look. Take a second and look."

She was quiet for a few seconds, then said, "Oh, those things, you mean? Well, sure, yes. I guess everybody sees those things. What did you call them?"

"Phosphenes. And I was just thinking, maybe that's what the blue light was all about."

"Phosphenes," Mother said, obviously liking the word. "I was hurt by the theatre too," she said, "but it's still in my blood. And it's in yours too, if you want my opinion."

"Theatre isn't in my blood. I was always more interested in the play-writing than in the theatre."

"I'll make a prediction. You're young, you're in a fallow period. You're going to write a play and it's going to have a great part for me."

I didn't want to argue. Mother's feelings are near the surface in this matter. "Actually," I said, "I am working on a little something. Nothing on paper yet, but I'm in the creative mode right now." I was secretly referring to the creation I'd born through my navel; thus in a sense I wasn't lying.

"I'm not surprised," she said. "And you'll take control of it and begin to shape it when the time is right." She was referring to something I'd said years ago, about the way the creative process works.

"In this case, I think the creation is in control of me."

"Well, maybe that's good."

"Maybe so," I said. "Maybe I was wrong about taking control. Maybe that's not what art is."

"When I did Ophelia, I made myself lose control. That's why it was the best thing I ever did."

I'd heard about Ophelia all my life. Before I was born, Mother was in a production in New Haven that had been intended for Broadway, but never made the move. There was even something about the actor playing Laertes and my father's being jealous, but I never heard the details. Clearly, the part of Ophelia was Mother's moment of glory, artistically speaking. Unfortunately, the show was also the pinnacle of her career and fell far short of the expectations of all concerned.

Mother and I could relate to each other. Talking with her left me with a strangely broad and nebulous view of life, hinging on the consequential basis that for me there have been no wars, no sudden catastrophes on a large scale, only the normal course of life and death, all changes in direction taken as the results of my own decisions: that things have gone as planned; and what could be sadder than that?

After we hung up, I wandered out to my office and found Robin asleep, curled up on my swivel chair. He's almost too big for that now. Rather than wake him, I quietly examined him. I noticed his right hand had a nasty little cut near the juncture of thumb and index finger. His hands were quite dirty, too. I made a mental note to ask him about it, then left him.

The day has faded to dusk. I didn't realize it was a holiday until Faye came home and mentioned the fireworks scheduled for tonight. The big hotel on the mountain sets off a display over the golf course. I may walk over there later and watch. Fireworks on a summer night—like phosphenes, but with your eyes open.

July 11

I've met Lilace.

I've discovered who Robin is.

Mrs. Stone caught me in the yard and told me that Mr. Stone has had a gall bladder attack. She tried hard to appear dispassionate about discovering him in the bathroom, but she seemed unable to stop adding detail after detail.

"He says to me he has a backache," she began, "and he goes into the bathroom. Then he doesn't come out for a long time. That's all."

She tried to smile but her face was too red for a smile and was full of pain. I was concerned for her.

"You know, I was making asparagus. Creamed, the way we like it, so I didn't worry. I was busy. But it was a long time, and then I wondered. You know?"

"Of course," I said. We were standing in my driveway, at the cusp of our territoriality, not exactly facing each other, but angled away slightly. Mrs. Stone seemed to notice all this and stepped back onto her own lawn.

She frowned at the middle branches of the beech tree across the street. "I wish I was worried sooner," she said, and tried to smile at me. It took me a moment to understand what she meant. "Then I would knock on the bathroom door sooner. That's all."

"Well," I said, "you took good care of him, don't you worry. He's lucky to have a good wife like you."

She frowned at the gravel around my feet. "The only thing I really don't like is he was on the floor." Here she looked at me imploringly, but I knew of nothing to say. "He has his eyes closed and I think, well, the old fool is dead now." Suddenly she hacked loudly, clearing her throat. "'Get me a doctor,' he says to me, 'my back is broken.' That's all. So I get him one and now everything is okay. You know?"

"Sure. Thank goodness for all the doctors in this town."

"But then I see he is all wet with press-piration."

"I guess that's part of a gallstone attack, huh?"

"Maybe so," she said, and gazed off toward the beech tree again, suddenly lost, unsure. "No no, Mr. Owen. The press-piration is the infection. I thought he's having a heart attack." Again she hacked, quick and loud. "But this is bad enough. My bathroom floor is clean anyway. I'm always cleaning. Not much else to do."

By now her face had turned red and her eyes had grown wet. Her chest began to heave, and she was trying to speak but her voice shook more and more violently until finally, on the verge of hysterical crying, she began to laugh at herself. I felt I should reach out and embrace her, offer comfort, but she turned so quickly and hurried back into her house that I ended up just standing there gawking after her.

The Stones are both pushing eighty, or maybe past it, so every sickness is cause for concern. They have a daughter who lives in Dallas and a son in Oklahoma City. The daughter, Lilace, showed up a couple of days after the attack, but the son is a Big Man, Mrs. Stone told me, too busy, so sorry, could send some money if needed.

Lilace and I met last Tuesday when I was in my backyard edging the azalea beds, and she came out to shake a rug.

"You must be Mr. Owen," she said, walking through the gate,

right over to me.

"Yes. Hector," I said, and we shook hands. "You're Lilace. How's your dad today?"

"Still improving," she said, nodding her head. Then she looked around my yard as though in search of something else to talk about. She looks about fifty, a compact, dark-haired woman who might be mistaken for a teenager from the back. "Your yard is lovely," she said, then fixed her gaze on me. I imagined her wondering if I, a few years her junior, found her attractive (which in fact I did).

"We've been trying for months to schedule an evening together with your folks," I said, "but things keep coming up."

"Yes," she said. "You were sick yourself just recently."

"Oh, that," I said. "A little paraquat poisoning is all." Why I said that, I have no idea, except that Lilace was dazzling me with the way her eyes darted around the yard and then kept landing back on me. Now she was laughing. She got the joke! No doubt she knew that I'd flipped out, but I guessed her parents would have couched the story in words friendly to me.

"We're available any time," I told her, "if you think some company would help."

"Thanks. I'll let you know. I'm leaving in a few days, probably Saturday. I kind of doubt Dad'll be up to socializing, but who knows? It might be just the thing."

"Let me know," I said, and I gave her my best smile, I hoped. She was a good daughter, this chick who knew of paraquat, to have traveled so far, leaving behind whatever usually occupied her in Dallas.

I'm afraid I spied on Lilace that night. I was sitting in my office, a room I constructed in the three-car garage which stands separately behind our house. As I flipped through a pile of neglected correspondence, I glanced out the window and caught a glimpse of movement through a window in the Stones' house. It was Lilace in the guest bedroom. I watched her for a few seconds, noting a natural elegance in her movements as she apparently measured some distance on a wall, using a yard stick. She was holding an open book in her hand, too, marking a place in it with her thumb. The book seemed to have nothing to do with the measurement of the wall. It was as though she'd been reading and suddenly decided to consider hanging a picture somewhere in the guest bedroom. There was something wonderfully feminine about what I was seeing, this two things at once. The Stones would have such a bipartite daughter, I stupidly mused; Mr. Stone is Jewish, and Mrs. Stone is Catholic.

Lilace leaned against the wall, reading the book, the measurement apparently forgotten. Something attracted her attention, and she was gone from sight.

I'd been at my desk sorting through some aging correspondence. I held two letters from Zane Green, the earlier one proposing that I write a one-man show for him based on his father's life, his father having worked himself to death behind a deli counter in Murray Hill in support of his large brood. That Zane wanted to play his father on the stage was both a fascinating and daunting idea for me; at any rate, it left me paralyzed, creatively, so I never got very far with that project. Efforts I made to begin it only spiraled into confused speculation based on my scanty recollections of my own father, and a creeping envy toward Zane.

The second letter, which I received only six months ago, contains no mention of the one-man show. It's full of elation at his having been cast in David Ribelow's *The Carney* at the Mark Taper Forum. He promised a post card from L.A., but never sent one. I don't blame him.

There was also a letter from Nancy Nickerson, a woman I didn't have an affair with (I never had any affairs), a skilled and pretty actress I first encountered when she read a part in my play *Plowman Dig My Earth* at an audition on Theatre Row. The whole first page of her letter revisited that play, which attempted to evoke sixties-style sexual freedom in a latter day setting of disease and despair. (And this was before AIDS!) Nancy then wrote that she had become engaged to an executive at a department store. Without saying so, she seemed to be asking if I approve, or maybe if I would care to rescue her. Actually I would, I ache to, I'm on my way, you drove me wild with desire, especially when you wore the short cotton dress at the rehearsal for the reading. I'll leave Faye, who no longer touches me, and marry you, Nancy, and we'll return to a life in the theatre together. Yikes!

Other unanswered letters, half a dozen or so of them, threatened me in the sense that I'm terrified of being reached, touched in any way by those people from my past; I barely glanced at the envelopes. Then I took the whole bunch of them, Zane, Nancy, everything, and tossed them in the wastebasket.

Why am I terrified of being reached? I would have to explain my retreat, my apparent failure. How would I explain that my intention was to hold my life in abeyance. Indefinitely, yes, in the face of dysfunction that precluded even such obvious solutions as divorce. It would sound absurd to my old friends and colleagues, who pursue careers with fervor. And now my homunculus, who at least brings the absurdity out into the open for me, would be even harder to explain.

This garage was built right on the property line next to the Stones' lot; the window of my office faces their house. I caught a glimpse of Lilace again, and I quickly turned off my light so I could spy on her. Robin was not completely off the mark, I admit, when he called me a voyeur. I would never go creeping around the bushes looking for an opportunity, but I would never pass one up if it presented itself, either.

The window was wide open, the shades pulled up. She was moving around the room—no yardstick or book now—picking up objects, clothing, something, moving things from one place to another. Sometimes she would disappear for a moment, then return. I watched steadily, not taking my eyes off the window for a second even when she wasn't in view. Yes, I would have enjoyed immensely watching her undress, but apparently she did that elsewhere, because she was gone for a while and then re-entered the room in a nightgown.

The door to my office opened suddenly. I jumped, almost fell out of my chair. In the guilty instant that followed, I assumed the intruder was Faye, but it was Robin. I switched on my desk lamp as he came into the room and shut the door behind him.

"Whatcha doin'?" he said. "You look like your mother just caught you pounding your pud."

"I was just in a deep reverie," I said. "I'm not used to being interrupted in my office."

He wasn't interested, and I was relieved. He wasn't even listening to me, but was reading the suicide instructions on my wall (moving his lips as he read, I noticed).

"Hey," he said, grinning. "This is good. This is funny."

On the wall, off to the side of my desk, I have a neatly printed sign framed and hung. With black Helvetica letters on a white board, it has an official look to it. (I had it hand-lettered professionally downtown.) It reads:

TO COMMIT SUICIDE
1. Close all windows tightly.

2. Close all *outside* doors.

3. Make sure door from office to garage is *open*.

4. Start engine of at least one car. (Both cars should be started for maximum efficiency.)

5. Take position at desk, sitting comfortably if desired.

6. Take liter of Jim Beam from lower right-hand desk drawer.

7. Sip from bottle as desired.

8. Optional: write note to survivors.

This sign is just a joke I made up on a whim, although Faye has told me that it wouldn't be at all funny to some of her friends.

Nor mine, come to think of it. Zane Green, who played the lead in my play at the Peterborough Players in New Hampshire, told me he once tried to *back* his car off a cliff. There was a concrete and steel guardrail and the drop from the cliff was only about eight feet, Zane admitted, so all he did was put some bad dents in the rear of his car. Although that struck me as an example of someone trying to *fail* at his suicide, other things Zane said and did convinced me he was capable of killing himself. For one thing, he was a heavy drinker back then. "You can certainly drink yourself to death if you forbear on all other methods," I told him when we were both drunk. For another, Zane remains one of the most brilliant actors I've ever known, having the interesting ability to appear physically big in one role, then physically small in another role—this on stage, no camera tricks. Not that his brilliance derives solely from that one chop. My point is, sometimes extreme, artistic talent grates against the survival instinct enough to pulverize it.

Zane and I talked about suicide and talent for quite a while one morning up in New Hampshire. That was the day I noted that there are two kinds of people—those whose last resort is suicide, and those who have no last resort. Among the latter kind I count myself. That's why the sign in my office is a joke.

The liter of Jim Beam is there in the drawer, however, its paper tax stamp untorn.

"You've changed clothes," I said to Robin. He had on a new outfit of blue jeans and a black T-shirt emblazoned with an action figure.

"Got 'em off a clothesline," he said.

"Where?"

"About two blocks from here. Not a bad fit."

"You did this today?"

"Tonight. I move around pretty well in the dark. Gotta watch out for dogs and cats, though. No telling what they might think I am. Edible, you know what I mean? A moving rawhide toy."

He peered into my wastebasket, riffled nonchalantly through the letters without reading anything, then sat on the floor. His eyes seemed to have cleared somewhat, the whites no longer yellowish. His elbows were still bony, but the bones didn't seem to be poking through the skin as before. His bare feet looked almost soft.

"You look better," I said.

"It helps when you can eat, sleep, clean up, use a bathroom. Basics, Hector. Could you get some more of that Brie, by the way?"

"I accused Faye of eating that all up. It was you."

"And why don't you get some cantaloupes. And cut it up small so I can manage it. I crave cantaloupe."

"Yeah. Okay. Next time I go to the store."

"What are you staring at? I look that good?"

"I'm not staring."

"Looking at me with a bemused smile, then."

I was staring because he looked different. And he acted differently, too. I was trying to put my finger on what it was—more than just a cleanup and a slightly healthier glow. It seemed that his presence was larger, more imposing. I felt as though in some way he was crowding me.

"Do you like this kiddie shirt?" he said, pushing his chin down into his chest and pulling the action figure picture out into his view. "I think I look kind of cute in it. And I've got on briefs with pictures of cowboys on the front."

Suddenly I identified it. There was a lack of manliness in the homunculus, and for some odd reason, that was annoying me. I hadn't thought of it before, hadn't demanded or required that Robin be manly, but until now he had seemed manly in his own little way. I was too tired to deal with boyishness, too crotchety to watch out for tender feelings.

"Want to see a pretty woman in her nightgown?" I said. He looked up at me, surprised.

"Pictures or the real thing?"

"The real thing," I said.

"Okay."

"Just okay? Not *yeah yeah yeah*?"

"Hey, butt, what am I supposed to do, jump up and down?" He was taking his time getting to his feet. "Because jump up and down is what I'd have to do to reach a woman. I'm two feet tall, you dumb asshole."

"You want to see her?"

"I said yes. Unless we have to go to a lot of trouble."

I switched off the lamp. "Out the window," I said, and Robin crawled up into my lap in order to see over the sill. "In the window next door," I said.

"I see her. That's what's-her-name, Lilace. Too old for me anyway."

"But cute," I said, watching Lilace trying to get something out of her eye.

"Nice nightgown. Looks expensive. Nieman Marcus, I bet. Isn't she from Dallas?"

"Nice nightgown? You're more interested in the nightgown than in what's *in* the nightgown?"

Robin slipped down from my lap and scuttled off into a dark corner. I kept watching Lilace. Now she was scratching her elbow. Now she was gone. Now the overhead light in her room went off, but there was still light, must have been a table lamp.

I heard Robin pull open a file drawer; I switched on the lamp. He was pulling out a fat manila folder.

"'Notes and Midnight Essays,'" he read, and looked at me questioningly.

"Just thoughts about life, mostly, going all the way back to school days. Not worth looking at."

But he opened it and flipped through a few pages. "'The best gift a father can give his son is to butt out from the very beginning.'"

"I wrote that about ten years ago," I said. "My father did that, and I was trying to make it a positive thing at that time. There was no outside male force shaping my life, ever. There was my mother, a female force, but not the other side. I can't even imagine what it would have felt like."

Robin sniffed, shoved the file back into the drawer (in the wrong place), and said "Instead of raising azaleas, you'd want to shoot guns at animals now, work on car engines."

"I guess," I said. "And climb corporate ladders? Play on the team?"

"Piss on the campfire in concert with the other guys?"

"Yeah, I don't know; I have no feeling for any of that. I don't know male power, and other males recognize this instinctively the moment they meet me."

"Hector! What's this!" Robin was looking at a Bloomingdale's lingerie catalog I'd saved.

"That's a collector's item," I said. "Or it was supposed to become one when it was issued about fifteen or twenty years ago."

"Can I have it?"

"I guess." He sat cross-legged and started perusing the sexy photos. "Since they can tell I'm not playing the male game, men don't need to assert their own power over me, thus I see a side of them that other men don't see."

"Good," Robin mumbled, his eyes bugged at a photo. "You can use that to your advantage."

A lump formed in my throat, emotional upwelling because, I suddenly realized, I was opening up to Robin, and he was being receptive, a good friend. We were talking, for the first time, like a couple of pals. It took me a moment to find my voice again.

"Well, no," I said, "I have to disagree. It's not a revelation that gives me any advantage over other men. But it gives me a certain kind of insight. Over the years, I've seen that men block off their feminine sides—everybody knows that—in defense against women, of all people. Growing up, men were made to fear women."

"Get over it, Hec. Fear? Like afraid to ask them out on a date?"

"Yeah. Think about it. Why should that be scary? But it is. It's a rite of passage, getting your first date. Terrifying. Why? I'll tell you why. It's a taught response.We were taught to fear women. But now, these days, post-sixties, post-seventies, post-eighties, something's changed. The scary part of women has been systematically chipped away, to a large extent, over the past few decades. Women are more human, more humane towards men."

"Really?" Robin said, but he seemed engrossed in the catalog he was perusing.

"Take Faye, for instance," I said, and instantly everything in the room changed. Robin changed, the air changed, I changed. Would I really talk about Faye? Betray her to a buddy? My little buddy was all ears, I could tell, trying so obviously to appear nonchalant and uninterested.

"This woman is completely nude!" he said.

"That was a very artsy catalog." I glanced back out the window, letting Robin believe I would allow the subject of Faye to drop.

"So anyway..." he said. My my. Apparently he was listening after all.

"Women want to be in the army now. In military schools."

"Oh, that stuff."

"Manhood can no longer be defined in terms of doing unpleasant things with a stiff upper lip. Women now do these things too, and they don't hold it against men; on the contrary, they're still fighting to get to do more of these things, asking only that men be kind and let women define themselves. This independent attitude leaves men with little reason to hide their feminine sides, though they still do, of course, out of a tradition going back centuries. There's a certain uneasiness, though, in maintaining huge, cumbersome defenses against—very little."

Robin had stuffed the catalog into the front of the file drawer by this time. "I'll keep this right here," he said.

"Fine. You remind me of a squirrel burying a nut you're going to forget about inside of twenty minutes."

He said, "So Faye is joining the Army?"

I laughed. "No. I just mean, I didn't need to be afraid of her. Not that I was, really. But I don't think I ever would have had the courage to ask her out, except..."

"Yeah? Except what?"

"What I did have the courage to do was preemptively take her away from Karl Furst."

"And Karl Furst would be...?"

"Yikes, Robin. This is an epiphany for me. Maybe I am a man after all. I mean, a regular man, who competes with other men for women."

"But more sneaky, you mean?"

"Yeah. I guess that's right."

"Yeah," Robin said, "damn right that's right. So, knowing all of this, you're the man for the new millennium, I guess."

"What do you think?"

"Maybe so, except you're completely dysfunctional with women!" He started laughing, and I thought it made his face ugly, and I couldn't laugh with him, didn't even try.

"Hey, sorry," he said. "I know it hasn't been easy for you. You can talk to me any time you want to."

"Thanks," I said, feeling spent.

"How about turning the light off," Robin said. I turned it off and checked the view into Lilace's window across the way. She was out of sight still. I leaned back in my chair, let my head fall back, stared at the darkness clinging to the ceiling. This darkness was like tar, sticky and viscous, but okay as long as it didn't drip down onto me.

Robin cleared his throat softly and said in a husky voice, almost a whisper, "You don't have to love women in general to be normal, Hec. Just sort of like them okay and want to screw them."

I could just make out Robin's breathing, and heard him shift his position on the floor, bumping the filing cabinet softly.

"You know who I really am, don't you?" Robin said.

"Of course." I continued staring straight up, preferring to let Robin's voice remain disembodied.

"But I mean, you know, 'Robin,'" he said. A moment later he said quietly, "Robin. I'm *Robin*."

A chill ran down my spine, and then my eyes went out of focus. "My god," I muttered, sitting erect now. Until this moment, the name Robin had meant nothing to me, but now I remembered.

"I knew you didn't realize who I was," he said.

"Robin? Is it really you?"

"Squeak squeak," he said. "Yep, it is me."

I hadn't thought of Robin in forty years. The name had long since lost any special significance. I wouldn't turn on the light, but I turned to face the direction of his voice. "Squeak squeak, that's good," I said, "that's funny." Robin, when he'd been my favorite toy, did squeak when you squeezed him.

"Before we go any further," he said, "I want to tell you I appreciated your digging me back out of the garbage can."

"Oh, right. Mother threw you away that time because you were so worn out."

"'Preciated you saving my butt."

"Robin. *Robin*. I can't believe I didn't make the connection. It's you, isn't it?"

"Same soul, you might say. The toy is long gone, but the soul stayed with you. Inside."

"Whoa!"

"Pretty cramped and weird in there, Hec."

"I'm sure it was."

He sucked in a breath as though about to say something, then expelled it slowly.

"What?" I prompted him.

"Was there anyone besides me after I was gone?"

He shifted so that his face caught a dim shaft of light from the window. I could barely make out his features, but now I saw the face of Robin—my little Robin, my beloved doll of forty years ago, when I was a toddler, cloth and rubber image of an elfin woodsman. I stared at him, holding the perfect image on my retinas, though it tried to transmogrify in the dim light. Robin. He'd said his name first when I was locking him into the coal bin in the basement, but it hadn't registered.

"I asked you a question," he said. "Was there anyone else after me?"

He asked with undisguised jealousy, and I felt, for a moment, a menace from him and some guilt as I thought of Candace and the consuming passion I'd known with her.

"There must have been," Robin said, and he leaned back into the darkness. "You wouldn't be sitting there gaping like a guilty dog."

"No," I said. "I was thinking of Candace, but she was a grown-up lover. There really was nothing, no one after you."

I thought I heard him snort in disbelief, and I waited for him to argue with me, but he said nothing. "What's the matter, don't you believe me?"

"I believe that Candace was your next love after me. But I'm not sure she was really a grown-up love. I think you might have loved her with your whole being, the way you loved me. In which case, why am I here instead of her? Why isn't she the one getting locked into basements and hidden from the wify wife all day?"

"Well," I said, "I think you've answered your own question. It's you. It's always been you." I actually smiled at this conclusion.

There was a sound, distant, like boxcars coupling, or maybe it was a clap of thunder somewhere in the mountains, which had bounced from cove to slope until its final generation reached Asheville like a whisper.

"There's a kind of craziness," I said, "that happens when you first fall in love. As in madness, insanity. I think an individual can only experience it once, with one person. Later, we may have other opportunities to be in love, but those are different. Those are not insanity. For me, the insanity was with Candace. When we fell in love, it opened a big hole in my soul, if you will, and let out all the..." But I couldn't say what it had let out. I sat silently thinking about the hurt I'd felt growing up without my father. I remembered the painful insecurities, the awkward rate of growth that left me physically immature when most boys were beginning to grow beards, the complete absence of sexual mentoring—I learned about sex from reading girlie magazines and books and listening to my fellow ignoramuses. So it was mostly hurt that came flowing out of the hole in my soul, and Candace came flowing in to fill the emptiness. The infusion of balm where there had been pain was so extreme that I couldn't believe it, really. That was where the jealousy and other paranoia originated: it was just too good to be true, so ultimately, inevitably, I destroyed it.

It was clear I was lost in thought. Robin said, "Aren't you glad I've finally made it back to you?"

"I don't know," I answered. "I really don't know."

We were still and silent for a long time, an hour or more during which the light went out in Lilace's room and I stared into the patch of cloudy, town-lit orange sky visible through the canopy of trees. Finally I heard Robin stir, knock against the wastebasket. "I'm nodding off," he said. "I better get out of here." I heard him stand up and pad across the room to the door, which was now faintly illuminated by fragments of light floating in through the window. I saw him in silhouette as he stretched on tiptoe to reach the doorknob.

"Want me to get it for you?" I asked.

But he opened it himself.

"Where you going?"

"Maybe I'll roam the neighborhood a little," he said. "See if that mother's hung out any more kiddie clothes."

"Yeah, well, be careful," I said. I wasn't really worried about him. Robin, when he wanted to be, was virtually indestructible, if I remembered correctly. Of course, he'd changed a lot since I was four years old.

Robin slipped out the door, leaving it ajar so that I had to get up and close it. I went to my desk and tried to read for a while, but kept thinking about Robin, even considered going out to try and find him. I ended up staring into space instead. I began to nod off in my chair about one o'clock, but I couldn't bear the thought of lying down in bed next to Faye. I couldn't bear another day of being unable to touch, to connect with another prisoner of the universe in order to make our lonely cells larger by one.

I moved from the desk to the easy chair, resigned to sleeping there, if anywhere. Straining to keep my heavy eyelids open, I read the suicide instructions posted on the wall, silently editing certain small awkwardnesses in its structure. '5. Take position at desk, sitting comfortably if desired.' should read: '5. Take comfortable position at desk.' Also the parenthetical expression in step 4, (Both cars should be started for maximum efficiency) is unnecessary.

The office door opened. I swung around and saw Lilace standing there in the doorway—actually it was the doorway into the bedroom of my childhood, complete with the model airplanes on a small shelf against the cowboys-and-Indians wallpaper.

"You wanted to see me naked," she said, and I couldn't tell if she was offering or accusing.

"Lilace," I said. I was surprised, but my voice sounded flat, expressionless, like hers had.

"How about just my private parts?" she said. She reached down to the hem of her skirt, which came just below her knees. Taking it in her hands, she first looked up at me and smiled like a bureaucrat making me wait while the computer brings up my file. She pulled the skirt up, the hem up to her chin, fully revealing café au lait panties (a little color there, not black and white!) She wore no hose, just socks and sneakers. I felt my penis harden and strain against my shorts. I watched her, speechless, as she awkwardly held the skirt up around her armpits by pressing her elbows into her waist.

"Here," she said. Then breathlessly, again, "Here, here..." as she slipped her hands inside the elastic and worked the panties down her thighs almost to her knees. Breathlessly, again, "Can you see?" She executed a sort of plié, tilting her sex so I got a better view. I could see glistening wetness there, and a narrow slit of pink in the soft black nest of pubic hair. "Can you see it?"

I wanted to say yes, but I couldn't speak. I had an orgasm. I tried to stop it in the instant of my waking, but by the time I opened my eyes, it was too late.

"Shit," I muttered. I would have to go into the house to clean myself up, and I knew that once I'd done that, I would get into my pajamas and crawl into the comfortable bed beside Faye.

Robin disappeared for a few days. Not having him around was in some ways a pleasure, since he wasn't interrupting me in my reading, causing food shortages I had to explain, or leaving odd little messes around the house. Faye said she assumed I was "going through some changes." (Before, I would never leave odd little messes around the house, for example.) Robin's absence allowed me to act like my old self. But I missed him, too, and worried about what was happening to him.

Mr. Stone was feeling much better, and Lilace arranged a little evening at the Stones' for us. It was on that morning that I heard the phone ringing as I returned from my usual walk to the convenience store for coffee and the paper.

I hurried inside and answered. It was Faye, trying unsuccessfully to sound calm.

"Somebody broke in and vandalized the boutique," she told me.

"Oh god," I said. "What's the damage like?"

"Well, not too bad," she said. "The police are here."

"Are you all right?" I waited and there was no answer for some time. I imagined her unable to speak, holding back from crying.

"Sorry," she said finally. "What did you say? I was distracted. The police were asking me something."

"I guess you're okay?"

"Not really. It's got me upset. I want to come home and cry."

"Well, come on home. I'll put on some tea."

"Make it coffee."

"When?"

"I don't think they're going to take long, the police, I mean. I'm closing up when they leave. Inside an hour."

She was home slightly over an hour later, and we had a cup of coffee together. It was almost time for lunch, but I'd neglected to cook anything.

Faye was sitting on the couch in the living room. "It was such a feeling of being violated," she said.

"You saw it when you first walked in?"

"Oh, I saw it through the window before I got the key in the door. A whole rack was turned over right up front. I had to push it out of the way to get the door open."

"Was stuff taken, or was it just vandalism?"

"Stuff was taken," she said. "Mostly underwear, thank god. It's high markup and they didn't take anything expensive anyway." She stood up. "I guess I ought to go back and straighten things up. Maybe I ought to open up this afternoon."

"Can you do that? Straighten up? I mean, don't the police want to keep the crime scene intact?"

She snorted. "They couldn't care less. They couldn't even figure out how the burglar got in. I think they suspected it was an inside job, something for insurance or something. But nothing much was gone, and the damage isn't going to cost much of anything. Then when I told them there are no employees, they looked at each other like a couple of perches and shrugged their shoulders."

"A couple of perches, huh? I like that. So what else was there? Just racks turned over?"

"Racks turned over," she said, disappearing toward the kitchen with her empty cup, "all the plugs along the baseboard were pulled out."

"What do you mean?"

She came back in the room with fresh coffee. "I had the floor fan plugged in, the coffee maker, the cash register, my boom box, stuff like that. Everything was unplugged. Not taken, just unplugged."

"What about your video display?"

"They didn't touch that. It's plugged in up above the counter. For some reason they only pulled the baseboard plugs."

"Sounds like they panicked for some reason and left before they finished. Any more coffee in the pot?"

"Some."

I left the room not really for need of coffee but in order to think, to let my suspicions ripen. When I came back with my freshened cup, I said, "And they don't know how he got in?"

"They *the*orized," she gave me a big smirk, "that it was an animal. They found the little grate off, the one at the back of the store they put in for ventilation. A cat could get through there, or a raccoon or something. This was after they'd already found all the plugs unplugged. I had to point out that animals don't normally go around systematically unplugging things."

"Well," I said, convinced I knew what had happened, "sounds like a gremlin to me." Mr. Robin Gremlin.

Faye laughed. "I think that's what it was." Then she sobered and put her hands on her knees. "It leaves you with a kind of sick feeling. Yuck, you know?"

We fried some bacon and eggs, comfort food, for lunch, and she went back to the store and put in an afternoon.

That night, after Faye was asleep, I came into the house for a snack. I'd been reading in my office. Robin was rummaging through the refrigerator, inside it, holding the anchovy stuffed olives in one hand. He heard me behind him, didn't bother to climb out and look at me.

"Want an olive?"

"Please don't eat all of those," I said.

"There's nothing else good in here."

"There's tons of food in there."

"It all has to be cooked. Don't we have any cold cuts?"

I opened the door all the way and saw him on all fours on the top shelf. The way the interior light hit his face made him look unreal, shiny as the lacquered face of a puppet. He climbed down, grabbing a piece of cheddar on the way. I closed the refrigerator door and watched him as he climbed into a chair at the breakfast table. He had changed, continued to evolve. I watched him struggle to open the olives. I watched his face, especially, as he pursed his lips, wrinkled his nose, got frustrated and stopped, sighed, started again.

"Nobody ever gives me any help," he grumbled. He crossed his legs hanging them over the edge of the chair, wrapped his ankles around each other.

"I don't mean this to sound mean," I said, "but you're getting, I don't know, on my nerves or something." He looked at me, but then returned to the task of opening the jar. "I think I have mixed feelings about you."

He looked at me and grinned broadly. "No shit," he said, and the jar lid finally gave. "There!" he said. "Want one?" I did take one.

I chewed. We both chewed. I glanced at him and he was looking at me with a half grin.

"What," I said.

He took another olive, his hand so small he could reach all the way into the jar and fish the olive out. I winced, sure he never washed his hands. He popped the olive into his mouth, chewed it.

"What was this... this *feeling* that hit you," Robin said, "about... ummm, maybe halfway back in your life?"

Surprised by the question, I recovered easily, calculated half my age, early twenties, wasn't sure what he was asking about. "A feeling that hit me?" I said. "Not sure what you mean, but I'm curious. How would you describe it?"

"I don't know," he said. "It's hard to explain."

"I'll bet," I said.

"Why do you say it like that?" He was defensive now.

"I mean I'll bet it's hard to explain since *you* are hard to explain. Hell, Robin..."

"I wasn't having *thoughts*, okay? But I remember the feelings, every one of them, years of them. All the years of them. I can put them right in order. It's just that there aren't words for it because they're feelings, not words. You're stupid," he said, and turned his hurt face away from me.

"Don't be so sensitive," I said. "About halfway back? Like in my twenties or something?"

"Yes," he said, still pouting.

"Well, you have to give me some kind of clue. Feelings have names, you know." I was hooked and wasn't about to let go of it now, whatever he was getting at.

"Okay," he said, game all of a sudden. "There was a thrill, definitely. A surge of self esteem, too."

I thought for a minute. "College," I said. "I'm a senior in college, I've written a one-act play, *365 Ways to Prepare Capybara*. The playwriting professor loves it. He's producing it in our so-called Laboratory Theatre, a nice little facility in the basement of the Drama Building. The other senior playwriting majors are full of envy."

"This is it," Robin said, nodding. "Everything was kind of strange. What happened?"

"We use student actors, of course. The cute and chubby little sophomore who's playing the ingenue gives me my first beejay."

"I knew it!"

"I'm asked to write an article for the student newsletter. The whole department seems to have gained new respect for me. The entire final semester is an uplifting experience. I feel validated. I'll be going to New York with a production credit already under my belt."

"This is what I was talking about," Robin said. "Bull's-eye. Let's go outside so we can talk before what's 'er name wakes up."

He jumped down to the floor and scurried out toward the back-yard. I noted his little put-down of Faye, felt a momentary pang of defensiveness, then put the olives away and followed him.

I headed for the office, didn't see him but suddenly heard him behind me. "This was going on for months," he said. He'd been standing beside the back steps, in shadow.

I continued slowly out toward the back of the yard, consider-ing the ease with which Robin was seducing me into this pleasant reminiscence. I spoke softly as he hurried to keep up with me. "I graduate, spend the summer in Bridgeport working as a janitor to save up some travel money, then on September first, 1976, I take the train down to the city. I find a job as an order clerk at an en-cyclopedia-publishing firm. I get a fourth floor walkup apartment, one room, on the Lower East Side. First couple of weeks there, looking out my window I see people on the street brandishing guns, people setting cars on fire, unconscious people on the side-walks, and once, a man standing at the curb with his fly unzipped, jerking off."

Robin was nodding his head. "It felt like excitement with just a little fear, but mostly... I don't know, curiosity or something."

"I think so," I said. I was enjoying reliving the adventure, being reminded that I was once so alive. "I can walk to Katz's Delicatessen. I love to eat there, the knishes, the corned beef, hot dogs, knockwursts, big bottles of Knickerbocker, and I'm proud of becoming desensitized to the sight of bums and derelicts. I aban-don—wisely, I think—my three-act indictment of small town life in New England, working title *The Harkersville Hysterical Soci-ety*, which is half-written by now. I start a new piece, labor every night after work and every weekend until it's finished. It's a long one-act called "Bux," about a capitalist who falls in love with a hippy girl. This is 1976, remember."

"No, I don't remember, but I know you were full of confidence."

"Sure. I believed in my work. Didn't have enough sense or
experience to do otherwise."

"There was this huge hope, sort of *yippee*. It lasted a while.
Stuff had to be happening."

"Right. You must remember the general excitement, expectation... Let's see, I live near the Bowery, where several
off-off-Broadway theatres have made homes for themselves in
rotting old storefronts. I begin finding these places and walking in
through the front door. I always hold my script in my hand. It takes
less than a week to get someone to read the script. A man named
Harry Marx, who runs a little grant siphon called The Bowery Arts
Theatre, reads "Bux" and a week later he calls me and arranges to
meet me at Phebe's, a bar on the Bowery where off-off-theatricals
hang out. The place is crowded, and the walls are covered with
show bills for all the current off-off-Broadway plays. It's Saturday afternoon. We sit on stools at the bar. Harry has the script
with him; the brown envelope's gone, the cover page is dogeared.
He's fingering the edges of the pages, nervous, dragging the thing
through the wet rings left by our beer glasses on the bar. I sit there
wincing because I lack the sophistication to realize that a play always gets destroyed once it's given over to a theatre."

Robin grabbed my pants leg to stop me from pacing. We were
near the remnants of an ancient hedge that I imagine once extended across the back line of my property.

"That sounds kind of cynical," Robin said, "that a theatre *always* destroys a play."

I laughed. "I mean, the script, the paper it's written on, you
know. 'Nice writing,' Harry says. This is after we've tried for
some small talk. He seems amazed at how young I am. He's prob-

ably in his thirties. 'I'm not sure if it's right for BAT,' he says, 'but I mean I'm really *not sure*.'"

"I don't get it, Hec. Why did he say that? In that tone of voice?"

"He gazes so deeply into my eyes I have to look away and sip my beer. Eye contact too long, you know what I mean? 'It's not what I usually like,' he says. I go 'What do you usually like?' 'Blond playwrights,' he says. I look at him and he's staring into the bottom of his beer mug."

I sat in an Adirondack chair. Robin leaned against the front chair leg.

"Your hair is brown," he said.

"I know, but in New York that's still blond. Make no mistake, he was referring to me and I knew it."

Robin suddenly skipped off across the yard, like a little girl wanting to be chased. He disappeared in the shadow of the garage. It looked like he tried to climb into one of the other Adirondacks arranged against the wall there, but then I couldn't see him in the shadows. Shortly he reappeared and approached me with a tentative, maundering air. He finally leaned against the chair leg again.

"This was a sort of sick feeling," he said, his voice husky, almost a whisper. "Something new."

"Not without its own kind of excitement..." I suggested.

"Just some kind of flattery," Robin said, and suddenly he surprised me by touching my shin, stroking it sympathetically. "You didn't feel attracted to him, I don't think. There was nothing I can connect to anything like that. You felt kind of sorry for him, I think."

"You don't know?"

"They're just feelings. I didn't have the benefit of the senses and intellect. And besides, it was a long time ago."

"Well, you're right anyway," I said. "I tried to finesse it. I wouldn't lead him on—was very careful not to. But then and there, on the spot, I invented a trick I used throughout my career, and it worked. The trick is simply to treat a person kindly, with respect, and professionally. I gently avoided his remark and went on with a discussion of the script. If he had any fantasies about me, or what reward I might be considering for later, it was not on my account. He produced the play the following summer, just a few performances in a broiling box of a theatre. Very small audiences. Marilyn Stasio, who reviewed theatre for *Cue Magazine*, gave me a dismal review—hurt my feelings, but I was young and rebounded quickly. I fell in love with the actress who played Catherine, the sexually confused heroine bent on complete honesty with all her lovers."

"You fell in love with her?"

"You don't remember anything in that department?" I laughed. Robin was now sitting on the grass at my feet. "I've fallen in love with many, many women," I told him. "There have been times I've fallen in love with women whose names I never knew."

We heard a dog barking somewhere a few houses down. Robin stood, using my pant leg to pull himself up.

"Let's go back inside," he said. "I'm hungry."

To make him feel better, I picked him up and carried him. He relaxed into my arms like a baby, even snuggled up to my chest. Once in the kitchen, though, he was out of my grasp, onto the floor quick as a cat, and had the refrigerator door open. He gave the door a kick to swing it out wide, and then climbed onto the bottom shelf.

"Look, Robin," I said, "you can't stay here forever, you know."

He turned right back to glare at me. "Why not?"

Suddenly it was as though I was contemplating not my own sanity, but something like murder. Thinking quickly, I told myself that making the homunculus go away—assuming I could—was hardly tantamount to murder, and I forced aside the whole idea and the sickly feeling of guilt. "Oh man," I said, "I don't know."

He grabbed a block of Swiss cheese that had been carelessly wrapped in plastic, slid back out of the refrigerator, leaving the door for me to close.

"Slice this for me in little chunks," he said, holding the cheese up toward me. "*Please*," he said, and gave me a toothy little fake smile. I took the cheese and found a knife.

"And I don't want any of the dried-out part," he said.

"It's dried out because *somebody* didn't wrap it up correctly," I said.

"Don't be mean," he cooed at me.

I sliced the cheese into neat little postage stamps, carefully trimming the toughened areas where the air had reached it. Robin climbed onto the kitchen table via a chair, sat on it with his legs crossed under him. "Why did you say that?" he asked. "Am I in the way or something? Don't you like me any more?"

"You're effeminate," I said. I didn't mean it as an answer to his questions, but as the resolution of my own wondering. He'd been annoying the hell out of me and that was why.

"What?" he said.

"You're getting really, really effeminate," I said, and I knelt beside the table and scrutinized him.

"Just remember," he said, "it doesn't make you a homo. They're two different things."

I thought back, trying to recall any early evidence of his effeminacy, but all I could remember was how nasty a little fellow he had been. A nasty *fellow*, though, through and through.

"I'll tell you what *I've* noticed," he said.

"What's that?"

"I'm getting bigger."

"That's true," I said. "Why don't you get off the table now?"

Ignoring that, he said, "Funny it would bother you if I'm a little smoother, a little more refined now."

"I didn't say you were any more refined."

He nibbled at a postage stamp, imitating a mouse. I stared at him, my mind suddenly wandering to cartoon mice, to my childhood, to a summer when I was twelve.

I lay on a pallet in the living room late at night. I was there to make room in the house for company, relatives vacationing. It was a treat to sleep on the floor, under the air conditioner, so cool, hearing the motor humming me to sleep. I thought about Karen O'Connor, the prettiest girl in my school, and it didn't matter, as I repositioned my pillow comfortably beside me like a spouse, that she'd never spoken to me or even noticed me. I gently, softly slipped my hand around Karen O'Connor's waist and leaned up on my elbow to face her. We gazed into each others' eyes, then closed our eyes and I kissed her gently on the lips. Everything was slow, gentle, soft, tender. That's the way love was. Love was not a threat.

We kissed and kissed and I rolled on top of her, the way I knew it was done, and wrapped my arms tight around her. I reached beneath her and caressed the small of her back, tentatively letting my hand drift to her buttocks. She didn't stop me.

I heard stirring in another room and a light went on down the hall. Karen O'Connor was instantly just my pillow again, so accommodating, my confederate a hundred percent. She would never have betrayed me, because we were in love.

"Man, you look like you've gone catatonic," Robin said.

"Yeah," I said, and turned to check the refrigerator door, which was not completely closed. "Funny, Faye said something sort of like that to me the other day."

July 24

Yesterday was Sunday. I had a couple of beers. I believe it was the first time I've imbibed since my birthing pains. Our two Adirondack chairs are placed up against the garage wall to give a view of the azaleas. I had my beers about two o'clock while the chairs were still in the shadow of the garage. It was a hot, humid day, and the house, though cool, felt oppressive. Faye, however, had spent all day in the living room studying Sears, Spiegel, and Clifford & Wills catalogs. In deference to the heat, she was clad in bra and panties, black, as has become her wont.

Black undies. Why have I noticed? What's the significance? She doesn't seem to think she's a teenager. Maybe there is no significance. Maybe they came from her boutique, items that weren't moving. Maybe free samples from a salesman. I could ask her, but I haven't, and won't, because I can imagine, if I care to, and don't need to know.

I was enjoying the buzz off the second beer when she came around the garage, now in baggy white shorts and a faded red cotton shirt. She sat.

"Well well. Good morning," I said.

"Hot."

"Beer in the refrigerator."

"Staring into space?"

"Yep."

"Beer." She hoisted herself out of the chair and disappeared;

I heard the back door clatter and then I heard it again. She came back bearing a beer for herself. Nothing for me.

Again, why did I notice? I didn't actually expect her to bring me a fresh beer, did I? I didn't particularly care, did I? Notice Faye. Why?

"I heard what you said," she told the azaleas, then sipped at her beer. "At the mall. That you're cracked."

"No kidding. You heard? You didn't act like it."

"What am I supposed to do about it?" She tried to get comfortable in the chair, sipped again, then again. This was the way she drank beer, sip sip sip, sloshing away all the carbonation before she half finished the bottle.

"Nothing, I guess. You'd be crazy to do anything. End up crazy like me."

"Why?" Sip.

"Transfer my pain to you."

"You're in pain?"

"No. It's just an analogy. If it was pain I was feeling, pain would transfer to you."

"But it's cracked you're feeling, so I'd go crazy too?"

"I don't know."

"What kind of cracked?"

I was afraid to answer. I said, "I don't know."

"Not afraid you're going to die or something?"

"Not this time."

She sipped her beer. It had to have been flat by now, barely a third consumed. I thought of the convenience store where I got the beer. I thought of the morning clerk at the convenience store, a man about my age. I saw him almost every weekday morning, yet had never had a conversation with him. I had isolated myself from almost everybody, everything. Faye would not have sex with me. Why should she? She was not the one who'd changed, who'd given birth, who'd gone off the deep end. I was lucky she was talking with me. And I was suddenly very afraid she would stop even that.

Faye pulled herself out of the chair again, started back toward the house.

"Where you going?"

She hunched her shoulders, sipped as she walked.

I said across the distance, before she could round the corner of the garage, "Wait." She stopped, turned and looked at me. "I've never even talked to the guy at the convenience store. I see him every morning."

She held her beer bottle up at eye level and looked at it, swirled the beer that was left in it. "You have no connection with the outside world," she said. "I've noticed that. When we moved down here, you cut everything off."

"I talk to the Stones all the time," I argued, hoping she wouldn't walk away.

"Pretty hard to avoid that."

"Lilace is nice."

Finally Faye returned and sat in her chair. Sip sip. I wanted to attack her about the way she drank her beer, destroying it from the outset. But I didn't want to risk sending her scurrying again. We hadn't talked in months. Years, actually.

Sip. Sip sip. "She sure is staying a long time," Faye said.

"Yes. Seems to be a good daughter."

"You can have her."

"Thanks."

"What else?"

I looked at her and saw her foot wagging. I resented having to work hard to have a conversation with my own *covivant*. So I leapfrogged the conversation; I said "Why'd you get pregnant in the first place?"

Sip sip. Stall. Think. Then she laughed. Sip sip. "You don't even connect with Mother and Daddy when we go out there. You're completely cut off. How am I supposed to talk to you?"

"You mean because I put on a façade with them?"

"Mr. Nice Guy."

"Right, exactly," I said.

"What do you want, Hec? A beejay?"

"That's not an offer, right?"

"Right."

"We're supposed to go out there this Christmas, aren't we? To your parents."

"Probably."

"You want me to try and connect with them?"

She sighed deeply. "No, that's all right. Just be nice. I'm just saying..." and she looked over at me, "If you're okay the way you are, fine."

I nodded my assent, but I was desperate to strengthen, somehow, the tenuous connection Faye was allowing by being there in the backyard talking with me. "Business doing okay?"

"Yeah," she said. She got up and went inside. I was dumb; otherwise, I might have thought of something else to say to her, some way to keep her there a little longer.

The sunlight had reached my toes and would continue to engulf me as the shadow of the garage's roof receded. But I sat for quite a while longer—until the sun was up to my knees—trying *not* to reinvent the conversation this time. I had spoken with Faye, and while it was not the conversation I might have wanted or imagined, it was real, so I savored it. It was truncated, pared to the essential as only the conversation of old marrieds could be, but I began to realize that the few words we'd spoken reverberated with volumes of emotion. Faye's connectedness with her parents, my alienation from them. Encoded reference to my mother, by way of inference. It had been a conversation about the impossibility of divorce.

As always, it was not a fight, and it did nothing to clear the air; the air between me and Faye remained murky.

The air was murky between me and everything.

A fight might have broken something, done some harm to the fetid entity we labeled our marriage, and that could only have been good. Faye, the daughter of her parents, was as locked into the institution of our marriage as was I, the son of my mother. I felt hopeless.

I pulled myself out of the chair and went in search of a fight. I found Faye on the front porch, of all places.

"You never sit out here," I said. I barged ahead, sat on the top step, leaned back against the balustrade so I could see Faye in the wicker settee.

"Have you noticed," I said, "that we can't figure out any way to get divorced?" This grabbed her attention. Her mouth dropped open just a smidgeon.

After a moment, she said, "Now that you mention it." Then she looked at me and said, "Is that why you said you were cracked? To give me a reason to divorce you?"

"No, no. But it just seems like most couples would have gone their separate ways long ago."

"Probably," she said.

"Have you not wanted to?"

"You haven't really given me any reason to, Hec. And I've tried to be loyal."

"We've been loyal to each other, yeah."

"Well, haven't we?"

I nodded and said, "Yep." I watched Faye. She watched no cars passing. The air was still, hot, on our little street in our little neighborhood in Appalachia. A sparrow flitted up from a bush and lit on the power lines connecting our house to the big juice running along the street on creosoted poles. Faye looked up at the bird, followed it visually as it hurried, within a few seconds, into the uplifted branches of the Bradford pear tree growing untended in our front yard.

"Guess we could have made something of Merrien," Faye suggested helpfully. "You and her."

"Probably," I said. I was perfectly willing to discuss it, but I was shocked, inwardly, that Faye would bring it up. Did she think I'd had an affair with Merrien? Irrationally, I felt flattered. I purposely delayed telling Faye that I had not had an affair with Merrien. "You mean, after the Big Excision."

"After the Big Excision, yes. That's what I mean."

"That was all numbness, wasn't it? You and me, numb."

"I remember that," Faye said, nodding her head.

"Merrien was having her usual depression but in spades, as I remember it, so she was at our apartment very often, several times a week. Kept us sort of occupied, you and me, didn't it? When the subject of ourselves threatened to crop up, we'd talk about Merrien."

"I guess that's right."

"This is going nowhere, though," I said.

"Why? No affair with Merrien?"

"Actually, Merrien did become a little episode in my life. The weather was turning nice, so I began walking Merrien home."

"About thirty blocks."

"Right. I always gave her a hug and a kiss on the cheek when I got her to the front of her building. Then one night my kiss landed on her mouth and her tongue went right into my mouth. I wasn't expecting it, but I accepted it. We didn't linger long like that. She turned me loose, cast her eyes downward and, without looking at me, turned around and went inside. I felt a little surprised, a little delighted. I had a thirty block walk back home, then, to calm down."

Faye stood up and leaned on the balustrade, her nice buttocks suddenly the uppermost part of her anatomy—an unintentional Valentine from my vantage point. "That riles me," she said. Her voice told me she spoke the truth.

"But it's not really good divorce material," I said.

"No. Was that all?"

"Nope. Merrien continued to show up at our apartment, always with some kind of anxiety or depression she needed to get off her chest. The wet kiss might never have happened as far as her other behavior was concerned. I'd still walk her home, and we were back to dry hugs and friendly pecks on the cheek. But only for a while. Then one night at the front of her building, I aimed for her mouth and it was my tongue that darted out and felt her teeth part to let me into her mouth."

"And she let you."

"Well, yeah, but then she said it was wrong. Not fair to you. What do you think I did?"

"Probably apologized to her."

"Thank you, but no, I didn't apologize, since I didn't feel that was appropriate at all. I gave her the friendly hug, the friendly squeeze on the arm, and left her there."

"You know, the thing that kills me is that this was going on and she kept being my friend, acting like she depended on me emotionally."

"And what about me? How was I acting?"

"Hec, you always act so weird I wouldn't hazard a guess as to what's going on with you. Did anything else happen?"

"Well, I began to fantasize about her. I was temping all the way downtown in the financial district in that sleazy travel agency, and during the long subway rides to and from work, I invented erotic scenarios about Merrien and me."

"Do you think she was pretty?"

"Well, in my opinion she had an unremarkable but shapely figure, maybe a little wide at the hips, maybe a little modest at the bust, but a thin, comely waist—wouldn't you say?—and nicely shaped legs. That dark hair was too long, but if it had been shaped right, Merrien's face wouldn't have looked so pasty and round; her nose was perfect."

"I agree with you there."

"I liked the way it turned up. Her lips were thin but would have been fine with anything but the dark red lipstick she wore."

"That was horrible, true."

"Once, at our apartment when you were out of the room, she actually lowered her head and looked at me out from under her lashes, nailed me good with those round, dark blue eyes. I was struck by how seductive those eyes could be."

"You sure were paying attention, I'll say."

"So I fantasized, but I was careful not to make a move on Merrien in reality. Some months went by, it was late summer, and you had to go to North Carolina to see your mother."

"Her cancer scare."

"Right. Why didn't I go with you? I can't remember."

"You were in production at the Wonderhorse."

"That's right. They were doing *Brain Tempura* so I stayed in New York. Merrien showed up with a bottle of gin. I let her in the apartment, she stood there and looked at me for a few seconds, then burst into tears and fell into me."

"Fell into you?"

"Dropped the paper bag containing the bottle of gin onto the carpet, wrapped her arms around me, dripped large hot tears all over my neck, sobbing uncontrollably, squeezing me tightly, jamming her thigh into my crotch."

"Fine!" Faye blurted, surprising me. Then she said, "So Merrien was what, a damsel in distress?"

"I think all the tears were to say she'd given up trying to hold herself back. She was ready to party."

"So did you party?"

"Well, I started getting a hard on. And as soon as I realized that, I felt a shot of adrenaline empty out of my stomach into my heart. Then my brain took over, commanding my emotions to arm themselves and fight fire with fire. Guilt and shame led the charge, and within seconds the boner had subsided and I was guiding the vulnerable maiden to the recliner. I myself sat safely on the couch, across the room, and began offering her soothing words of reassurance.

"After a while, she dried up sufficiently to speak. 'Why don't you fix us a drink,' she said. So I did, and we got drunk."

"I take it that was when it happened," Faye said. She was grasping the balustrade. I could see the muscles in her forearms bulging.

"Depends what you mean. Let me tell you, Faye, something about myself."

"Please do."

"I've never cheated on you. You know what I mean by cheated—had sex with another woman. I mean, since we've been married. Actually, ever since I've known you, if you want to be exact.

Before that, yes, of course. But not since I met you."

Faye let go of the balustrade, walked across the porch and looked toward the Stones' house, facing away from me.

"Merrien was all over me. Drunk, she was even more aggressive. Drunk myself, I wanted to take her. She went to the bathroom, came out a couple of minutes later and proclaimed loudly, 'I want you to *fuck* me, man!'"

Faye turned around suddenly. "She did not!"

"Her exact words. This was because I'd been given every opportunity and hadn't done anything—hadn't tried to take off her clothes, or put my hands on her breasts or between her legs. We were kissing, rolling around on the couch, but that was it."

Todaro: But you say you 'wanted to take her.'

Owen: Part of me wanted to take her, but I knew there would be no point in taking off our clothes. My penis cringed, I say *cringed* at the idea of extramarital sex. Do you hear what I'm saying?

Todaro: Yes, I hear. How do you account for this feeling? How would you describe it?

Owen: Instilled guilt. Very basic, early conditioning. Something to do with the way my parents treated each other, and some early learning experiences. Nothing mysterious, same old crap all boys get and later learn to disregard. But in my case, it wields a powerful sword, cutting off the blood flow to my erectile tissue.

Todaro: A sword? You're referring to this moral conditioning as a sword?

Owen: It's a being, an angel, let's say, wielding a sword. Or a demon, however you want to look at it. It's an emotional package is what it really is.

Todaro: But this sword, does it hurt you?

Owen: You're taking me too literally. What I'm talking about is impotence born out of fear and guilt. These feelings 'hurt' in a sense, but not physically. Oh, but...

Todaro: Yes, finish your thought, Hector.

Owen: There has been physical pain. The stomachaches. The birthing pains.

Todaro: Manifestations of the sword?

Owen: Or are we getting a little carried away with the metaphor here, a little intellectual?

Todaro: Are we?

Owen: Yes, we're slipping away from my extramarital sex life.

"What are you thinking about? Where do you go?" Faye said. I was surprised to see that she'd sat back down on the wicker settee.

"I was having a session with my analyst," I said.

"So you're saying you didn't... have sex with her."

"Didn't have intercourse, no. If you require that I porked her, or anyone, this is not going to lead to grounds for divorce."

Onto Faye's face came the strangest mixture of emotion I've ever seen. She was both relieved and disappointed. It was there even though she was clearly trying to keep a poker face. Then she looked at me and there was both love—I mean it, I know it–and revulsion. She couldn't have mirrored my own feelings about myself better. And as for my feelings about Faye, I was attracted to her sexually at that moment, but there was an even stronger feeling that she was surrounded by barbed wire and ice.

Two young men, I guess students at UNCA, strode down the sidewalk. Faye and I watched them, heard a few words of their chatter. They were so involved in their conversation they didn't see us. For a moment I imagined myself falling in step with them, walking into their academic world, out of mine, safe from characters of my own invention that have become real.

Faye pulled herself out of the settee and wandered down the steps, around the house, down the driveway. I got up and followed her. I was beginning to feel heavy as the beer metabolized in me, but I needed the familiarity I felt with Faye. I needed not to be alone with myself or Dr. Todaro.

I caught her as she squatted to pick up a piece of trash, a discarded paper cup, at the back corner of the house.

"I wrote some parts just so I would eventually meet whatever actresses would be cast to play them. That might count for something. You know, if you could get a lawyer who could prove that, for a playwright, intent is tantamount to guilt."

"Depends on if anything ever came of it. You said nothing ever came of anything."

"I said no actual sex. What about crimes of the heart?"

"How bad a crime?" She was fumbling with the lid on the garbage can beside the garage.

"There was one time I could tell about, with one of the ac-

tresses, the rolling around on the couch—different couch, same
scenario–burning desire, cringing penis, negative results. She was
incensed. Can't blame her. She never spoke to me again."

"You want me to guess which actress it was? I think I can."

"No, that's okay."

"What about Merrien? How did she react when you didn't...
fulfill the role that seemed to be called for?"

"She tried to act like the whole thing never happened. You
came back from North Carolina, everything was like before."

Faye walked on back to the Adirondack chairs. I followed after a moment. She sat in one chair, I took the other.

"You seem more upset about Merrien than I thought you would
be," I said. "I didn't mean to upset you. I really didn't."

"No," she said, "it's not that. I mean, it hurts, but it's been a
long time. I just wonder..."

"What?"

"When I was at Mother's for the cancer scare, I was thinking
of something else. I mean, I was thinking about her, concerned for
her and everything. But I was thinking about something else too.
I didn't discuss it with her, of course."

"Didn't discuss what?"

"Well, I mean, give some thought to the timing of your affair
with Merrien. Your rolling around on the couch with her. When I
was in North Carolina, that was when we would have been having
our baby."

Owen: Yikes.

August 6

Faye started getting suspicious the night we visited the Stones. She'd been preoccupied all day with some problem at her boutique—a shipment of lingerie had arrived even though she'd cancelled the order; the vendor denied the order had been cancelled. Faye was trying to put the workday out of her mind, abandon her dark mood as we walked across the side yard to visit our elderly neighbors.

Asheville is hilly, mountainous at its edges; houses sit on lots that slope. The Stones' house looks from the front like a small bungalow, but like a two-story house from the back. And because the streets in our neighborhood wind through steep, twisted terrain, the lots are oddly shaped. The Stones' backyard abuts the next street over, across which there's a little park, nothing more than a triangular copse too small to build a house on. At the near corner of this park, a street light blazes, attracting a host of summer insects and repelling, theoretically, human intruders who might otherwise haunt our quiet, under-policed neighborhood.

I stood at the window of the Stones' parlor, looking down at this streetlight, giving myself a rest from the conversation. Lilace left the room to check the teapot in the kitchen. Mr. Stone was telling Faye a story she and I had heard before.

"This would have been, oh, a few months after the *Kristallnacht*," he said, his voice dropping in pitch and volume on the final word, as it did when he said 'pogrom' or 'extermination.'

"By this time our marriage was illegal, *ex post facto*. Mrs. Stone wanted to travel with me, but I tried to convince her we should travel separately."

"We barely escaped the Nazis," Mrs. Stone said. "We came to America... oh, it was like going to the moon..."

"We were married but little more than children," Mr. Stone continued. We settled in New York City and lived there through the forties, fifties, and sixties. Every day, waking up, for a minute I thought I was still in Germany, then I felt so good, so safe."

"Of course I could have stayed in Germany safely if I pretended not to be married," Mrs. Stone piped in. "I looked quite the little Fraulein."

"But she chose instead to travel with her husband, at risk of arrest and incarceration," Mr. Stone said, glancing at his beloved, his eyes softening in spite of the dispassionate edge he was trying to keep in his voice.

As the Stones continued their banter—their love having known no bounds, even until today—I moved to the window and looked out. I saw Robin walking along the street until he reached the utility pole which supported the street light. There he stopped, poked around in the weeds growing along the street, disappeared into the copse, and then reappeared and looked up in my direction. He couldn't have seen me at the window in the dimly lit room, since he was standing in bright light some several hundred feet away, but he did stare up toward me. I resisted an urge to wave him away, get him out of sight.

"You certainly seem distracted, Hector," Lilace said, bringing me suddenly away from the window. She had brought coffee and a plate of petits fours and another of sliced bananas and kiwis.

"I'm sorry," I said. "I was thinking about my childhood."

Mr. Stone laughed loudly, for him, and Mrs. Stone blushed

visibly even in the dim candle light.

"It was all before you were born," Mrs. Stone said.

"But he needs to know this," Mr. Stone said.

"Everyone needs to know, and not forget," Mrs. Stone said.

We all nodded in agreement and began sipping our coffees in silence. I felt a yearning to return to the window and see Robin, though by then he would have been gone, no doubt. While he's a little sloppy about covering his tracks, he's been discreet as far as actually showing up where he might be seen.

Lilace was wearing a white silk blouse and a black skirt which hiked above her knees when she was sitting. A stolen glance confirmed that her legs were shapely, slim but not bony. The silence in the room grew longer, punctuated by the tinkling of Mrs. Stone's spoon on her cup as she stirred in mounds of sugar. I caught Lilace looking at me; she didn't avert her eyes, but gave me a gentle smile. I felt slightly embarrassed, looked across the table to Faye, and she too was watching me. I glanced at Mrs. Stone, who was staring into space, no doubt to a place in Germany many years ago. Finally I looked at Mr. Stone, and he was glaring at me.

"You of all people need to know this," he said to me, not even trying to disguise his disappointment in me. Suddenly smiling, he said "If you are to call yourself a writer, you must know what a pogrom is." He looked at his daughter and said, "He didn't know what a pogrom was."

"Actually," I said, "I did know but had forgotten momentarily." This was the truth, but didn't help in any sense.

"Let's eat fruit," Mrs. Stone said.

"And although I used to write plays," I added, "I don't call myself a writer now."

Mr. Stone laughed quietly. "Then you are beyond reproach," he said, "and that is more comfortable for you."

"Dad," Lilace said, "Hector is not Jewish, and there are plenty of good Jewish writers to write about the Holocaust."

He looked at his daughter with what seemed to me a patronizing indulgence. "I'm afraid you miss my point," he said, and smiled into his coffee cup. "A writer, *any* writer, should be familiar with the major..."

"Isn't it a good thing that I'm *not* a writer!" I interrupted brightly, laughing long enough to try and cover my rudeness, of which I was cognizant, thank you.

"Faye," Mrs. Stone said, trying to brighten things, "how's your coffee?"

"Fine, thanks."

"Faye would like, perhaps, to talk panties," Mr. Stone said.

"Dad!" Lilace said, rolling her eyes at Faye in apology.

Faye laughed. "Well," she said, "it would be all right with me, but I don't want to talk shop here and bore the lay people."

Mr. Stone was forcing himself to smile now, trying hard to come down to our level, make himself accept that we were trivial people, unable to converse on a meaningful level.

"They gave him something in the hospital," Mrs. Stone said. "It made him, I don't know, he..." and she looked at her husband for help.

"Nothing," he said. "Grumpy. Okay?"

"It's okay, Dad," Lilace said.

"You never know the side effects of some of the drugs they use these days," I said. "Most of us could use something to shave off a layer or two of inhibition. Nothing wrong with saying what's on your mind."

Nobody knew what I was talking about. I hardly knew myself. It occurred to me that this conversation was silly, pointless. I wondered why I even bothered befriending the Stones. I wanted to be with Robin, alone with him, talking with him about anything at all, matters important or trivial. I wanted his company.

At ten o'clock we said good night to the Stones. Lilace walked Faye and me to the door, where she embraced first Faye and then me.

Walking across the front yard, trying to keep in step with Faye, I glanced up the block, thinking I might catch a glimpse of Robin, but he wasn't in sight.

We'd forgotten to leave the front porch light on and we had to feel our way to the door. Faye fumbled with her keys, but I got mine in the hole first and opened the door. Robin was on the Queen Anne, apparently waking from slumber, disoriented. To stall, give him time to get out of the room, I pretended my key was stuck in the keyhole. I shouldered Faye back onto the porch.

"What's the matter?" she said, irritated.

Robin had assessed the situation and scurried out of the living room toward the kitchen.

"Damn keyhole..." I muttered, extricated the key, and let us in.

"Are you feeling all right?" she said.

"Fine. How about you?"

She shook her head. "Not talking about me." She pulled off her low heels. "You're not acting the way you used to."

"You mean I'm behaving abnormally, or what?"

"Not abnormally. Just not *you*."

"Something specific?"

"Tonight. Tonight was very specific."

"The Stones need to vent. I've just heard it before."

"No, it's not that. Do you realize you stood at the window for about fifteen minutes, staring out? No, not staring out, looking at something."

"I couldn't bear to hear that story again. That minute by minute account of their escape from the Nazis."

"He wasn't telling that story."

"He wasn't?"

"He finished telling that one. He was telling about Lilace's first boyfriend, when she was a teenager. He very skillfully made me wonder if maybe Lilace had gotten involved with a black man. He let me wonder for a while, and then he cleared it all up."

"Making you feel guilty for wondering..."

"No. Not that. He was creating suspense, that's all. Purposely made it an interesting story."

"All right. I admit I didn't hear a word of it."

"That's what I mean. You've always taken in everything. You would never miss a story like that. He kept referring to the boyfriend as being of 'another persuasion.' It was confusing. You would have seen right through it, but I couldn't."

"And how did that make you feel, Mrs. Owen?" I said, imitating Dr. Todaro.

"I kept wishing you would come back and sit down and listen. No, not listen... help *me* listen."

"Oh," I said. I was touched. We were a married couple, after all, and these small interdependencies would crop up from time to time.

"You're right," I said. "I let you down."

Faye sighed deeply, leaned her head back. I looked toward the kitchen and saw Robin peeking around the counter. I gave him my sternest look, and he ducked out of sight.

"And what is this Melba toast?" Faye suddenly said with an exaggerated scowl.

"Oh, I don't know. Thought I'd try something different."

"You've hated Melba toast ever since I've known you," she said. "And I'd appreciate it if you wouldn't leave the wrappings everywhere."

"I'm getting absent-minded," I said, and resolved, then and there, not to buy Robin anything else to eat except items I myself would choose, no matter how he begged me.

I wandered into the kitchen, furtively checking to see that Robin was gone. Once I was satisfied, I turned on the light and took a packet of Melba toast from the box on the counter. I began envisioning Lilace as a nubile teenager, getting it on with a black boy in the back seat of a car.

Nonchalantly munching the toast (which I do detest), I strolled back into the living room. Faye was sitting on the Queen Anne in her underwear, her legs spread wide, her hand resting on her crotch.

"Dr. Todaro and I spoke this morning," she said.

"You talked with Todaro? You mean, on the phone?"

"You were supposed to call and set up an appointment, and you didn't."

"I was to call him *if* I felt uneasy or anything. I feel fine." I had removed my shoes and trousers. We were still in the living room. I plopped down on the couch next to Faye. "He called you?"

"I called him. From the boutique. We had a pretty good talk about you. He mentioned hypnosis. I told him I'd see if you were interested. Sounds like sort of fun, don't you think?"

I certainly did not think, but I was careful not to react too strongly. "Hypnosis. Well, I think it would be more interesting for him than it would be for me. I might not even be susceptible to it. But I'll think about it."

Until now, I'd been sure that my behavior appeared reasonably, if marginally, normal to Faye. Now I began to question whether

Robin's presence in the house could be effectively hidden. After all, Faye lived here; she would notice things. For example, I've never cared for melons, but have been buying cantaloupes lately for Robin. And the Melba toast. Small things. But they add up.

She was pensively working her pantyhose down, stopped at the knees. "Hector," she said, "the way you act. It's hard to describe. It's like there's somebody else in the house."

"Maybe there is," I said. "Maybe the homunculus is loose, coming out at night, hiding in the attic, that sort of stuff."

"But you don't see him, do you?" she said. "It was just that one episode, wasn't it?"

"Episode? Is that Dr. Todaro's word?"

"Yeah, it is, now that you mention it."

"Well, it was not an episode," I said. "It was a stomach-ache and a dream. Look, Faye, I don't deny I'm still overcoming some of the stress from New York, and then there's my retirement. You know, I'm dealing with not working. Lately I've been thinking I may need to get some kind of work going. Not writing, nothing artistic. Something entrepreneurial, maybe. I've always had that urge, you know." This was all a lie.

"But at the mall, you did say you were cracked."

"Yes," I said. For the next few moments, I seriously considered telling Faye that the homunculus, Robin, was indeed manifest. I leaned my head back on the Queen Anne's brocaded upper curve, stared into the space beyond the ceiling. "I may need to see Dr. Todaro, but I'll do it if and when I decide it's going to be helpful."

"Okay," Faye said, suddenly sounding hardly interested. I sat up and saw that she'd picked up a *Glamour* and was scrutinizing an advertisement. She put it on her lap and looked at me. "I don't get the feeling you're being very honest with me," she said. "I don't think you're cracked anyway."

Standing up, I gave her a sidewise smile and said, "Well, you're right."

Faye pulled off her pantyhose and then her panties, dug her heels into the edge of the couch seat, hunched over immodestly to examine something about her genitalia. I looked away, hurried out of the room to the kitchen.

I drank a glass of water slowly. I was about to return to the living room, estimating that Faye would have finished her gynecological tinkerings. I put the glass into the sink, and happened to notice a claw hammer lying on the floor next to the trashcan. I didn't recognize it as one of my tools (I have very few) so I leaned closer to examine it. Then I saw a very large flathead screwdriver behind the trashcan. I pulled the can out from its corner and revealed four old bent nails and some splinters of wood hardly larger than toothpicks.

I had a choice. I could ask Faye about the tools and evidence of woodwork, and risk alarming her if she knew nothing of it. Or I could assume it was Robin's affair and pretend not to have noticed anything. I chose the latter, and kicked the tools farther behind the trash can, out of sight.

Faye was reclining on the Queen Anne, her panties back in place, her pantyhose removed except for the toe of one foot. I thought she looked comical with the pantyhose hanging there, the job of undressing so nearly completed but not.

"Find anything in there?" I asked.

She didn't seem to catch the reference to her self-examination. Instead, she turned her head to look at me, frowning. "Did you notice the skirt Lilace was wearing?"

"I think so," I said. "Black, wasn't it?"

"It may have been a very dark brown," Faye said softly, her

voice trailing away. She lolled her head from side to side for a moment, then pulled herself up from the couch, said "I noticed you did notice," and retired to the bedroom.

I sat on the Queen Anne and considered whether to go out to my office, or stay in the house until I got sleepy, or roam around the house and yard and my office looking for Robin. I was tired, and after a while I went to the bedroom and lay down next to Faye, who was fast asleep.

I woke up in the middle of the night. It was as though I'd heard something, but I listened and there was nothing. Still, I was wide awake. I looked at the clock. Three fifteen. I rolled over, tried to find a comfortable position. As I rustled about in the bed, I thought I heard something again — a thump or a knock. I lay perfectly still, heard nothing more. I couldn't fall asleep, so I got up and padded to the living room. The homunculus, I thought, up to no good somewhere around here. He ought to be sleeping like a normal person. I was so wide awake I mentally checked off my caffeine intake from the previous day. That coffee Mrs. Stone served. That must be the culprit, I thought. Old German remedy. Will bring you sweet dreams. My ass. I padded on into the kitchen.

Creak, thud.

A sound was coming from somewhere in the house. It was a small house. I would find it. I went through the kitchen, onto the back porch. The trap door to the basement was open and the light was on down there.

"Stop!" he cried out, his voice thin but urgent. "Don't start down the steps!"

I stopped, leaned forward a little to peer down. He came into sight from underneath the steps, hurried to struggle up toward me. When he was halfway up the steps, he stopped, breathless, and looked up with a sheepish grin on his face.

"Didn't want you to hurt yourself," he said. "I've been doing a little work on the stairs. Haven't finished."

"How did you get this thing open?" I asked him.

"It wasn't easy," he said.

"*Why* did you get it open?" I said.

He hesitated, nervously tried to chuckle, but obviously didn't have an answer for me. I started to step down toward him.

"No!" he said, holding a tiny palm toward me.

"What's going on?" I said.

"That first step is a killer. I noticed it was loose, so I'm working on it. But right now it's dangerous."

I leaned over to examine the first step, which was poorly lit from the light in the basement. I reached down and pressed on it with the tips of my fingers. It easily gave way, seesawing on the center runner.

"What I was doing," Robin said, waiting then until I looked at him, "was I was going to make myself a nice little nest, a comfortable nest down here. Very unobtrusive, of course. I was going to use the little room you had me locked in. I was going to clean it up, put in a few little items, you know. Just for a place to sleep or retreat to. But I had to, you know, fix the stairs so I wouldn't get hurt coming and going."

"There was nothing wrong with these stairs," I said. I was still looking at the top step, beginning to see what work had been done on it. It had apparently been removed and placed back about two inches off—just enough so that the left side missed the runner by a fraction of an inch. That was why the plank seesawed. "Good work," I said wryly. I stepped down, skipping the loose top step, and brushed past Robin.

"It's not finished yet," he said lamely.

I was barefoot and didn't want to walk on the dirty basement floor, but I peered across to the little room and could see that the door was closed, the lag bolt in place.

"I haven't started on that part yet," Robin murmured. Then more vehemently he said "I told you I want to get this stairway safe first."

He was a terrible liar. I decided to go back to bed and think about it tomorrow. I turned to go up the stairs when I saw a jumble of gardening tools leaning against the basement wall just to the left of the stairway. I recognized the tools as my own, which I kept in the garage.

I looked at Robin, who averted his eyes. He said, "If you don't want me down here, just say so. I didn't think it would be any trouble to anyone. I was just..."

"Oh shut up," I said. I inventoried the gardening tools. There was a leaf rake, a yard rake, a hoe, a spading fork, my new hedge clippers, and a shovel.

I heard Robin yawn. I looked at him and he was sitting on a step, his legs folded and crossed in front of him, his arms also crossed in a gesture of patient waiting. Suddenly I was overcome with a stampeding fatigue. I thought I was blacking out.

"Go back to bed," I heard Robin saying softly. "You're tired. We'll talk about it in the morning."

It was all I could do to make it back up the stairs. I was afraid I would not be able to step over the loose tread at the top, but I did manage to.

I woke up in bed when Faye got up at seven, but I don't remember walking back through the house to get there. In the morning the trap door was closed. The gardening tools, I later noted, had not been returned to the garage.

I note a similarity between my inability to scrutinize and understand what Robin was up to, and my ruining the relationship I had with Ginger. After I had repeatedly and brutally refused to let Ginger come to New York and be with me, after I had neglected her for long periods, turned a deaf ear to her pleading, and finally to her insinuations that she was seeing someone else but would still come to me if I would just let her, finally she broke it off. It was only then that I saw everything clearly, broke down in front of my friend little d don and cried for days, phoned Ginger and begged her to take me back, all to no avail because it was too late, way too late. I had meticulously burned every bridge back to her, and never knew what I was doing. It was as though a part of my mind had gone to sleep, or into a coma, and would not revive until the damage was done. Certainly on one level I was determined to rid my life of Ginger. But on what level? I loved the girl. She was cute and wonderful and good for me.

Now, that part of my mind has blacked out again. What am I watching the homunculus doing? Why can't I focus on it and see it? Is there something I want, on some level, that he's accomplishing for me? And when it's accomplished, will I regret it the way I regretted losing Ginger?

I'll speak with him about it, try to get him to open up. And I'll keep a watchful eye on his activities—to the extent that I can without behaving any more strangely than I have been.

The morning after our visit with the Stones, Lilace caught up with me as I started on my usual walk. I was heading away from the Stones' house, but she'd been sitting on their front porch and saw me.

"Hector," she said brightly, coming up behind me. I stopped and turned, dumbly drank in her intoxicating smile.

"Where you headed?"

"Nowhere in particular," I said. "Care to join me?"

She glanced back at the house. "Well, I guess they'll survive without me for a few minutes. You're not going far, are you?"

"No, just a block or two," I said, and we walked side by side.

"Actually I have a favor to ask," she said. "Maybe two favors. Related favors."

"Far out," I said, and she accepted it seriously, so I fell in love with her.

"It's about their car, Mom and Dad's."

I nodded. "I didn't know they had a car."

"They don't drive it, but they have one in the garage. They've asked me to drive it a little, and thought it would be a good idea to use it when I go out to the airport. I've got to get back to Dallas pretty soon."

I found this information so depressing it surprised me. "No," I said. "I mean, I hope not."

She looked at me, met my eyes as I tried to explain myself

wordlessly. She smiled. "I thought we could take the car for a spin today, just to make sure it's running okay. I wouldn't want to break down on the way to the airport."

"You mean, you and I?"

"If you wouldn't mind," she said. "And then the other favor will be for you to go with me to the airport so you can return the car."

"Of course."

"I'm not much with cars, and if there's a problem, well, you know, two heads are better than one."

"I'm not very mechanically inclined," I said, "but right, two heads are better than one."

"You think you could find time to try it today?"

"Sure," I said. We walked on along the sidewalk for a few moments. I stopped suddenly so Lilace stopped too. "How about right now?" I said.

She smiled and said, "Far out."

The car was in an attached garage on the far side of the Stones' house. We had some trouble getting the garage door to slide up. It was the solid-plane type of door and at first would not move more than a foot. Finally Lilace went inside the garage through the door connecting the house, and she spotted the trouble — a mop that had been hung over the track on which the door slid.

The obstacle removed, I lifted the door open. Lilace stood before me, facing me with her arms lifted as she followed the motion of the door. I was struck by the line of her body, stretched in that posture, and I'm afraid I stood staring at her thin waistline. My stare seemed to stop her in the stretched position for a moment. When, embarrassed, I met her gaze, she blushed and quickly let her arms fall to her sides. I saw the car behind her and directed my attention there.

"What in the world is it?" I asked.

"I have no idea," she said. We looked for a chrome nameplate. I found it first.

"Barracuda! Not what I would have predicted." I sounded impressed, and was, with the car's sporty musculature.

"Oh, I remember now," she said. "Barracuda. I laughed when they told me they'd bought it. It was the first car they looked at when they decided to leave New York and felt they should have a car. They thought it was very nice, so they bought it. Had no idea it was sporty."

"Looks in good condition," I said, assessing the interior through the window.

"It was not very old when they got it." She opened the passenger door. "Let's see if it'll start."

I got in and adjusted the seat. The key was in the ignition. I looked at the array of instruments. "I feel like I'm in an airplane cockpit."

"Go ahead, try it," Lilace said, and she pressed her knees together with her hands and watched my hand turn the key.

The battery was a little weak, but the engine cranked and started. Lilace clapped her hands together and smiled. "You're a genius," she said. Flattery beyond reason! And as such it pleased me very much. It told me that Lilace was not too hard to read, and wasn't trying to be.

I let the engine idle for a minute or so, listening as it gradually smoothed out and the exhaust, initially a burst of black smoke, thinned and finally became transparent. I looked over the instruments, trying to see what information they would give me. "My god, look at this," I said, eyeing the odometer. "Sixty-seven thousand miles."

"I think Mom and Dad put about twenty thousand of those on," she said. "Shall we?"

I backed out to the street and headed toward Merrimon Avenue, which I took south toward downtown. The car was obviously in good running condition, but I knew that we both wanted to go for a ride for its own sake. It was a pleasure driving the strange, powerful vehicle.

"Care to stop somewhere for a cup of coffee?" I said. "I could use one."

"Sure." That smile.

We found a spot to park downtown. Two young men admired the car as I got out. They let me see them admiring Lilace's legs as she got out. I was in high school. This was the girl I wanted on my arm, walking to classes. These were the hot wheels I wanted waiting for me in the parking lot.

"There's a great coffee shop next door to the library," I said, leading the way up the narrow, tree-shaded back street. "Actually, it's a book store called Malaprops, but it's also a cafe."

"Sounds nice," she said. The street was steep and we walked it silently. I didn't talk because I didn't want her to hear me huffing and puffing from the exertion. Teenagers don't huff and puff.

We sidled through the narrow aisles of bookshelves in Malaprops. I led the way to the back of the store where a stairway descended to the lower level. A vast, cluttered bulletin board at the foot of the stairs attracted Lilace's attention for a moment, and I stood with her, perusing the index cards, Xeroxed notices, scribbled scraps of this and that—all the wants and needs of Asheville's underground posted in one place—all things holistic, hip, student, gay, lesbian, desperate, impecunious, green, comforting, unproven, free and very cheap, and wanted.

The cafe had the feel of the womb, warm, comfortable (though the chairs were hard), protected from the corporates looming above and to the side of this very building. We ordered tea, found a table in the corner and waited for our drinks to brew.

Once we had the cups in our hands, Lilace suggested we go outside. She'd noticed the screen door near the bulletin board, and beyond it some picnic tables on an ancient loading dock. Like many structures in hilly Asheville, the lower level opened at the back to the outside, while at the front it was under the ground.

The dock overlooked a stark alleyway and parking lot, but was itself shaded by a row of trees sagging with wisteria. The platform was pleasingly deserted. We sat at the largest of the tables because there we could lean back against the building.

Lilace sipped her tea, frowned, finding it too hot.

"There's something very liberating about knowing you'll soon be gone from a place," she said. "I mean, I may come back to Asheville some time. Probably will. I don't come every year. Not even every other year. I don't know. They're getting very old." She gazed off across the parking lot.

"I find it very depressing to think you're going to be gone from here," I said. It was much too much. Far too strong a thing to say, but I felt it. It was backed with emotion that welled in my throat. I expected her to laugh at me, but she didn't. She didn't even look at me.

"I like you too," she said. "They both think your hair is ridiculous, long like that. When they said that, the day I got here, when we were making small talk about the neighbors, including you—that put you in a good light for me." She looked at me and smiled wickedly. "I'm still a teenager at heart, you know."

"I can't believe you said that. I've just been feeling like a teenager myself."

"Really?"

"Well, the car, you know. And..." I hesitated, couldn't say what had popped into my head.

"Go ahead, say it." And she poked me with her elbow. "Go on."

"Your legs, getting out of the car. Mmm, mmm, mmm." We both laughed.

We sipped at tea too hot.

"But you're right," I said. "It's wonderful, the freedom you mentioned. But at such a price. To be free, but only because you'll be gone soon."

"Well, I'm not sure I really meant... I'm not sure that's what I meant. I mean, hell, Hector, I'm not free to *do* anything. It's just a feeling. It's the feeling that makes a vacation refreshing, even though this is not a vacation."

"I know what you mean," I assured her. "I wasn't misconstruing what you said."

We were quiet then. I caught myself chewing my lower lip—a habit I thought I'd abandoned twenty years ago.

"My husband collects pistols," she said.

"No kidding," I said, trying to sound politely uninterested.

"That's all I'll tell you about him," she said. "I hope it's enough." She touched my hand. "Is it?"

I nodded. It was all I could do. Then I realized it was time, possibly, for me to try and sum up Faye for her. I began trying to formulate a four-word sentence, and had just begun to realize it was impossible, when Lilace spoke again.

"Was it long? Your hair, back in the sixties?"

"Oh, sure," I said. "I was right in the middle of everything."

"Me too," she said. "It was ruined for me, though. In seventy-one. My boyfriend OD'd."

"I'm sorry. He died?"

She sighed deeply, sadly. "Sort of."

"I'm sorry for you," I said. "Where were you?"

"Oh, at Columbia. It was a wonderful scene." She convulsed in laughter for just a second, then tried her tea again. "God, listen to me."

"I am listening to you," I said. "Keep talking."

"Not much to say."

"Anything more about your marriage?"

"Pooh," she said. "I've adopted one main disillusionment: that no marriage of mine could ever live up to the one my parents have. Perfect love. Do you see it? Have you noticed it? Or is it just so obvious to me because I'm their daughter?"

"No, it's obvious to the general public too."

She laughed. "Kind of sickening, if you ask me, but hey."

"Well," I said, "I'd rather see that than two people quietly at each others' throats in not-so-subtle public ways all the time."

"Like me and my husband," she said, and laughed again to try and mitigate the effect. "Try your tea," she said. "It's good stuff."

I did; it was.

"It's not as perfect as they pretend it is," she said.

"Their marriage?"

"The marriage is fine. But their history, well, I don't know. I guess you don't go through what they've been through and come out clean, no matter what."

I wondered, but didn't ask, didn't want to press.

She went ahead, "My brother was the one who started digging and asking questions. From what we've pieced together, her decision to travel with him, in 1939 inside of Germany, was not so impetuous as they prefer to paint it. Mother was more than a little resistant at first. She didn't think it made sense to risk her life just so they could ride the same train at the same time."

I nodded, glad, in a way, for the smirch on the Stones' story. Lilace said finally, "Well!" and picked up her tea, poked at it with her spoon.

"Do you ever wonder what happened to all of us flower children?" I asked her. "I mean, where the hell did everybody go?"

She shrugged her thin shoulders, sighed deeply, drank some of her tea, looked at me and smiled worriedly upon catching me staring at her. "I can't believe you live next door to my parents."

I took that as another compliment. We finished our tea and judged there to be plenty of time left on the parking meter, so we walked down the steep side street to Lexington Avenue. We explored a row of small shops and boutiques so reminiscent of the sixties it was almost laughable. Incense abounded, heavy jewelry made from the byproducts of the industrial age—belts and buckles made from car seat belts, hash pipes (people still smoke dope!) fashioned from everything, and made into erotic shapes, take your choice! Waterbeds. Quaint, flowing, sheer clothing. Rough fabrics from foreign lands. We even saw the hallmark of the era: black lights illuminating Day-Glo posters.

During our romp through the past, we carefully played at pleasing each other, agreeing with each other, finding the same things delightfully evocative, giving each other slack, probing and finding places on our minds that fit together comfortably. When we came to the end of the block of shops, I found myself shivering with the pleasure of making a new friend, and not just any new friend, but a *chick*.

The most direct route back to the car would be up a curving incline along which we could see several prostitutes stationed.

"What do you say?" Lilace winked toward the street in question. "Think we can make it through that way?"

"All right," I said. "No toying with them, though. Okay?"

"No, of course not," she said. "And if they try to approach us, you make sure they know we're not interested. I'm holding onto you and keeping quiet."

We set off up the hill, on the opposite side of the street from the hookers. Poignant backdrop for the working girls, a two-story motel squatted just beyond a level, graded blacktop parking lot. It announced itself as a product of the MBA-driven 80's, all business. It faced, conveniently, the quirky achitecture of the convention center up the hill, but with no shine of its own, no glow. The dust of a decade seemed to have abraded its surfaces. It was so squared-off, so utilitarian with its metal access stairs and cinder block walls, with only a nod to aesthetic appeal—alternating subdued shades of orange, blood, and yellow distinguishing the square cubicles.

"We're real adventurers," I said, and she laughed. At the top of the hill we stopped to catch our breath and looked back on the row of hippy stores down on Lexington. "Knowing the sixties are long gone," I said, "do you ever catch yourself yearning for those times to somehow be embodied in one person? To find that person, I mean."

She gave it some thought, nodding to show her understanding more than her assent. "I guess we'd better get back so Mom and Dad don't worry," she said.

I remembered what she'd told me about her boyfriend's misfortune with drugs. I felt stupid to have made an inadvertent reference to it. Suddenly I was awkward, and I remained awkward as we walked back to the car. I still felt cowed and tentative when I pulled the car into the garage and quickly turned off the engine, mindful of carbon monoxide. I hesitated before moving to open the door, looked at Lilace. She was with me, didn't move to open her door either.

"I've always been able to express myself in writing," I said, "but it seems the trade-off has been that I can't talk without putting my foot in my mouth."

"Is that what you think?" she said. "I don't know what you think you said, but whatever it was, I certainly didn't notice it. All I noticed was you kind of crawled into your shell right before we got back to the car."

"About your boyfriend. The one from the sixties who... I didn't mean to bring it back up."

She gave me a nice smile. "I'm not sensitive about that, Hec. Hell, that was a long time ago." She held her hand across the seat toward me and I took it in mine, squeezed it. We smiled at each other, let go our hands, but still didn't move to get out of the car. "Our favorite way to trip was to drop a tab and then start making love." She looked across at me once again.

"I'm interested," I said.

"Interested?" she laughed. "I've got you by the lips!"

"Okay," I said, and laughed too. "You've got me by the lips. I want to hear."

She leaned her head all the way back, stared at the headboard. "If we took our time," she said, "really let the feelings flow between us, gave the stuff a chance to get into our brains, the rush of blood when we climaxed would cause the acid to kick in at the same moment. The effect was an orgasm that seemed to propel us into another universe and leave us there for about eight to twelve hours in ecstasy.

"Our robots would lie in bed, which was a piece of foam rubber on the floor, and watch the movies on the ceiling. You know what I mean by 'our robots'?"

"Of course," I said. "Sort of like your bodies, as opposed to your minds, which were by then separate entities."

"Hey, you've been there, Hec."

"Hey," I said.

"We didn't have black lights or much in the way of psyche-
delic posters or the other hip decor. We didn't need it; we were seeing the real thing. We played Hendrix, Doors, Creedence, Traffic,
Spirit, Joplin, Mothers, and sometimes Dan would want to hear
things like Carole King or Crosby, Stills, Nash and Young. His
taste in music ran a little mellower than mine, but I enjoyed all of
it, especially stoned.

"Sometimes we'd stay in our robots, but other times we'd
watch them from across the room or up on the ceiling. Dan's robot
was so soft and firm. Well, eighteen years old, what do you want?
Mine was very skinny, like pipe cleaners. Later on in life I filled
out some, but I cringe when I see photos of myself back then, a
gangly skeleton covered with skin, not a tit to my name, great
wavy mane of hair, and of course the hip-hugging bell-bottoms
even though I had hardly any hips to hug."

We both laughed. "I bet you were irresistible," I said.

"There's one photo of me and Dan standing together outside
a coffee house on Amsterdam Avenue. This photo is really comical because Dan was kind of plump and he was pretty tall. I look
like his little kid, like maybe he's taking his daughter to her dance
lesson or something. It was taken right before he OD'd, but I do
look at it once in a while because it's such a perfect picture of the
two of us together."

Lilace sucked in her breath, put her hand on the door handle,
but then shifted in her seat and sat still.

"It's up to you," I said. "I'd like to hear it if you want to tell
it."

She smiled at me because I was reading her so well. "He told me one day that he was going to trip by himself. It was like telling me he was leaving me, but I tried to be cool. I asked him where he was going. Reminded him you're not supposed to trip by yourself. Told him he needed to be with somebody he could trust. All that stuff. Really I was trying to get him to talk about it, tell me who he was going to be with. Let's see, he said he was going to 'start out' over at Kevin's place. 'Start out,' you know, which sounded kind of evasive to me. I was jealous. I said what do you mean 'start out?' and he told me how Kevin was an old friend but sort of freaked him out sometimes so he might move on if he got uncomfortable over there. So I told him if he starts freaking out he could come on back home. 'No. I don't want you to be waiting for me. I'll be worried about it if you're waiting for me.' So I said I'd be there but I wouldn't be waiting for him. I'll never forget the way he turned to me with this worried little smile on his face. He said, 'The thing is, I'm doing this without you.'"

Lilace wrapped her arms across her bosom. I nodded and said "I have to wonder why."

"I didn't ask him why. I wanted to, but it wouldn't have been right. People were free in those days. Love was free.

"So the next day Dan took his trip without me. He hung around the house all morning, and we didn't say much to each other. He would have left earlier but he had to wait for the dealer, who was out of town scoring. I never smoked if I was down about something, but I did start drinking Chianti at about nine thirty, so by noon I was sloppy drunk and depressed, mostly to show Dan how much I was bothered by what he was doing.

"He was drinking chamomile, trying to stay calm, I imagine, so he wouldn't have a bum trip. I know my drinking was making him nervous, but he didn't say anything—just tried to be cheerful. He was trying on different outfits, his fringed leather jacket so he'd look like Steve Stills. That's what he finally wore. I wanted to ask him why he needed to look so good, but I didn't. I was afraid of what the answer might be, even if he didn't answer at all."

Lilace let herself go, placed her hands on her knees, leaned her head forward a little and shook it back and forth. "I'm sorry, Hec. You don't want to hear this."

"Yes I do," I said, almost urgently.

"Anyway, the point is, it was a hell of a way to end things. Until that day, I didn't have a clue anything was wrong between us. And I don't know—and will never know—that there really was. Maybe he was just feeling the need to experiment without me. It could have been an assertion of his freedom because he was getting ready to really commit to me. He might have intended to... I don't know. Maybe he would have gotten high and decided it was better with me than without me. He might've called me or come home.

"The phone rang, he talked to the dealer, and after he hung up he tried not to act like he was in a hurry, but he couldn't hide it. He was out the door, Steven Stills if I ever saw him, clonk clonk clonk in those suede boots. And I never saw him conscious again."

She looked at me and smiled. "I could never tell my husband that. He doesn't even know about Dan. It was a different world completely."

"I know," I said.

"Well, you must wonder what happened to Dan finally. I don't know. After a while I couldn't keep going out there to visit him— visit his robot, that is, which was all that was left of him. For all I know, he may be lying there still. It's strange, but I don't feel guilty about losing contact. It was needless pain and bother for me, and wasn't doing him any good."

"You're right," I said.

She had her hand on the door handle again; I put mine on my door handle, and taking note of this, we both opened our Barracuda doors at the same time.

August 7, afternoon

Much of my time in Asheville has been spent staring into space. Staring out the window is one form of that, but often I sit in the easy chair in my office and stare toward the wall, my eyes out of focus. My mind is simply resting, finding its proper shape again, I hope.

It was mid-afternoon when Lilace knocked at the window. Snapping into focus, seeing her smiling in at me, I realized I'd been daydreaming about her all day since we'd gone for the drive. I quickly went to the door and opened it.

"Open for visitors?" she said brightly.

"Sure. Enter my humble domain."

She stepped inside and surveyed the room. Almost immediately her attention went to my suicide instructions. Until that moment, I'd never realized how prominently that sign was displayed, how starkly the black and white stood out against the pale green of the walls. I didn't want Lilace to read it, but she'd already finished it before I could think of anything to distract her.

"That's interesting," she said too quietly.

"A joke. That's all."

"Oh."

"In reference to something else. Something back in New York." She smiled politely, tried to find something else in the room she could comment on. "It's not about me," I struggled on. "It's about people whose last resort is suicide. While I, on the other hand, have no last resort." I felt so stupid.

"It's funny," she said. "Listen, are you working?"

"No! I don't work. I stare into space."

"Well, maybe that's part of working. I don't want to interrupt..."

"No. It's not part of working. I really don't work."

"Not ever?"

"Not really. I write in a journal sometimes. Lately. I used to do that in New York, and worked there. But no work now, here. Well, right after we came to Asheville, I was commissioned to do one short dramatic piece. A one-shot deal. But that's over. I'm retired. This office is just for staring into space. Once in a while I read in here. But not work."

"Retired, huh?"

I was afraid she would say I was too young to be retired, as others have said. But she smiled, or maybe it was a wink, and spun around to look at my desk.

"You've done something different with your hair," I said. "It's fluffier. I love long hair. Chestnut hair, I'd call yours. It's beautiful."

"I just washed it," she said, turning again toward me, leaning her bottom on the edge of my desk.

"It must be clean, then," I said. I felt like an idiot, nervous beyond imagining in her presence. She wore faded bluejeans, a gray flannel shirt from which the sleeves had been pinked off and allowed to fray. Her white sneakers glowed with factory freshness.

"My hair? Yeah. I guess it's clean. Since I washed it." She laughed at me, and I loved her for it. It let me laugh at myself. It let me be funny, and I hadn't been funny for such a long time.

"I thought about washing mine," I said, fingering the ponytail, then passingly smelling my finger. She laughed harder.

My mind raced. I kept thinking of things to say and ruling them out because they contained references to Faye or to people's ages or might be construed as sexual innuendos—though by now everything seemed a sexual innuendo. "Had scheduled a hair wash," I said, but it fell flat. Lilace stopped laughing, just smiled at me.

"Look at you standing in the middle of the floor," she said. Then she pushed off from the desk, stepped to me, stood close, facing me. The top of her head, the lush brown hair, was just under my nose. It smelled like the bubble bath I'd used as a child. I felt her breath on me at my open collar. She looked up at me, and we kissed. She slipped her hands around my neck. Tentatively, I placed my arms around her waist, but didn't pull her close to me. The kiss ended. She looked at me again, and we let each other go.

"Felt like it," she said, "so what the heck?"

"Glad you did," I said.

She moved away from me, picked through some magazines lying on the lamp table next to the easy chair. "You come out here at night? Reading and staring into space and things?"

"Usually," I said. I allowed my gaze to linger on the lovely line of her buttocks as she leaned over the chair, licking her finger and leafing through a few pages of the *New Yorker*. I was careful to look away when she turned toward me again.

"I do that too," she said.

"Do what?"

"You know, come outside after dark. Roam around the yard."

I nodded stupidly.

She moved to the door. "I need to get back. Dad's waiting for me to make him a chicken pot pie."

Quickly she was out the door.

"See you!" I said, but already she was passing by the window, through which she smiled and waved at me.

I was so distracted it was impossible even to stare into space. I paced the office for a while, gave up on the idea of reading a magazine before I even tried it, walked outside, walked around the block, walked to the corner and walked around another block. Lilace, *who comes outside at night and walks in the yard*, had invaded my mind. She was romping there, making a mess, making my eyes roll skyward, my wings flap as though I could soar into that blue and white air, weightless, powered by Lilace. The hour or so I walked seemed like no time at all. When I rounded the corner onto my street, I saw that Faye was home from the boutique.

I walked in through the front door, said hello to Faye, asked her if she'd had a good day at the boutique.

"I'm tired," she said, not looking up from *Mademoiselle*. "I don't feel like talking."

I hesitated, about to go back to my office but feeling a pang of hunger.

"It was Nancy Nickerson, wasn't it?" Faye said. "One of them, anyway. Right?"

The leap I had to make, from swimming in swirling Lilace thoughts, to remembering and discussing Nancy Nickerson with my wife, struck me as impossible. But then it seemed fortuitous that Faye would bring it up, since otherwise I would have been hard put to explain the agitation, which must have been evident in my demeanor.

"I'm hungry," I said. "Let me get a snack. Want anything?" Faye shook her head, still staring at the magazine while her *Nancy Nickerson* floated through the room like a day old helium balloon. In the kitchen, I found a banana needing to be eaten. I peeled it and stood in the doorway to the living room as I munched it. "I'm at the auditions," I said. "She walks into the room. I'm immediately stunned by her beauty, but that's nothing unusual for me. I look away from her and try to listen to the director, who's whispering something in my ear about the actress who just finished auditioning for us. I can't hear a word he's saying. I'm looking at Nancy Nickerson."

"I knew it," Faye said. She put down her magazine. "You started it, then."

"I don't know."

"Sure, Hec."

"It was chemistry. She says to me, 'Do you know why a dog licks his own genitals?' Actually she yelled at my ear, over the noise of dozens of other voices trying to compete with the hyper-amplified juke box music."

"At the audition?"

"No, later. We were having drinks at the bar in Manhattan Plaza, along with the rest of the cast and the director. We'd cast Nancy as the ingénue in *The Mamelukes in Great Neck*, which I'd based to a large extent on the smidgen I knew of her life, though I wouldn't admit it."

Faye tossed the *Mademoiselle* to the floor. "What do you mean? I thought you'd only just met her."

"No, well, I've skipped ahead a year or two now; this was the second time I'd worked with her. In a week we were opening across the street on Theatre Row. Why are you nodding?"

"It just makes sense," Faye said. "That was when it looked like your career was taking off."

"I guess so. Anyway, you're right, this was a heady night. We'd just had our first rehearsal in the theatre. Up until then we'd been working in a dark and dusty space on the top floor of the building."

"She always struck me as sort of trashy. Trashy mouth, anyway," Faye said.

"There were other people touching and bumping me and Nancy on all sides, but we were still essentially by ourselves, encapsulated in the matrix of noise and drunken disinterest. We had to yell at each other to be heard, but no one else could hear over the noise. No one knew or cared that our bellies were rubbing each other, except of course us."

"Why are you talking like that now? 'Matrix of disinterest.' Is it that exciting, remembering it?"

I continued anyway, swallowing a mouthful of the sweet ripe banana. I *was* excited—not by the memory, but by the act of telling all this to Faye. "Nancy held her white wine so that the rim of the goblet was almost touching the corner of her eye. We were scrunched in the crowd, elbows pressed to rib cages, you know. I could see her wonderful fingernails. I guess they were red, although the light in the bar obfuscated real colors. But the nails were long, perfectly shaped, darkly colored, accentuating the white lissome fingers of Nancy's delicate hands."

"Oh good Lord," Faye said.

"No?"

"Go ahead," she said, and leaned over to retrieve *Mademoiselle*. She pretended to read it again.

"At that time there was a commercial running on TV and radio for Mateus wine. 'Hey hey hey, Mateus Rosé!' Remember? I had reworded the tune for Nancy after she'd received a review in the *Daily News* for her performance in a children's play at Circle Rep. The reviewer had noted Nancy's retroussé nose. I now liked to sing *Hey hey hey, retrousse nosé*. I didn't want to run it into the ground, but I'd sung it to Nancy a couple of times, hoping to get the courage to then lean forward and kiss that very cute button nose."

Faye sat still, staring through the page on her lap.

"So in response to her question about the dog, I sang *Hey hey hey, retrousse nosé* and leaned forward, puckering hard, my sights locked on the center of her face—and knocked her wine glass into her cheek. Sloshed wine right into her ear."

"She loved that," Faye said.

"It was odd; there was this burst of laughter nearby, but it wasn't for us. We were still alone."

"In the matrix of disinterest..."

"Right. I managed to grab a napkin off the bar with one hand and wrapped the other hand around Nancy's waist, feeling her warmth through the shirred bodice of her gypsy dress. I quickly blotted the wine off her cheek and neck and then dabbed at her ear with a dry corner of the napkin. I didn't apologize—it wasn't necessary, she was giggling—but I shook my head in disdain at myself, my awkwardness."

"Okay, Hec. This is all well done. Disdain. That's great. You wouldn't be building it up like this if anything had happened."

"Are you sure?" I was having fun now. I waited for Faye to admit she was interested in the details. She finally did.

"Meanwhile she was heating up in her shirred bodice," Faye prompted.

"I guess so. She yelled 'We could get a room.'"

"What, right then?"

"Right then. I still had the napkin, dabbing at her. Without thinking, I looked at her, and she gazed back at me with a touch of shyness, leaving no doubt that I'd heard correctly."

"You know, Hec, I wonder why I've ever doubted my perception of things. How much contact did I ever have with Nancy Nickerson?"

"Not much."

"That's right. That one party at her boyfriend's apartment, and that was it. But I knew exactly the kind of person she was."

"Nancy was a joker. She used to order Pouilly Fuisse champagne by asking for 'Fussy Pussy' and act like that was the correct pronunciation. But she wasn't kidding around that night."

"Well, I know you didn't get a room. You wouldn't have had the money."

"Actually, I thought the reason had something to do with loyalty to you," I said.

Faye slapped her magazine down on the floor at her feet and looked at me. "She probably got a room and paid for it," Faye said. I smiled. "Well, did she?"

"Not that night. Throughout the run of the play, she flirted with me. Kissed me one night in the dressing room backstage when we happened to be in there alone. I acquiesced, enjoyed it very much in fact, but didn't pursue it. And finally, after the production was history, Nancy came up to the apartment one afternoon when you were at work, ostensibly for me to explain how to work the computer. I had my chance that afternoon, but didn't take it. Sometime later—a month, a year, I'm not sure—I began to realize that it was not out of loyalty to you that I opted out of that affair and others that might have happened. It was out of some deeper sense of dread, which must have been instilled in me at a very early age, because I haven't been able to remember being much indoctrinated against adultery."

I looked at Faye. She had her hands clasped behind her head and her feet on the coffee table. "I hope you don't expect me to feel sorry for you," she said.

"No. Of course not," I said. "In another sense, I was acting out of self-preservation, pure and simple. It was the first time I was actually afraid of getting AIDS if I had sex with anyone but you." I was still holding half the banana I was snacking on. I took a bite; now it was tasteless, but I chewed anyway. "The last time I saw Nancy in person was when we met surreptitiously to go to a movie together. We held hands throughout the movie—I did enjoy naughtiness if it didn't go as far as actual sex. After the movie, I walked Nancy to her subway stop and said goodbye at the top of the stairs at the entrance to the station. I'm sure there was a sort of finality in the way I said goodbye. 'You know why a dog licks his own genitals?' she asked again, and I remembered the riddle from the night at the bar. 'No, why?' Have you heard this, by the way?"

"I don't think so."

"Why does a dog lick its own genitals? 'Because it can,' she said. You had to see her eyes sparkle, looking at my reaction. I laughed. It was funny, but I've heard funnier. She was insane. It was like she was telling me something. You know?"

"Her eyes sparkled."

"Okay. It's hard to explain. Anyway, she turned abruptly and hopped like a puppy down the subway stairs."

"We saw her on TV that time, remember?" Faye said.

"Right. An episode of *Hill Street Blues*." I popped the rest of the banana into my mouth and turned back to the kitchen to rinse my hands under the faucet.

"Hec?" I heard Faye call.

Drying my hands on a dish towel, I returned to the doorway.

"You don't think I believe that load of crap, do you?" she said.

"Why would I lie?" I said. I tossed the towel across the kitchen onto the counter, then turned to the bookshelf, giving Faye my back.

Every word about Nancy was true. I wondered what it meant

that Faye needed to be sure, that she cared what had happened.

"She played a prostitute," Faye said.

"What? Oh, on *Hill Street Blues*. I don't remember."

"Type casting," Faye said.

"Very funny. Actually, yes, she did play a prostitute. All legitimate actresses who get parts on TV crime dramas play prostitutes. There's some rule in the Actors Equity code or something."

Faye watched me fumbling with the Harvard Classics, several volumes of which had been mysteriously replaced on the shelf upside down. "What's the matter, Hec?" Faye said.

"Hmm?" I feigned reading a passage from Dana's *Two Years Before the Mast*.

"Forget it," she said. "Anyway, no sex of any kind with Nancy Nickerson."

"Right. She did give me a beejay in her dressing room after the show one night, but I do not consider that sex."

"What?"

I replaced the volume right side up and sauntered out of the room, heading for the back door, finding it funny to have teased Faye with that last comment, but also sad that I had made it up, that it should have really happened and then could have been my wonderful shameful secret.

I could smell the fragrance of Lilace in my office. I sat and breathed it for a while. I watched the light in the room evaporate as twilight deepened. The subject of AIDS niggled around in my brain. Was I neurotically trying to work up some fear?

Before moving to Asheville, I'd written letters to the theatre groups here, having identified them by calling the Chamber of Commerce. I introduced myself, sent my resumé to the head of each group, suggested I would like to meet with them just to get acquainted once I'd moved into the community. One small group

was impressed enough to commission me to write a vignette to be
included in a show they were planning to open on World AIDS Day
and later tour the state. They offered six hundred dollars for a piece
to run no more than ten minutes. It was to be a profile of a young
man here in town who had lost his lover to AIDS and was himself
HIV positive. I was to interview him, of course. This seemed like
easy money to me. Working an hour or so every day, I completed
the project inside of six weeks, and the theatre group paid me for it
promptly. Though they were a small group, they were well funded
through a single private source—one of the members.

Tim Schmidt was grieving for his lost lover, Bob, who'd died
less than six months earlier. The interview was colored with that
grief, and yet Tim was able to talk with me forthrightly about the
impact AIDS was having on his life.

I was mainly interested in fear of death, which I guessed he
must feel. When I finally had the courage to ask him about it, he
told me that yes, he'd thought about it plenty, but was not actually
afraid of dying. 'There are certain very unpleasant opportunistic
diseases I could get,' he told me. 'Those I worry about, but not the
dying itself.' Bob had died of Kaposi's Sarcoma. 'I took care of
him right here, twenty-four hours a day, for about a year. When
it was time for Bob to die, I called an ambulance and we went to
Solace House. When you go to a bed in Solace House,' Tim said,
'you don't expect to come back out.'

I asked Tim if he would consider suicide. 'Why not? There are
some things I wouldn't want to suffer through, knowing it would
end in death anyway. I don't want to live the end of my life blind.
If I got CMV, that's cytomegalovirus retinitis, I don't think I'd
want to go through that. Or AIDS dementia. Going crazy doesn't
sound to me like much of a fun way to wrap things up here on
Earth.'

All these statements of Tim's appeared in the vignette I wrote. But my own thoughts were more difficult to dramatize. I didn't know Tim. I didn't want to tell him what I was writing, but why not? Why not tell him I put myself, with all my fears and prejudices, into the vignette, as a vehicle for telling his story.

I earned my six hundred. I'd lived this nightmare in New York, even if it was mere anxiety and depression. I needed to stay away from the landscape of AIDS for my own sanity.

But where is that landscape? Is it only in places I'm afraid to go? Solace House. Gay bars. The back seats of boxy minivans owned by bored housewives? Even remote possibilities are enough for my paranoid mind. The landscape of AIDS is not just made of places, but also of happenings. Cautious movements of hemophiliacs. The accident—the tiny puncture of the skin. Bleeding gums after brushing teeth. Health workers. And feelings. Feelings maybe even more than places or happenings. The yearning of the freshman coed, away from home at last, away from hurtful moral tones, free to search for love. The child whose life is too short on love to get him high enough. And at least for now, AIDS exists in the frustrating landscape of the unknown. Perfect, in short, for my irrational fear.

I could not stop thinking about AIDS, the force which represents the culmination and the damnation of a revolution I always felt had saved my life—the sixties, the sexual revolution.

If a woman would have an extramarital affair with me, was it not reasonable to suspect that she might have done the same with some other man—a man who, by the same token, might have had affairs with other people? Was this not precisely how the virus was spread? Single women were now the segment of American society in which infection was spreading most rapidly.

I don't know Lilace.

I didn't know Tim. I never knew Bob. And I'm too afraid to try to know them.

Sitting in my swivel chair, I stared not into space, but blindly at the white cardboard and black Helvetica lettering which adorned a prominent spot on the wall.

My mind wandered on.

Bob and Tim enjoyed their sex. Tim made that quite clear to me. If I knew I was going to die from a sexually transmitted disease like AIDS—first thought, here—I would be so afraid and shriveled that I'd never get a hard on again. Yet Tim told me that it was during sex, long after Bob had tested positive for HIV, that Tim first saw a greenish lesion on Bob's back. During sex! (The lesions, Tim said, are green at first but later turn purple.) Did they finish sex that time? Did they go ahead and have orgasms? Or did Tim see the lesion, his eyelids drooping with passion as he must have been thrusting from the rear into Bob's anus, and suddenly lose his erection? I didn't ask. Too timid, scared myself, to ask if Tim was scared. I only asked him, in another context, about his fear in general.

But what if Tim, from under his drooping eyelids, saw the green blemish heralding Kaposi's Sarcoma, and it brought him to orgasm at that instant? What if the adrenalin rush of fear was twisted into eroticism, just as guilt is processed in that way? Guilt was never sexy; fear was never sexy.

Or was it?

A garter belt, a pair of shoes, panties, snakes, flies on feces, dead bodies—Kaposi's Sarcoma.

Were you horrified, Tim? Did you stop, pull out, put three fingers to your slightly parted lips? Or did you cream, Tim? Was it maybe the best load you ever dropped.

I had to walk again, get outside for some air, clear this half-baked psycho-bunk from my head. By the time I'd paced slowly around the block, I realized that I'd spooked myself when I let my feelings for Lilace fly in their own direction, and had found a convenient, because familiar, home for the fear: AIDS. The laugh, uneasy and scornful, was on me.

I rounded the house and went inside through the back door. Faye had prepared a light dinner for us both. She'd reheated some leftover pork barbeque and made it attractive on an old dish she'd inherited from her father's mother. She'd made a salad, placed some sliced bread on a plate, set the table for us. It was kind of her, thoughtful. I usually do the meals.

As we ate, I offered some slight reminiscences of a trip we'd taken long ago to Nova Scotia.

"We should paint our house sky blue," I joked, referring to cottages we'd seen in Nova Scotia.

"Lavender," Faye said. "You should write a play set in Nova Scotia." There was some clinking of flatware on stoneware as we both ate and stared at our plates. "You should consider doing some writing," she said quietly.

"It won't happen," I said, as lightly but finally as I could manage, and that was the end of that discussion.

I did the dishes. By the time I was finished, Faye was reading a magazine in the living room.

The screen door off the back porch squeaked. I passed from the thick air of the house into the dark ether of the backyard. Faye was relaxing on the Queen Anne with a Vogue, finishing the bottle of wine we'd opened with dinner.

A withered sliver of moon tilted in the western sky. I stood outside the house, hands jammed into my trouser pockets, breathed deeply the moist air, caught the rubbery scent of the boxwood blossoms, a hedge of them growing untrimmed, wild along the back property line two doors down. I glanced at the Stones' house. The mystery of window lights held me. She was in there some-where. How long would I have to wait until she came out? (Would she really?) I walked past my office, to the back of the yard, into the deep shade of the althea crowding along the fence between my yard and the Stones'. There I stood, trying to make out a silhouette of the flowers against a sky that was too dark.

I jiggled the items in my pocket—a few pieces of change, my keys, lip ice. Faye would fall asleep on the couch, I knew. I was not worried about her coming to look for me.

I pretended to be a ghost, tried to walk soundlessly across the dry grass, but it crunched softly under my tread. I walked up the driveway to the front sidewalk, passed the front of the house, then back down the narrow side yard and into the backyard again. I considered going next door and knocking. Surely Lilace would answer the door. It was past ten o'clock. Maybe the Stones were already asleep. Yes Lilace, and not Mrs. Stone, would answer the door. But I didn't do it.

I walked ghost-like to the fence, the spot where I'd first met Lilace. I stopped there, suddenly unsure, suddenly feeling foolish.

The back door of the Stones' house rattled. It was stuck, some-one was urging it past the friction. It opened. The small bug light over the back steps remained off. I saw Lilace's slim figure de-scend the steps. I panicked at the thought that she might not see me standing there, might never see me, never. She disappeared behind crepe myrtle. She was disappearing!

I was unused to going into the Stones' yard, had never been more than a few feet into it, in fact. But I felt I had to go there, find her.

"Good evening!" she said, making her voice sound like a horror movie somewhere off to my right. She giggled, and she appeared. "What are you doing out here in the gloom of night?"

"I often come out for a breath of air late at night," I said. Why wasn't she standing close to me? Why didn't she walk into my arms, place hers around my neck, like this afternoon?

"Do you really?" she said. "Do you often come out for a breath of air late at night?" She leaned against a fence post, bringing her smile into view in the faint amber light from the kitchen window. I could have taken one step, stood directly in front of her, leaned my face to hers, kissed, lost my tongue in her mouth, taken hers into mine. This I was sure of. But the center of my body was tensed with an expectation that sent sparks to the surface; I shivered as though the night were cold.

"It's all right," she whispered, and I felt her warm hand slip over mine, each finger finding a place between fingers, clenching, letting go, turning loose, coming back and finding warmth again. Warmth rushed up my arm, into my neck, made me dizzy. Lilace leaned away from the fencepost and touched the collar of my shirt. Now I found myself leaning against the fencepost, she still holding my hand, gliding her other hand down my shirt sleeve, taking my other hand, placing it in the small of her back. Now the coiled energy inside me released wild shudders into my torso. She absorbed the tremors into her warm breasts.

"It's all right," she said again.

"If it is, it would be the first time," I said, surprising myself with the hoarseness of my own voice. "You excite me well beyond the level I've ever been able to handle."

"You don't need to handle anything, Hector," she whispered. "We're friends. I know we are."

Whether she knew it or not, this was an evocation of the old days, the sixties. *If you can't ball your friends, who can you ball?*

we used to say with the weight of irrefutable logic. And an old song lyric came to mind: *If you can't be with the one you love, love the one you're with.*

But out of habit—oh listen! out of *habit*—I pounded down the sixties-style sexual elation with latter day AIDS trepidation.

Suddenly we were walking, hand in hand, toward the back of my yard, then across the yard and up toward the house again. She spoke to me quietly. "This night, the air, it's so much like the way I remember Austin."

"What was it like?"

"Oh, always humid, for one thing. Always warm and wet. Campus always dominated by the Texas Tower, a huge male symbol. Across the front of the building was inscribed 'Ye shall know the truth and the truth shall make you free.' I always wondered what the difference was between ye and you."

"Subjective and objective cases," I said, and hated myself for it. "What were you doing in Austin?"

"Graduate work. Never got my master's, though. Got married instead."

We were walking up the narrow side yard, the darkest, most secluded spot on the lot. I stopped and took Lilace in my arms, kissed her, pressed her body into mine, took her tongue into my mouth and sucked it. Then I held her, felt her breath on my ear.

"Now, what do you say?" she said to her young child.

"Thank you," I managed, grateful to the point that I almost cried.

"And thank *you*," she said. She sank to her knees, urged me down beside her. The grass was dry, but it was thick like a cushion. She lay back, one knee cocked up. I carefully found my place beside her, lying on my side, propping my head up on the palm of my hand. I gently placed my other hand on her belly. Quickly she took

my hand in both of hers and moved it up to her breasts, helping me
to feel their shape, small, softly empty.

"Can't you come to me?" she said, her voice now swelled, fit-
ting her throat tightly.

I leaned over her, kissed her, but was unable to relax for fear
of crushing her under my weight. Helpful, she turned on her side,
facing me. It was a position of less passion, but allowed us to
relax, to gain intimacy. The very awkwardness we struggled to
overcome was exciting. No comfortable old partners, we were
teenagers longing for the perfection we'd imagined through our
pubescence, picking through every moment for the good parts,
trying to ignore the elbow-jabbing earth beneath us, its unwel-
come pull on our bodies. We wrapped our arms around each other,
kissed, I pulled her very breath into my lungs, let it escape only as
slowly as I could, not wasting it, not wasting the precious smoke
of the expensive joint, the longer I could hold it in, the higher I
would get.

"Did you ever do that?" she whispered, pulling her face away
from me, taking a break.

"Do what?"

"Share smoke."

"My god. You knew that's what I was thinking!"

"You were doing it," she said, and kissed me perfectly, lightly
on the lips.

"Yes, I was. But getting higher off you than I ever did off
smoke."

She relaxed away from me, lying back on the grass. I stroked
her hair. My eyes had become so accustomed to the dark that I
could make out her profile, that of a child, the nose pug, the face
small.

"Are we safe here?" she asked.

If Faye had gone to bed, then we were less than twenty feet from her, but the wall of the house was there, and besides, Faye would have fallen asleep in the living room with her bottle of wine. I knew we were safe from intrusion. More than that, I felt it. "Yes," I said. "We're on another planet."

I lifted myself, leaned over and kissed her again. She wrapped herself around me, found my sex with her thigh and gently pressed there, giving my hip the warmth of her own sex.

"Can I tell you something?" she said. I put my face to her hair and listened to her. "I need to be me, now. I need to have this for myself, not for a pretend person, not for who I was thirty years ago."

I listened, but she said nothing more. I lay back, we held hands. Stars were twinkling through from eternity as the earth's hazy air crystallized above us. I began to understand that there was no hurry; there could be a relishing of this time—there must be, in fact—this time beforehand. She meant that we must not waste it, and we need not; we could own it because we were fiftyish—own the tenderness, the gentle, unworried touching that played between us, that thoughtlessly wandered from public places on our bodies to private ones.

"Something is very different with you," I said.

"Do you need to tell me?"

"No." But I needed to sort it out if I could. Unlike Nancy Nickerson, or Meredith or any other woman I'd had sexual opportunity with since I'd been married, Lilace was truly there for me. I would not be impotent, no moral scruples would cause me to back off. I desired her, had the opportunity, and was able. Even the danger of being outside the house would not interfere. Any semblance of privacy would have been enough. All the fears I'd known with other women—that we'd be caught, that I'd contract

HIV, that the woman would grow possessive and reveal the adultery to Faye and the rest of the world, that the woman's husband or boyfriend would find out and hunt me down and kill me, and on and on—these fears evaporated, only manufactured manifestations of the real fear—that this sex was loveless, or that it was full of love and would have to end.

Would anything else stop me? Could anything else? No, nothing. I was free to love, if only for tonight. I need only try and make it last until the light of day, last as long as possible, give Lilace as much time as I could, and give myself the same. A profound relaxation swept over me, something completely new to me. The spring-loaded energy within me uncoiled in an ecstasy that caused me to gasp.

"Are you okay?" Lilace said.

I breathed once deeply, twice, stared wide-eyed at the stars as though I'd never seen them before, and I had not. "Yes," I said. "Suddenly I have a super boner."

Lilace giggled quietly. She snuggled into my side, began stroking my thigh. She whispered so quietly I could barely hear her. "We have forever. Don't wait longer than you can. I'm so happy."

I was sorting out these statements, thought I knew what she meant. It was all disjointed, but it made sense. I relaxed on my back, let her brush her lips along my cheek and ear. She pulled my shirttail up and stroked my soft belly, kissed it, reached down my leg and ran her hand up its length. Slowly, everything slowly. I filled my hand with her hair, felt the shape of the back of her head.

I had the sensation of a tugging at my shoe. I thought yes, I'll take off my shoes. Plenty of time. Tugging, tugging. The toe of my shoe. She was kissing my shoulder, her hand in my hair, her other hand on my belly again.

Tugging at my shoe.

Tugging at my shoe?

I tensed. She felt it. "It's okay," she whispered. She relaxed, snuggled into my side again, stopped touching me with her hands. "It's okay. I *want* to stop and start. I *want* that."

Tugging at my shoe.

Tugging.

I lifted my head, sighted down the length of my body.

It was him. It was Robin. He saw my face, saw he had my attention. Stealthily, noiselessly he crept on all-fours up to my head. I turned my face away from Lilace to see him. I could make out his expression—excitement, fear, and worry all overridden with a nervous grin. He held his finger to his lips as if I needed to be instructed not to reveal his presence. I felt his tiny fingers push my head away so that I was gazing straight up again.

I felt his hot wet breath entering deep into my ear canal, and I had to wipe it away with the back of my hand. He then moved even closer, so close his lips brushed against my earlobe and I jerked away involuntarily.

"Sorry," he whispered, but then moved as close again. "I just have to tell you this. Go ahead and ball this lovely lady. That's what I wanted to tell you. I'll leave you alone now so you can enjoy it. Ball her and I won't bother you again, Hector. Do you understand?"

There was an involuntary quaking in Robin's whispered words, especially evident on the word 'understand.' I nodded once, discreetly, to show him I heard.

"I'm not sure you do," he whispered, anger now burnishing every word. "Not sure you *savvy*. You ball this chick, you'll never see me again."

He crept away like a crab, sidling on all fours toward the front yard. I turned onto my stomach to watch him. When he reached the corner of the house, he stood up, looked at me for a moment. He was in silhouette, but I'm pretty sure he shot me the finger before he disappeared around the front of the house.

I raised myself uncomfortably up onto my elbows. I looked at Lilace, and though in the darkness I could make out little more than her wonderfully feminine shape and the lush, fragrant forest of hair falling partly over her face, I saw also, as in the light of a sudden flash of lightning, the lie that screamed TRUTH: SEDUC-TRESS, ADULTERESS. The lightning flash blinded me; all was dark for a moment. Then, as the shades of black began to reassert themselves around me, I saw the darkness crawl out of every corner of the yard, every cranny in the bark of the trees, every damp, cold place around the foundation of the house. It slithered to me, entered me, coiled up inside me, wound around me tighter than ever before, and left me breathless, my fever broken, the sweat already drenching my clothing.

Suddenly a thought invaded my mind like a knife into flesh. The trap door to the basement—I knew what he'd been doing. The trap door would be open now. He would have opened it himself somehow. The loose step was balanced precisely to topple the Unsuspecting off the edge of the stairwell onto the gardening tools below. The spading fork would have been turned with its thick, sharp tines pointing upward.

The Unsuspecting would be lured toward the back of the house by noises—whispers, giggles, faintly animal, human, human animal sounds. The Unsuspecting would see the open trap door and decide to investigate...

Lilace was sitting on her knees beside me. I hadn't seen her move to that position. I'd lost track of time as well as space.

"You can't, can you?" she whispered. "I'm sorry. I'm so sorry."

I wanted to tell her that the truth had hit me. The clouds had suddenly evaporated, the way they had when I realized Ginger was gone, that I'd pushed her away from me mercilessly without letting myself see what I was doing. I saw things only when it was too late to change the results.

I turned to try and say some of these things to Lilace, but she was gone.

"It's too late!" I said, panic cutting through my chest and stomach. I tried to stand up. The blood rushed out of my head and I found myself—how much later?–awakening on the grass a few feet from where I'd been.

"Don't!" I said as loudly as I could, trying to warn Faye, though I did believe it was too late, else my mind would not have cleared and I would not have seen the truth.

I struggled to my knees, took a few seconds to let the blood come into my head, then gained a standing position carefully. Again, my vision began to blacken, but the sensation passed. Quickly I took steps toward the back door. When I made it to the door, I could see that the basement light was on, glowing up through the open trap door onto Faye's face as she stood over the gaping hole, gazing down curiously.

"Don't!" I cried, exploding through the screen door.

"Oh," she said drowsily, drunkenly frowning in confusion. "I thought I heard you down there. I was just..."

By then I was at her side. I took her elbow and pulled her away from the death trap, none too gently.

"Hec, what are you doing?" she said, much annoyed at the rough manner I used to pull her to safety.

"I was working on that top step earlier," I stammered. "It's loose, you could have killed yourself. I forgot I left the thing open like that. Scared me when I saw you there..." I was panting, trying to catch my breath and could not seem to do so.

"Well for god's sake," Faye said, turning to leave the scene.

When she was gone, I slumped to the floor. After a while, I caught my breath. I leaned over the trap doorway, saw the spading fork perfectly positioned, tines up. I carefully crawled over the loose step, made my way down, disassembled the death apparatus.

He had the gall to show up at my office door the next day. I was in the middle of a reminiscence, and was damned if I'd let even Robin bring me out of it. Holding my anger in check, I let him come in and find a place for himself. He chose the floor next to the filing cabinet, occupied himself drawing circles in the dust on the floor with his finger.

I'd been remembering my computer, a PC of the old 8086 type, slow by today's standards, but reliable and uncomplicated. I got rid of it when I left New York. It had become a demon for me; even the smell of the manufacturing residues, normally a pleasant "new plastic" aroma, was enough to tip me into nauseous waves of paranoia and fear. Leaving New York was tantamount to admitting failure, I felt in my heart, regardless of all my rationalizations. The sight of the monitor staring at me with its one giant eye was an insult. Its teeth, the keyboard, grinned at me, sinister, accusing me of worthlessness. Who needed the grief? Not me, so I gave the thing to Vida, the seventeen-year-old girl who'd just signed on with the Ford Agency. She's on TV commercials now. Her mother Puerto Rican, father, Irish, they lived in the apartment just below us. I told myself that by giving her the computer, I was encouraging her to continue her education. She accepted the computer gratefully, but let me know that she made a thousand dollars for her first day's work as a model. That didn't help my ego, but I couldn't resent it, because in telling me about her fortune, Vida was struggling against her natural inclination to hide her pride. She was growing up beautifully. And physically, she was absolutely perfect by today's standard—far too thin to be sexy to an old codger like me.

I sat at my desk ignoring Robin. I was tapping the letter "b" on my old Smith Corona portable, seeing if I could tap it with just the right pressure to make the key swing up exactly halfway to the platen. I was finding I had to give it a pretty good little pop to get it up there.

"Working on a new piece?" he said after a while.

It wasn't the right thing for him to have said. I hadn't realized how mad I was at him. It was as though he was responsible for everything I hated about myself. What I hated most was my not having made love with Lilace, for which I blamed him directly and fully. I picked up the Smith Corona and, from my position in the swivel chair, hurled it at him as hard as I could. I saw the shock on his face just before the typewriter hit the wall, missing him by inches.

He jumped up and made for the door, but I was already on him. "Not so fast, little pup," I said, spitting the words at the back of his head as I grabbed the elastic waistband of the corduroy shorts he was wearing. He tried to wriggle out of the shorts to make his escape, but I grasped the waistband with one hand and his ankle with the other.

He relaxed, face down on the floor, and said, "What are you doing, Hector?"

I jabbed down on the small of his back to hurt him, still not letting go of the waistband. He barked in pain, then groaned, then began whimpering. "I'm sorry," he said. "Please don't hurt me again."

I wanted to hurt him more, but he was so small, so helpless. I almost gave him another jab for good measure before releasing him, but I didn't. I rose from my kneeling position and walked across the room, leaned on the windowsill and looked out at the backyard.

I heard him moan some more, huff and puff as he righted himself. I was waiting for him to leave, but I didn't hear the door open. I turned around and he was poking at the typewriter where it lay, upside down, on the floor.

He noticed me watching him, and said "Can I have this? It's broken now anyway."

"I'm going to have to kill you, Robin," I said. "You've become a tragedy in my life."

Backing away from the typewriter (and me), he countered, "She was going to screw and leave. You would have had one more unfulfilled longing from then on."

"In other words..." I said, but he interrupted.

"In other words, she was going to hurt you, Hector."

I knew he was wrong, but I didn't want to be sucked into an argument. I still just wanted to beat him up. But he took my silence as the beginning of acquiescence.

"Hey, man," he said, "she ain't even that good-looking."

He had no idea how angry he was making me. He misjudged my restraint as another step toward reconciliation. He edged back over toward the typewriter and tentatively poked a finger at the part he'd found so interesting. Daring now to take his eyes off me for an instant, he smirked and muttered, "*Old* mama, too."

Quickly he checked to see my reaction. I smirked back at him, finding this last comment pitiful and ironic. Lilace had been beautiful, didn't look to be out of her thirties even though she was, of course. She had been my chance of salvation, my one possible doorway back to sanity, and a lovely person, an articulate hippie for me to talk with, to join with, to heal with in the face of the millennium and free love's final death throes. It didn't matter that she would be gone soon, back to Texas. It had been the moment, the night before, that counted. It had counted for everything, and he had ruined it.

I moved to my desk and picked up the stapler, turned toward him and threw it at him as hard as I could. He dodged it, but barely. I quickly moved between him and the door. He started trying to calm me down, saying my name again and again. "Hec, take a breath, man." "Hec, give this a minute and let's talk." Things like that. Maneuvering around the room all the while. Suddenly he made a lunge for the window. I stepped toward him and had him around the waist by the time he'd hit the windowpane with his fist, trying to break it, but unable to exert enough force.

I was going to hold him down on the floor again and really give him some punishment, but now he flew into a wild rage, flailing his arms, kicking so furiously that I let him slip from my grasp. I chased him like a wild dog after quarry, and he ran with the instincts of prey. He pulled the floor lamp down in front of me, trying to buy time to open the door. I did fall over it, smashing the shade and bending the stand, but he could see he didn't have time to get the door open. Running to the corner, he yelled, "Please!" I was already coming at him. He darted past my desk and pulled a drawer out into my path. I slammed it shut with such force that the front panel cracked loose at the joint and several pencils and an old pair of sunglasses clattered to the floor.

I was moving fast, giving myself to the rage swelling behind my face. He was trapped now just below the window next to my desk. His face was contorted with terror as I dived at him, hurting both my knees when I landed at his level. He tried desperately to jump aside, but I got him by one wrist and one ankle.

He was struggling but helpless against my superior strength. I stood up, squeezing with my hands as hard as I could, determined not to let him escape. Suddenly he turned his head toward my crotch and thrust his mouth at me so hard that I instinctively let go of him to protect my balls. He bit savagely into the hill of my bluejeans, the vestigial codpiece that jeans manufacturers don't seem inclined to eliminate. I have no doubt that Robin thought he was biting through to my penis, but he just had hold of those several thick layers of denim. Once I realized that, I grabbed both his ankles and held his wildly flailing feet away from my face.

He grabbed at my balls with both of his hands and had a solid grip on my left one. He also maintained his bite on my jeans. The sudden pain of his squeeze sent me into a frenzy. I let go of him again and jumped away, falling into my antique magazine rack and breaking off the dowels at the joints. I screamed and cursed at him and threatened to kill him if he didn't let go, but he held on and squeezed even harder. I fell to the floor and cried out in agony, all the while trying to hit him with my fists as hard as I could, but to no avail; and then it was my turn to beg. "Please! Please let me go, Robin!" I was crying, sobbing great sobs. I felt the pressure ease just slightly, then tighten slightly again. "Please," I cried, "we can talk. We can talk about it. We'll come to terms." I broke into uncontrollable sobbing, and by degrees he eased off his hold.

He moved away from me and I continued crying, pulled into a tight fetal position on the floor.

I made the effort to dry up, took some time, let the throbbing in my testicle subside. I sat up on the floor. Robin was pouting in my desk chair. He did not know my mind.

I'm an actor of sorts—did a little acting, a few improvs in college. I decided I'd do a little acting now.

We sat silently for a while, sneaking glances at each other while I rehearsed in my mind. Finally I smiled at him ironically. Grudgingly, he smiled ironically back at me. I laughed. He didn't quite buy it, so I laughed even harder. He began to smile and look down at his feet, which were dangling off the edge of the chair.

"Hey," I said, "we have some choices here."

"What ones?" he asked.

"The way I see it, I had a right to be mad at you. Okay, I was mad, I let you know. Now it's time to say I'm sorry, since I let my anger get out of hand. If you'll accept my apology, but also acknowledge that you understand why I was mad, then I think we can go on from there. What's your response to that?"

He took a while to answer. I saw his lower lip quiver a bit as he started to say something, then shifted his position in the chair, sucked in a breath, and swallowed. "I guess we can go on now," he said.

"Good," I said. "Now listen to me, Robin. We go on as *friends*, you understand? Nothing more than that."

"What do you mean?" he said.

"You don't own me, and you have no interest in my love life. Let's get this out in the open. You were jealous of Lilace, were you not?"

"Okay, okay, okay," he said, with a measured amount of resignation. Suddenly I wondered if he, too, was doing some acting.

"Friends, then," I said. I held out my hand to him. "Shake on it."

I saw just a hint of suspicion flicker across his face, but he took my hand to shake it.

I jerked him as hard as I could, hoping to pull his shoulder out of its socket. He screamed in pain, a shrill, girlish wail, and in a second I had him face down on the floor, both his hands pulled sharply behind his back and forced upward almost to his neck. I had my knee in the small of his back, pressing down as hard as I dared. Now, I had him in a helpless position, and we both knew it.

"You bastard," he choked out. "I'll never trust you again. You know that, don't you?"

"Doesn't matter, Robin," I said. "I'm going to break your spine and then watch you die."

I waited for him to argue, or tell me to go ahead, or something, anything. But he said nothing. I could tell it was difficult for him to breathe, but I kept the weight of my knee pressing into his back. There would be no escape for him this time.

Long seconds passed. I felt the heat and tightness on the skin of my face where my tears had dried. I felt a slight soreness in my chest, the result of the unaccustomed pounding of my heart, now calmed.

Then I looked at the little hands whose blood circulation I was cutting off. The hands were dark red, almost purple. They were childlike hands. In fact, I realized that the entity I was holding so brutally to the floor was, in a sense, a small child.

My child.

My only child.

Ultimately, I leaned over to get a look at his face, and saw a glistening, silent tear roll down his cheek and puddle at the flare of his pink nostril; and I saw pain wrinkling the corner of his eye.

I let him up.

It took a few minutes for him to work the kinks out of his back. "You really hurt me," he muttered, limping around the office.

"You ought to be glad you're alive," I said, still sitting on the floor, now cross-legged.

"I am glad I'm alive," he said. "But you really ought to do something about your self-control. You're a *maniac*." He spit the word at me venomously.

"Just get out," I said quietly.

He reached the doorknob and turned it, with some difficulty. Then he was gone, and the door was left ajar just barely the thickness of his little body.

I was thinking about cleaning up the battleground of my office. Strangely, I felt a sense of disappointment that there was so little danger of Faye coming out and discovering the mess.

September 6

I went into something of a stupor through the middle of August. I refused to speak to Robin for several days after Lilace left for Dallas. I felt doubly humiliated that she took a taxi, didn't even say goodbye to me. The day of the Barracuda might never have happened.

Robin spoke to me politely, tentatively, once or twice a day, then left me alone. Alone with my problem.

And my problem was that I longed, I *ached* to be with Robin, to talk with him, to inquire of his activities, but I was still too angry.

It was the blackmail—the ultimatum he had whispered to me about Lilace—that infuriated me. I needed to set aside the anger, though, and concentrate on Robin's apparent desire to do away with Faye.

I considered ways of separating Robin from my spouse while keeping him available to me. I wanted to rent a small apartment for him, but knew it would be hard to hide such an arrangement from Faye because of her sharp eye on our finances. I do receive very infrequent royalty checks when *The Animal Fair* is produced in regional theatres, but I couldn't depend on that.

I decided to go for it anyway, using a Visa card I acquired without telling Faye. I found a very small, one-room garage apartment in the neighborhood just south of downtown on an alley off Boxelder Street, and paid the landlady six hundred dollars—two months in advance and one month security. My plan was to use the card for the apartment, then change my address with the card company to the apartment address. There would be some correspondence, initially, at home, but I'm always there to get the mail anyway. The chances of Faye running across the Visa bill seemed small.

I intended to squirrel away household money in order to pay the Visa bill, and possibly get some kind of regular income myself so eventually I could pay the rent directly.

I took possession of the apartment before the end of August, but I didn't tell Robin about it immediately. Instead I just enjoyed my secret excitement.

We were sitting in the living room about an hour after Faye had left for the boutique. He was filing his nails.

"Nice pants," I said. He had somehow acquired some white bellbottoms, the kind sailors wear.

"Mmm," he said. "I got these a month ago, but they were way too long." He hopped off the couch, stood posing in the middle of the room. "See how they fit?"

And they did. Adrenalin, meanwhile, was pouring into my system, my heart beating so fast I thought it would burst. I knew that when the moment was just perfect, I would tell him about the apartment. Just now, though, I simply looked at him.

He was easily three feet tall now, and his buttocks were round, plumper than before. His arms were still slim, almost stringy, and had taken on a porcelain sheen. The wiry black hair that had covered them was now reduced to a light brown fuzz. He'd acquired quite a collection of T-shirts, and chose large, loose-fitting ones even though I know he had some that fit snugly.

"I hate these stupid kiddie T-shirts," he said, frowning down at a faded rendering of Bart Simpson.

"Didn't used to bother you," I said.

"Well, it does now. I don't guess you could actually go out and buy me something if I described exactly what I wanted. Just a plain sweater, basically."

"I don't have money to buy you clothes. You'll have to steal them like you've been doing."

"You have money to buy me clothes if you really *want* to," he said, and then he lay down prone on the floor and started poking his finger through the mesh of the fireplace screen.

"Come on and get in the car," I said. "I've got something to show you."

He looked at me suspiciously. "*Your* car? You sure it'll run?"

"It runs fine," I said, though with my old Skylark it was always a gamble. "Come on."

I walked through the house to the back, not turning to see if he was following until I reached the door. I had to wait a moment, but soon he appeared from the kitchen and coyly peered around the door frame.

"Come on," I said.

"What if somebody's around?"

"Who?" I said. "Mrs. Stone? Let her see you. See how she likes it."

He smiled in acquiescence, sighed and hunched his shoulders a little, and followed me out the door, through the yard to the garage, which was, as usual, open.

He'd never ridden in a car—at least not to my knowledge—but he waited as I opened the driver's side door, then quickly climbed in ahead of me and settled into the passenger seat. He was fiddling around with his seat belt as I got in and closed the door.

"This will be a new experience for you, I guess," I said, still trying to conceal my excitement.

"I almost rode in a car the night I..." he trailed off. He knew I knew he was the vandal of Faye's boutique, but we'd come to an unspoken agreement not to discuss it.

Pulling away from the house, then turning onto Charlotte Street, leaving the neighborhood behind, I kept breathing deeply, kept quiet, afraid I would blurt out my secret and spoil the surprise.

He rode silently, the top of his head coming just below the open window. I glanced over at him frequently, noting that his hair was finer than before; silky brown, it played in the wind with little resistance. He squinted against the gusts and the bright, late morning sun, and I noticed the long lashes framing his round, soft eyes. In the few months he'd been alive (and free of me), he had actually become quite pretty. Driving over the interstate between the south and north sides of town, I allowed myself a fleeting moment of pride in having borne such a creature.

"Can you see anything?" I asked, mostly to keep myself from hinting about the apartment.

"The top of an occasional tree," he said. "I really don't feel like standing up in the seat so I can watch the wondrous beauty of Asheville float by."

I laughed giddily, an involuntary release for my bubbling anticipation. Asheville was indeed wondrously beautiful this day. I sucked my lips and drove through downtown, the bright sunlight splashing off the copper dome of the Baptist Church, the taller buildings jutting into the hard blue sky with utterly stupid and gorgeous dignity against Asheville's backdrop of graceful, elderly mountains.

Boxelder runs along the foot of a steep slope. The apartment is accessible through an unpaved alley running behind a harum-scarum cluster of houses. I urged Robin out of the car, grinning

broadly as I watched him slide across the seat and climb down. I
stood watching as he poked around the tiny driveway. We could
see little but the garage apartment and dense vegetation, much of
which (I noticed for the first time) was tall bamboo. The garage
itself was empty, its door inoperable.

He looked at me. "You've taken me to an apparently remote
neighborhood in Asheville, an alleyway to be exact. Are you going
to do something to me?"

I laughed. "No, I'm not going to do something to you. Look," I
said, pointing to the wooden steps leading up the side of the garage
to a small landing, "go on up those stairs." I realized, as soon as
I said it, that the stairs were somewhat too steep for him to climb
easily. "Here, I'm going to carry you," I said. He allowed me to
pick him up, putting his hands gently around my neck to hold on,
and twisting around so he could see ahead. I took the stairs two at
a time and set him down at the landing. He looked off; from this
height we could see the backyards (weeds and dog runs)of several
cracker box houses.

"Seedy," he said.

"A little disheveled," I conceded.

Robin turned around to look at me. I produced the door key
from my pocket and proffered it to him.

"The key to the door, I bet," he said.

I used the key. The door stuck a little at first, but then it opened.
The place smelled musty, so I hurried to a window and opened it.
Robin followed me inside tentatively. I stood in the middle of the
room.

"Kitchenette," I said, pointing. "Bathroom right through
there."

"What is this furniture?" he said, hands in pockets, eyeing the
single bed in a corner, then the mustard-and-green-striped love

seat. There were two other chairs and a dinette set as well.

"Comes with the place," I said, now anxious for some sign of approval. My little friend climbed up onto the bed and pulled the spread down to examine the sheets, mustard colored ones I'd bought at the mall.

"The pillows are brand new too," I offered.

He gave the pillows a token perusal.

"So what do you think?" I said finally. He gave the room another quick once-over from his vantage point on the bed. "Cute," he said, but still tentatively.

"It's yours."

"But you'll be here every day, more or less."

"Of course," I said, beaming again now.

He slid off the bed, turned a slow circle in the room.

"Cool," he said, and cocked his head and gave up the smile I needed.

There was a garage apartment much like this one down the street from the little frame house where I grew up in Connecticut. My brother Roger once claimed to have smoked cigarettes inside the apartment when it was vacant. He offered to prove it, to show me the butts where he'd thrown them into the toilet, if I would pay him. I was tempted, but not enough to give up the dime he wanted. And I was scared of the place because it was different from other houses in the neighborhood. Perched atop an earthen-floored, one-car garage, it was accessible only via a thinly constructed wooden stairway perpendicular to the garage wall, landing in a crabgrass yard strewn with dog feces. (I could almost be describing *this* place!)

Our neighborhood was working-class back then, has long since been claimed by developers building homes for the affluent. That mysterious garage apartment, which I could see from my bedroom window, but into which I never set foot, was occupied by many different tenants over the years, and usually they were scarcely to be seen. They probably worked nights or graveyard shifts.

Scarcely to be seen.

Standing there watching Robin checking out the place, I felt connected to that childhood mystery; now I was inside it. I stayed for a while, took a seat on the bed while Robin tasted the water from the sink, looked into the kitchen cabinets, the refrigerator, out the windows, under the sink, into the bathroom...

It was easy to imagine that I was a man in the nineteen-fifties or -sixties, a man scarcely to be seen, having hired onto the graveyard shift, thus separated from the little boys and girls going to school, the moms and dads working to make ends meet, and the rest of the people, grannies, whatever, who filled up towns and cities and what was left of the countryside. Invisible, working nights.

I felt like smoking a cigarette, a habit I gave up along with other smokes after college, but which seemed strangely attractive in that place of invisibility. Unseen, a man could do unwonted things. The taste of tobacco just before dawn, the burn on the throat, the benign defiance of death before breakfast, all seemed relevant to the garage apartment.

October 10

The summer ended rainy, but the autumn has been dry. To me love seems to be the force turning Asheville's leaves into fiery reds, oranges, yellows, deepest royal purples, blues, pinks. Love burnishes my every feeling, clinging to my breathing like the leaves to the limbs. The leaves, emblazoned with death, still refuse to fall, insisting on dazzling, on stealing my attention with their brilliance.

This cut on my face has set everyone off, and I'm tired of lying, covering up Robin's existence. Yet this is better than before he came out of me, when he was a fetid mass, a demon tumor occasionally scratching to get out, finding ways of making me hurt on the inside, never allowed consciousness or corporeality. Now, he may be a pain in the ass, but he is not a pain on my soul.

In the few weeks he's had his apartment, I've awakened every morning with a sense of relief. While he was here in the house, I worried that he would show himself to Faye, or she would stumble across him. But now I wake up and there's nothing to worry about. He's across town, and he's quite content.

A few days after I gave him the apartment, he started asking for things. "I can't live with these awful shades," he said. "I want yellow jabot curtains with white eyelet lace."

"I have no idea what you're talking about," I said. He went to the dinette table and took a piece of paper off it and handed it to me. He had written down, in a childish yet florid hand laden with curlicues, exact window measurements and item numbers from the Penney's catalog, which he also handed to me, opened to the page showing the curtains.

"I don't have a Penney's account, and I don't have the money to buy stuff like this," I told him. "Faye would notice it in a minute."

"Then I'm going to sulk and get depressed looking at these stupid shades," he said. He crawled up onto the bed and curled up facing the wall. He was wearing a baby blue terry cloth robe; in fact, he'd worn nothing but this robe since his second day in the apartment. Watching him there on the bed, I noticed how his hips had widened; it was accentuated by the way he was lying on his side, of course, but nevertheless, one would have mistaken him for a small woman at that moment.

"I'll see if I can come up with something," I said to his back.

Instantly he rolled over and gave me a pouty smile. "Just *something* is all I ask," he said, mollified.

Working together, we had the apartment to his liking within a week, and I'd spent little more than twenty dollars. As far as I could tell, he hadn't been going outside, and didn't want to. He'd seen large dogs running loose in the neighborhood. As things were, he felt secure inside the apartment, and so did I.

Of course I visited every day. I was there virtually all the time Faye was at the boutique, making sure to be home before her. I supplied him with the meager groceries he required. He cooked a delightful meal for me, Thursday's lunch, skillfully using a foot-stool in the kitchenette to reach the counter top. He deviled some eggs, julienned some ham and mozzarella, made mint tea, and even created some clever little roses out of tomato skins for garnish.

Yesterday the sunny morning gave way to black thunderheads. Faye ran a little late getting out of the house, so I didn't make it to the apartment until almost eleven o'clock, right in the heaviest

downpour of rain. I sat in the car, waiting for the deluge to subside.
I looked up through the windshield at the apartment just in time to
see Robin pulling a curtain aside to peek down at me. I waved but
he didn't see me.

As I sat in the car, an inexplicable melancholy swept over me.
In spite of my good spirits up to that moment and the way everything with Robin was working out nicely, I found myself choking
back tears. Then I could not choke them back, and one huge drop
rolled down my face and I sobbed and convulsed. I was thinking
of an odd set of coincidences that had occurred the previous day.
Odd, yes, but to think of it as depressing seems far-fetched, so I
don't know why it would have brought on tears.

I'd been neglecting my morning walk, hurrying instead to
drive over to the apartment. I'd decided to take my walk, just for
the sake of good health. Robin could wait an hour or so for me, I
thought, feeling a throb or two of independence. I set out toward
the convenience store, stopped in for a cup of coffee and the morning paper. Fighting an annoying impulse to hurry to Robin, I tried
to strike up a conversation with the clerk. He was laconic—stupid, it turned out. Maybe it was a mistake, after all, to fight my
impulses. But when I left the convenience store, once again I felt
damned if I would cut short my constitutional.

I headed into a neighborhood I've usually avoided because to
get there I have to walk across busy Merrimon Avenue. It's a quiet
neighborhood of old farmhouse-type dwellings built harum-scarum in the small hollers and along the low ridges of the folded
terrain.

I was noting the gingerbread on a vacant house when I saw a
pair of cardinals on a tree branch that hung just below the eaves.
The male was mounting the female, his wings all aflutter as he tried
to balance, she hunkering down a bit and trying to provide some

stability on the thin, bouncing branch. Voyeur that I am, I had to stop and watch the act completed. Yes, I felt aroused, disappointed at how quickly the copulation was completed, and the birds flew away—as though I had any stake in the affair! I walked on.

A block later—and these blocks twist and turn as they try, however unsuccessfully, to follow an elevation—I happened to glance down the side yard of a bungalow with a notably unkempt lawn bordered fecklessly on three sides by warped and buckled chain-link fencing. In the shade of the house, two dogs were going at it, situated with their heads toward me. The male was a mid-size cur, I guess with some beagle and some terrier in the mix, not a pretty dog, head too small and markings muddy and nondescript. The female was a bit smaller and may have been a breed. Her proportions were nice, and she was a uniform gray color with short curly hair all over, ears that flopped over her face. Again, I had to stop and watch. Get her, that's a boy! She loves it, yes! See her tongue hanging out. They finished just as I was about to check and see if her eyes would be drooping with passion. The male smelled of her sex when he was out of her, and she turned and wandered away toward the back of the house. The male then noticed me, didn't seem to care, trotted into the street and away. I walked on.

Quite a sex show in this neighborhood, I was thinking. I continued along the twisting, crumbled pavement, knowing that it eventually ended at the four-lane highway connecting Asheville to Tennessee and points north. I passed stretches of woods, wondered why nothing had been built on these lots, speculated it must be because they're steep. That's a surmountable obstacle, as evidenced profusely in the upscale developments on Town Mountain in the north end of the city, but the real estate value in this quarter wouldn't warrant the expense.

When I first saw the horse, I wasn't sure what it was. I had to back up and look through the trees carefully. He was a bay stallion, standing in a shaft of sunlight angling through the jack pines. From the street I saw him broadside. His huge penis was extended; I noticed it was retracting slowly, then it dropped down again. He stamped the earth, tossed his head, moved a step forward. Then I saw what was holding his attention. She was black with a white face and a star at her breast. I'd missed seeing her because she was standing in shadows, but now I saw her clearly. The horses were no more than fifty feet from the street. I remembered the birds and the dogs. Surely, I thought, I'm not in for yet another show.

But I was. I don't know how horses court—some ritual, no doubt, involving male urine and lots of intoxicating pheromones coming from the female's rear end—but for whatever reason, the stallion stood quite still, looking at the mare, for several minutes. She stayed in the same shady spot but turned several times, offering views of herself from each side, the front, and the rear. Her tail was slightly cocked up, as though opening her sex to him. After a while, he approached her. She was standing sidewise to him, but when he reached her, she moved to face him, and they smelled each others' muzzles. They seemed affectionate, and remarkably calm with each other. The stallion did not smell of her rear end, but simply moved around to her back and, with a great crunching of sticks and leaves on the ground, reared up and placed his front hooves on her back. She moved considerably under his weight, stepping unsteadily to gain stability. Her movements put them profile to me, a development I silently cheered, as it offered me a magnificent view of his penis extending to what appeared about a foot and a half in length.

As he adjusted himself further up onto her back so he could hunch closer to her vagina, she again had to adjust and struggle under his weight. Soon she was still, and he was thrusting toward her. He tried to enter her several times but couldn't seem to get in. He fell off her, but she stood still and waited as he mounted her again, and again she had to catch her balance, steadying herself by splaying her front legs.

A shaft of sunlight had found them by this time. The stallion's penis now glistened with wetness. I remembered to look at the mare's eyes. Her eyelid (the one I could see) was indeed drooping, even though she was gently tossing her head now and then.

Just as I looked back at the stallion, I saw him thrust toward her, and this time his penis buried itself several inches into her. He adjusted again, his hind hooves crushing sticks with a violent crackling. He thrust again, snorting loudly and tossing his head up. He was in now, and thrust hugely and violently, uttering low huff-huff-huff sounds and snorting. He thrust several more times, not as rhythmically as I would have expected, but more and more frequently until it was almost rhythmic.

I was so excited I had to adjust my own hard penis in my pants, checking up and down the secluded stretch of street to make sure no one was spying on *me*. The horses finished, I surmised, since the mare walked out from under him. But he followed her away adamantly, and I wondered if maybe they were going to continue elsewhere. At any rate, they disappeared deeper into the woods and I walked on, now worried that someone had seen me. I was anxious to walk and lose my erection.

If this strange coincidence were not enough, I then began to see other animals copulating wildly in yards, on street corners, and amongst the trees on vacant lots. Some of these other animals were clearly not indigenous to the area—there were lions, pelicans, wild pigs, for example. The pelicans, in particular, paid no heed to their nature, just lay down like a couple of humans and went to work face-to-face. I half expected them to light cigarettes when they were done. The show didn't stop until I wound my way back to Merrimon Avenue and nervously crossed the overheated traffic back to my neighborhood.

So as I sat in the car, waiting for the rain to play itself out, I was thinking again about those animals, wondering if even the cardinals, dogs and horses were hallucinations. I kept craning my neck to look up at the apartment to see if Robin was looking out the window. I felt tears running down my face, burning the shaven skin of my cheeks. Ever the mental playwright, I began inventing a speech, constructing a metaphor to describe my tears, using the way the raindrops were following the path of least resistance down the windshield.

At that, I forced myself to laugh. I said out loud, "This is ridiculous. I'm *happy*." As if in response, a rampage of wind whipped the rain laterally against the windshield.

"To hell with it," I said. I let myself out of the car and ran up the steps to the apartment. At the instant I reached the landing, Robin opened the door for me and I hurried inside.

"You could have waited another few minutes," he said, fetching me a clean towel from the hamper.

"I couldn't wait," I said. I took the towel to my face and then worked it through my hair. Robin stood in the middle of the room watching me, the hint of a smirk curling his lips. "What's so funny?" I said.

"You were crying," he said.

"Was not," I said.

"Was done it," he said, mimicking a local dialect.

"Wasn't done it," I argued, and let myself fall back onto the love seat, still panting from my run up the steps.

Robin sat beside me. He had grown so much taller that he no longer had to climb, but could lift himself into a seat in a more or less adult fashion.

He waited as my breathing returned to normal. I noticed he had rearranged a few items in the room, and that the air was fragrant with a delicate potpourri.

He placed his small hand on my elbow. I didn't react, and he let it rest there.

"Life's a bitch," he said softly.

"I don't know what came over me, but yeah, I was crying in the car."

"Could be you've been too happy, and the shock's been too much."

"I wouldn't doubt it."

"Want a drink?"

"What've you got?"

"A little bit of wine, milk, apple juice, gin, tea. I think that's all."

"Nothing, thanks," I said, and patted his hand, which he then withdrew from my elbow. "It's not that I'm sad," I said, "it's more like that so many things in the world are sad."

"Like what?"

"Usually love, for starters." I stopped, uneasy with the reckless way my mind was wandering.

"Such as what, for instance," he said. He sprang up from the love seat and went to the kitchenette. Filling a glass with ice from the freezer tray, he said, "You ever been in love? Don't try to tell me you love Faye."

"Well, I do..."

"Come on, Hector. You're playing with words. Whatever feelings you have for Faye do not amount to what you just called 'love' and you know it."

Rather than tell him how wrong he was, I chose to let the conversation drift in this alternative, more superficial vein. I chose to engage my teenager's mentality, and found it surprisingly easy to settle into it.

Robin had poured himself something amber to drink, and sat back down on the love seat, his hip touching mine. He then shifted slightly away from me, and I sat up just a bit straighter, and yet in these movements, which were really acknowledgments, we somehow gained a degree of intimacy beyond anything we'd had before. He was wearing a subtle perfume that reminded me of swimming naked in the lake I lived near as a boy. And the lake was on my mind, and walking by it with Candace, and later walking out onto the dock by myself, without Candace.

"There was someone, wasn't there?" he said.

"You know what's sad," I said, "is seeing the stars in the sky, you know, on a clear night, when you can see to the ends of the universe, and you're looking up there and you are sober."

He chuckled at this, relaxed, laid his head onto the back of the love seat. "Sober?"

"Yes, because, Robin, think about it: drunk as a skunk, you walk out into the night, the cool air hits your face, let's say you're walking out on the boat dock by the lake, and the breeze across the water carries an exhilarating fragrance to you, and you stand at the end of the dock and let your head sort of fall back, and that carries an extra dose of alcohol-laden blood to your brain just as you open your eyes and behold the stars above you. That moment, unquestionably, does incalculably more to sharpen your perception of the universe than does a moment of sober observation."

"Mmm. I think I follow you."

"Which is more real? A mildly exhilarating look at the sky on a pleasant summer night, or being blown out of your ever-lovin' mind by it?"

"You're right."

"This was real, what I'm telling you. I'd never been drunk before. I was, let's see, seventeen. Ecstasy had been Candace. She was blonde, beautiful, a year older than me, actually, but so much in love, both of us."

"Doomed, though," Robin said, "and you ended up hurt and scarred for life."

"Well, of course. What else do you expect? When I was with Candace, the heat of our passion was broiling. When I wasn't with her, I was writhing in agonies of jealousy. So inevitably I ruined it all one night in a rage when she went out with a boy in her class. Her mother made her do it. I tracked them down at the movie theatre and made a tremendous scene, ended up crying on the sidewalk in front of the theatre."

"I know," Robin said, very softly. "I was there, inside you. I couldn't see and hear, but the feelings were all washing over me like an acid bath."

"Is that true?" I asked him.

"You have a sense beyond the five physical ones, you know. You can feel pain that has nothing to do with the sense of touch. I sensed your emotions, and I remember them, but they were disembodied as far as I was concerned. You were the one with sight, hearing, touch..."

"I understand," I said, though I knew Robin's whole situation, his very existence, wouldn't stand up to very much scrutiny. "She was forbidden to see me again," I said. "A few unbearable nights later I stole a fifth of whiskey from my mother's liquor cabinet, went out to the lake and got righteously embalmed. Walked out onto the dock, and there was ecstasy, right up there in the heavens. All I had to do was get rid of this awful, world-class, status-quo state of mind we call sobriety."

I looked at Robin and tried for an ironic smile.

"Don't dismiss it," he said. "You're talking about something that's shaped your entire life." He placed his hand on my arm, but withdrew it when it seemed to stop me from talking.

"One matures, of course," I said, "and learns that adults love each other in quite different ways than the adolescent insanity I knew with Candace. A person eventually stops hoping that love like that will come along again some day, and finally starts telling himself that it wasn't really love at all—that love is this thing we get into with all its respect, responsibility, genuine caring and concern, commitment."

"And it doesn't ring true?"

"Not quite. Never quite, Robin. Because when you pare away all the adult gilding, love is completely selfish."

"Now wait a minute. That's not true..."

"Everything else, the responsibility, the respect, the commitment—it's all laid on, glued on, tacked on so we can control love, tame it so we can live with it."

"Lust, you're talking about."

"Love, I'm talking about. With luck, we end up married to a decent person."

"You're just feeling cynical," Robin said, and stretched his arms over his head, flexing his wrists back.

"No," I said, giving Robin a very reasoned, rational look. "Love is selfish, and that's a good thing. That's the way the universe is constructed. It's lots of fun."

"And where does that leave me," Robin said, "the toy you slept with every night when you were little?"

"Well, I don't know that that's who you are, and if it is, it's not completely who you are. Not even a very important part of who you are. I'm not a little boy any more, that's for sure. I'm going to be forty-six next month." I stood up abruptly, sadly and suddenly no longer a teenager, and went to the refrigerator. I heard Robin go into the bathroom and shut the door as I searched the cold wire shelves for the wine. I found the bottle, a cheap but decent white, about a third full. I took it back to the love seat and pulled out the cork. I saw Robin's glass where he'd left it on the floor at the corner of the love seat. I picked it up and sipped. It was apple juice. For some reason this made me smile. I put the glass back on the floor.

I felt somewhat purged, glad to have had Robin available to unload my feelings on, and now ready to make small talk and while away some of the afternoon.

It was not to be. Several long minutes later, Robin emerged from the bathroom. I heard him before I saw him, and looked up only when I realized he was not coming into the room, but standing at the bathroom door.

He had changed clothes, now wearing a lavender cotton dress, black patent leather high heeled pumps, and a full complement of makeup and jewelry including dangly golden earrings. He was obviously wearing a brassiere, too. The effect was grotesque, and I could not avoid revealing my shock and dismay, although once that reaction registered, I broke into a laugh that must have sounded hysterical.

"Fuck you," he said. He turned to go back into the bathroom, but spun back around instead and headed for the cupboard in the kitchenette, scowling and trembling. With the high heels, he was close to four feet tall, counting the clownish little bow he had tied in his hair. Using the step stool, he had no trouble reaching the bottle of gin on the top shelf, which he jerked toward him so violently that he tripped over his heels and fell down.

His increased anger and his position, like a discarded doll on the floor, struck me as hilarious, though I wished it hadn't, because my laughter, I could see, hurt him.

Purposely pacing himself, he stood back up, still holding the liter of gin, which was almost full, and faced me. I tried to stop laughing, but when I really looked at him, I was overcome by an impulsive fit of honesty, and I blurted out, "Hey babe, you're not half bad!" Then I giggled and the giggling soon turned into more hysterical laughter. I hated myself for laughing, but couldn't stop. The intimacy had been building since I'd arrived, and all its energy had suddenly exploded. Robin had exploded it with this giant overstep.

I was barely aware of him moving toward me, but he came right up to me, touching my knee with his thigh. His serious countenance chilled me into silence.

"I'm a woman," he said.

"You're in drag, Robin," I said, and the giggling threatened to bubble up from my chest again.

"When did you *assign* the male sex to me?" he said, scowling. "Was it when you were four years old, when I came out of the wrapper?"

"No," I said, grinning sheepishly, trying for levity that was impossible. "I didn't think in terms of gender when I was four."

"Haven't you seen me turning into a woman?" he said.

My eyes involuntarily dropped to his hips and the folds of his dress covering his sex. He saw this and placed his hands, holding the gin bottle, protectively over the spot in question, backing away from me.

"Yeah," I said. "Let's see what's under there. If you've turned into a woman, I'd like to see it."

"Get away from me," he said. It was clear to me that he knew very well he had not turned into a female, however effeminate he was turning out to be. "Whatever is under my dress, I'm a woman. And I want you to admit it to me, and accept it and accept me as I am and let us get on with our lives."

"You may imagine yourself to be whatever you want," I said, "and you may pretend to be a woman, and I'll pretend along with you. I really don't care. But you're a little man, in reality. I ought to know."

"When did you ever actually see a penis on me?" he asked.

I was ready for that. "I saw your penis when I was nursing you back to health after I pulled you from under my bed. And also when you stood on the dictionary that I brought you so you could take a leak."

This seemed to frustrate him, because he knew it was true. I turned away, looking out the window at the sky, which was now as black as I've ever seen it at midday. I took a swig from the wine bottle. This must have insulted him on top of everything else he was feeling, because at that moment he threw the bottle of gin, which hit me on the forehead. I believe it knocked me out momentarily, and when I opened my eyes I was sitting on the floor and he was standing in front of me, the gin bottle back in his hands but held up against his face. He was petrified with fear and horror at what he'd done to me. I felt blood trickle down onto my right eyelid.

I took a moment to run a check on my senses, and they all seemed to be working. I said, "Relax, I'm not going to die." It was enough to jar him loose, and he began crying, sobbing freely but never taking his eyes off me.

I let him cry for a few minutes before I stood up—no problem there—and went into the bathroom. There, I examined the cut— superficial, but with some swelling already—and began cleaning it with a washcloth. It took some time to stop the bleeding. I let the blood act as a glue to keep a pad of toilet paper stuck to it. It was beginning to throb when I returned to check on Robin.

He was sitting on the bed, leaning against the wall with his knees pulled up under his chin, his dress hiked up so that I could see the black nylon panties covering his bottom. I looked away quickly, and he noticed that I did so.

I heard a subtle swishing of cloth against flesh, and then he was standing next to me. "Here," he said. I looked at him. He was holding his panties in his hand, proffering them. "Smell them."

"Why?"

"Because I think you can tell the difference between a woman's smell and a man's smell."

"For one thing, I don't think that's necessarily true," I said. "I've never tried it, anyway. And besides, you probably stole those panties from some teenage girl's laundry hamper."

Before we could argue any more, I left.

On the way home, I worked out an explanation for the cut on my forehead.

Faye: [walks in the door after work] What's that?

Owen: What's what?

Faye: That bandage on your forehead.

Owen: [feigning amusement] Oh, that. Lucky I didn't vent my anger; we'd be less one cabinet door in the kitchen.

Faye: Oh. [goes about her business]

Owen: It's called 'projection.'

Faye: What is?

Owen: When you hit a cabinet door that you've just creamed your head on. You 'project' your anger to the inanimate object, which of course is not responsible for what happened to you.

Faye: You hit it?

Owen: No. I repressed the urge.

Faye: So the anger'll come out some other way.

Owen: No doubt.

BLACKOUT

The actual conversation went nothing at all like that. When I got home, I applied a regular sized Band-Aid, which didn't quite cover the whole cut, so some of the still bloody laceration was visible on my forehead. When Faye walked in, she didn't even notice it.

I was in the living room, through which she passed wordlessly on her way to the bedroom, the circuitous route her acknowledgment of my presence.

I put down the book I was pretending to read and followed her into the bedroom. She already had her skirt and jacket off and was pulling the red silk slip down. She looked up and saw the bandage.

"What happened?" she said.

"Bumped a cabinet door," I said.

She stepped out of the puddle of slip at her feet and, unbuttoning her blouse, came to me and peered closely at the wound. "Really?" she said. There was positively a note of doubt in her voice.

Her clothes looked like blood, especially her underwear. I wanted to cover up that red slip with sand, like a cat hiding its dirty. I stood petrified, my knee lodged against the side of the bed, watching her take off her earrings. She was undressing in a studied way, a feminine way, a certain way that had to do with my being there. It was a striptease, in a way, although I'm sure she wasn't doing it on purpose or even consciously.

I hurried out of the room, denying something powerful in me. Desire for her? Anger at her?

I was in the living room wondering if I should try and face whatever was compelling me away from my wife. Maybe I should go back in there and watch her strip, see where it led. What could happen that would be so bad? We might make love, which might change my relationship with Robin (not to mention with Faye, of course). I was loathe to risk Robin's anger. In fact, I was suddenly dizzy with the thought of my precious Robin being taken away from me—*thrown in the trash!*

But maybe I would not make love, not be able to get it up, have to admit impotence with my own wife. Well, that might be a good thing, might open things up for discussion and psychotherapy sessions—real ones. Maybe even marriage counseling.

At this last thought I stood smirking toward the fireplace, when Faye came into the room in her bra and panties, asking me to unhook her bra for her.

"It's stuck," she said.

Sure it is, I thought. She hasn't needed help unhooking a bra since before we were married. I unhooked it easily—it wasn't stuck.

"Thanks," she said, and started, it seemed to me, to turn around and face me. But after just a slight hesitation, she walked back toward the bedroom.

I followed her. Facing it; that's what I was doing, I guess. Well, I must have been facing it, because there was no other reason to follow her into the bedroom.

"Maybe what we should do," I said, sitting on the edge of the bed and feeling uncomfortable, "is go ahead and get an amicable divorce. That way, we let the pieces fall where they may. The historical pieces, I'm talking about. If the bad ones sink and the good ones float to the top, we could always get married again."

She didn't look at me, say anything, or move away from the mirror where she'd been doing something with her makeup. I could see her face in the mirror, and her breasts. The face was expressionless. The breasts were exceedingly round, like basketballs, huge, incomprehensibly erect for their size. I had to blink to bring them back into perspective. No, they weren't the size of basketballs—just large and lovely.

She turned away from the mirror and went to the bathroom, closed the door, locked it. She stayed in there for a long, long time. And all that time, all last night, I felt both stupid and right.

This morning Faye and I were standing in the kitchen at 8:30, the time she usually leaves for work. She was wearing her black suit, turned away from me, wrapping a blueberry muffin in plastic. I was admiring her shapely—and, in the suit skirt, well-defined— buttocks, purely out of habit. Sipping my coffee, I formulated a modest compliment. It was to have been 'You fill that skirt nicely.'

"So she whacked you on the head," Faye said, her back to me. I heard the encapsulated muffin go into the purse.

"What? Who..." I was off guard.

"The cabinet door," Faye said, and then she affected a fake Mexican accent. "De door she whacko you en la cabeza, no?"

"Oh," I said, trying to smile a little, "it'll be all right."

She turned around, closing her purse, returning my forced smile, and saying, "A cabinet door can be a nasty affair."

I agreed, nodding, humming my assent, trying not to seem interested.

She whisked a shopping bag off the kitchen table as she hurried out the back door toward her car, leaving her final word *affair* hanging in the toasty kitchen air.

This afternoon when she got home I was in the kitchen. It was as though the day had not happened, she had not gotten into her car in the morning, but had only stepped outside, remembered something and turned around and had come back in. And although I visited Robin today, it was an awkward and forgettable time. Except for some muttered apologies, we both pretended the fight had not occurred.

Faye breezed past me and disappeared into the bedroom. I stepped out to the back porch, poked at some boxes with my foot, jammed my hands into my pockets, stared out through the screen wire. I bounced my weight on the trapdoor to affirm that it was solid. (I'd nailed the top step securely in place and kept the door closed thereafter.)

The door to my office appeared to be ajar, but then I could see that it was just an illusion, the effect of the late afternoon light.

I heard Faye in the kitchen behind me. "No olives?" she said.

"Look in the door shelf," I said.

"How could they all be gone?" she grumbled. I heard her unwrapping something. A moment later she came to the porch and stood beside me, munching a bagel. "I talked to the mall this morning," she said. "Ross Perkins. He came to the boutique. You think that means they're desperate for tenants?"

"Could be," I said. "I didn't notice any empty spaces at the mall, though."

"That doesn't mean anything. You don't know how many stores might be on the verge of going under or moving out. Things happen way in advance."

"Negotiate. Be tough."

"If I can," she said.

"You can."

Then she was quiet, but continued to stand next to me. I looked at her. She'd put on faded jeans and a drab, baggy sweater. She looked back at me. Embarrassed, we looked away from each other, into the backyard scene, hazily through the screen.

"Matthew and Simone," she said softly.

"Yeah," I said. "I was thinking about them the other day. Wonder how they're doing."

Faye let my attempt to trivialize the subject fade for a few moments. "They scared me," she said. "They scared me to death, later, when I'd think about them, like a grizzly bear charging at me in the woods, just the thought of them."

Todaro: Matthew and Simone? Who were they? Why would fear be part of the dynamic?

Owen: We'd met Matthew and Simone once at a dinner party. Matthew was an actor, Simone a court reporter. They were in their fifties. They were nice enough, but forgettable in the endless parade of new acquaintances. It had been five or six years since that dinner party, when suddenly one day we heard from them again. It was March, the year I realized that I suffered from SAD—Seasonal Affective Disorder...

Todaro: I knew that.

Owen: ...that I had suffered from it for years. I was temping at the Time-Life Building in a research group, and on my own time I was working with a director staging a series of readings, one of which was a one-act I'd written.

Simone phoned, wondered if Faye and I would like to go with her and Matthew to Central Park this weekend and fly this colossal kite that Matthew had built from scratch. We set a time on Sunday to meet at the west side 72nd Street entrance to the park. When I hung up I felt discomfited, pulled unwillingly back into the cold of March, which I'd planned to sleepwalk through to the warm weather. Simone had made the outing sound like fun, and now I remembered how I'd liked Matthew and his frantic style of ingratiation, and had liked Simone, too.

Sunday was sunny and blustery. Faye and I walked all the way to the rendezvous, both of us filled with trivial fantasies about Matthew and Simone, wondering out loud if we remembered them in the same way. Simone was attractive, yes, and Matthew was tall and gaunt. No, Faye remembered nothing of Matthew's overpowering need to be liked; wasn't he something of a wallflower? I reminded her that it was Matthew who took off his shoes and thrust his bare feet into the ice chest containing all the beer. Yes, she remembered now. He was a nut, wasn't he? And Simone, Faye recalled, had some sort of French accent, or maybe it's a mild speech impediment.

They were waiting on a bench when we arrived ten minutes early. I'd forgotten the extreme triangularity of Matthew's head, the wide forehead and long, pointed chin. The shape was accentuated by the graying sideburns he probably thought softened the lines of his face. Simone had the unexercised softness of a sexy woman on the downhill side of life. Her appearance was warm and comfortable, made you want to crawl into bed with her and melt into her flesh. Her eyes were round and puppyish on a face a little too small for the rest of her—she looked almost pixieish.

Even unassembled, Matthew's kite was formidable in the gusty park, extending seven or eight feet so that Matthew asked me to hold one end of it when we started walking into the park. We chattered about our jobs, lack thereof, life in New York, as we made our way to the sheep meadow.

I recognized a surging need in Faye to find a friend, a female friend, one with whom she could share her female secrets. Simone seemed to fit the bill. Faye's only female friend at the time was Merrien, who was more like her child.

Matthew and I were assembling the kite, an unusual design, something like a Wright Brothers bi-plane. He began to dance and hop around the kite, holding it down as the wind tried to snatch it away.

Faye and Simone laughed and laughed, and I thought I saw them touching each other's forearms with their fingertips. The kite soared, Matthew letting out string almost as fast as the kite would take it. Out of habit, I thought I would enjoy a drink about now. But then something in me relaxed, and I didn't need a drink. I sat up, placed my arms over my knees comfortably, and gazed upward at the kite. I forgot about wanting a drink.

Matthew, now at least a hundred feet away, began a hilarious routine of "trick flying" the kite—behind his back, through his spread legs, flying it while doing a somersault–not a bad one for fifty-something. I joined the women to watch Matthew, and the three of us worked hard to project our laughter across the distance to where it was needed.

It was Simone who, a couple of weeks later, supplied Faye with a pill, smuggled in from France, which would end the new life growing inside her.

[Here Owen stops talking, his face suddenly blank.]

Todaro: Faye had been pregnant?

Owen: Yes.

Todaro: Had you known at the time?

Owen: No. I only found out later. The pill made Faye sick. She told me a few days later what it was. They called it a "morning after pill."

She was so certain that I needed to be childless, that a child would kill my career, that I would be an unfit father because of my bitterness at losing my career—she went ahead and aborted without telling me beforehand.

Over the next year, I gradually accepted culpability. Every time I felt free to spend time writing, or rehearsing, I had to accept the clear fact that a baby at home would have prevented it, because, you see, Faye was bringing home the paycheck any time I was spending my days at the theatre, so she could not have stayed at home to care for a baby.

So a new dynamic grew in our relationship. As I accepted blame, Faye sought fulfillment from the City, the way Matthew and Simone seemed to find it. She became more interested in her job, made a number of shallow new friendships, went to more shows, more nightclubs, did a lot of things without me. She started taking business seminars, fashion seminars — she was interested in fashion — she considered enrolling at the Fashion Institute of Technology. Life itself became her baby. Life in New York City, in particular. And she became cold, but in a way that only I could see.

[Todaro checks his watch.]

You better help me, Todaro.

Todaro: I'm trying.

Owen: Doesn't seem like it.

Todaro: And that day at the park, you don't think there was a child in Faye?

Owen: No. I think she got pregnant that night, when we went home sober and stayed sober. In fact, it had to have been that night.

Todaro: Do you think she did it on purpose?

Owen: Yes, I'm sure of it. But then, after lots of talks with Simone, she changed her mind.

Faye was still gazing through the screen wire, apparently lost in thoughts which I assumed were about Matthew and Simone.

"Scared you to death? Like a grizzly bear charging at you in the woods? I wonder why," I said.

"They were so happy. I mean I think they were really happy, don't you?"

"I think so. A little insecure. But as far as happiness goes, I think they were that. Why would that scare you?"

"Well, I was thinking about that. Wondering. It's simple, really. Now that I've thought about it. The reason they scared me so was because their happiness was perverse."

I smiled at this, and Faye looked at me. "You don't think so?"

"I do think so," I said. "It was totally perverse. New York City was their child. Their baby."

"That's it exactly," Faye said. "They were a married couple, and as such they had a biological drive—or whatever you want to call it. They should have had a baby."

I felt a wave of dizziness pass through me. I reached out and pushed the screen door open, but let it fall back. I stood silently.

We were both thinking of pregnancy, abortion, perversion, career, city—this I know. We stood silently, and in our silence, we said more to each other than we had in many years.

When Faye finally spoke, it jarred me, because my thoughts had drifted to Boxelder Street, to Robin.

"I didn't know it at the time," Faye said, "but how I saw myself, my role as a woman, as a wife..."

When she didn't finish, I tried to do it for her. "The pregnancy. And the abortion."

"Both of them," she said.

If Faye was filled with emotion, I couldn't tell it. She spoke coolly, and when I looked at her, she wrinkled her brow as though to scrutinize something in the backyard that was of passing interest to her.

"But anyway..." I said.

"Well, I just..."

"No, I appreciate it." I pushed the door open again, and this time stepped down onto the bare patch of earth where our habitual treading had worn through the grass. I held the door open, but

Faye didn't follow.

"But you're cracked, you say?" she asked.

"I'm cracked," I said. "Sorry."

We were still for a moment. I let the door close.

"At this point," Faye said, "I almost feel like calling Merrien and inviting her up to see us."

Merrien had moved to Alabama, was staying with her mother at last report. We'd lost touch with her long before we left New York.

"There's a thought," I said.

"I guess my maternal instincts are kicking up."

"Writhing around in their death throes, maybe," I said, and tried for a laugh.

Then Faye pulled up the baggy sweatshirt she was wearing and fully revealed her breasts. I was quite surprised; it was completely unlike her to dress without a brassiere. She made no pretense of any ulterior motive; she was showing me her lovely breasts. "These would still be nice for some baby," she said.

"Oh, I know," I agreed. "You've got great ones."

She let the sweatshirt back down and smoothed the bottom edge of it with the flat of her hands.

"Should we think about it?" she said.

I really wanted to say something, just say something to keep the conversation going, but I was speechless, literally unable to utter anything at all. I just stood there, looking in the general direction of the bottom edge of Faye's sweatshirt. She was asking this question of the man she married—not of me. I wasn't the man she married. I was a different man. I stood, my head hung, staring at her sweatshirt, feeling around inside for the man she married, and he was out to lunch. Out for more than just lunch. He wasn't coming back.

Finally I sat on the step, my feet on the bare patch, my knees held together. I tried to think what I should say. All I knew was that I could not hold this in abeyance. It had to be settled. So that's what I said.

"We need to settle this."

"I agree," she said. "Well, I still have my period, still fertile, you know."

"What else?" I said. I still hadn't found much of my voice.

"You had that hard-on the other day."

"Right."

"I can tell you I was... for a few days I'd been..."

"Flirting?"

"For lack of a better word."

"I thought maybe you had. So it wasn't just me off the wall."

She sat on the stoop right next to me, mimicked my posture—knees together, chin on knees.

"Hec?" she said.

"I'm trying to find him," I said.

"Any luck?"

I sat up straight, put my hand on Faye's back. I stroked across the broad of her back, affectionately trying to be good to her, trying to find right thinking.

"No," I said finally. "He's gone. Somewhere back in New York, I guess."

Faye was frowning, but tried for a smile when I looked at her. A brave smile, I'd say. I wanted to reward her bravery by lying to her, telling her it was me, after all, sitting beside her, and that there were no extenuating circumstances we couldn't deal with. I wanted to make a pact with her: we'd forget New York completely, forget lost dreams, lost babies. We'd pick up and go on. I wanted to run my hand up under her sweatshirt and take a nipple between my thumb and finger ever so gently and feel it slowly harden. I wanted to let the rent lapse at the Boxelder Street apartment, and for Robin to leave town and never come back. But it would all be lies, and lies take tremendous energy to sustain, and I was all out of that kind of energy. The Hector with energy for lies, however ecstatic the lies may have been, was gone.

"Most people would try to put the blame somewhere, wouldn't they?" she said.

"We never have done that, though," I said. Then I strolled out to the back of the yard. When I turned and looked back, Faye was no longer on the porch.

There was still plenty of daylight. I took an unusually long walk then, down to Charlotte Street, across that commercial thoroughfare separating my neighborhood from a cluster of woodsy vacation homes, then up the steep slope of Town Mountain. I was thinking at first how blame had nothing to do with anything. Faye had always acted with the best of intentions, and so had I. Why, then, couldn't we go on? I could see that she was a good person, a pretty, sexy woman, and that she hadn't even given up on me. Clearly she did still attract me in every way I could think of. To be honest, she was even more attractive now than she was when I met her and felt the impulse to compete with Karl Furst for the attention of a woman who could have been anyone.

It was too late to go back to her now. But why?

The answer was that there was something attracting me much more strongly. It tugged, with a perfect touch, at the ever-longing libido I'd stifled for so many years. And it assuaged, with all the right answers, the devastated fragments of my ego. In short, it had seduced and possessed what was left of the man who was the playwright. Now, that Hector Owen would not be denied, and Faye had long ago left *his* world completely.

Something had set all this in motion months ago, and I had by now accepted it fully, having dropped all reservations one by one. It was Robin, of course.

Throughout my life, I've wondered how a person can know a thing, wish to change it, yet be unable to. Walking near the crest of Town Mountain, I recalled the frustration, mostly during my young adulthood, of *knowing* I was filled with debilitating anger at my father's absenteeism, and wishing to empty myself of it, but being unable. I even remembered angrily kicking over a potted plant on the front porch when I was a tot because I *knew* how to ride the bike, but *could not*—at least not at that time.

The walk up the mountain had exhausted me, and my legs were quivering as I started back down the narrow switchback road. Golden leaves more than once fluttered down and brushed against my face, having given up their tenacious but futile holds.

November 9

Lainie Wishnick has been elected mayor of Asheville. I was hardly even aware that she was running, though I knew it from seeing the yard signs around the neighborhood. The news of her election stabbed me with the recollection that I'm in love with her. I had completely forgotten, but now I'm overcome with yearning and desolation. It's hopeless, obviously.

I think it's funny that I treat myself to miserable frustration like this. She could just as well be the girl who boarded the A train at 175th Street at rush hour on the way downtown to catch the crosstown to Grand Central–the one I mooned over for a year, but never saw again, never spoke to, never knew. It's not the torture I pretend it is. It's toying with my own emotions.

Todaro: Why would you do such a thing?

Owen: Because I can. It's a special skill, developed, honed over many years of playwriting. Think of it, Todaro. The ability to actually feel like you're in love, feel the yearning, desire, do the mooning, the whole emotional package. And at the same time know it's all bogus.

Todaro: It sounds more than bogus. It sounds...

Owen: Insane? I'm completely aware of my insanity, and yet I do own it, and it owns me.

I took a walk through a golf course in the sudden cold today. The back nine skirt the nicer neighborhood that abuts ours, and on blustery days the deserted course makes for fine contemplative walking. The cold was chomping on my cheeks with cat's teeth before I even reached the course, but I walked on anyway. Along the cart path, thousands of earthworms, lured to the surface by recent warm rain, lay as though flash frozen in three dimensional shapes like chow mein noodles. They looked like they might be good sautéed in butter and garlic.

The wind kicked up, the sky bulged down, ocher bruises on grey. I saw steam rising off the ponds; chemistry came to mind, and the old complaint that we're all made of chemistry, and the quality and state of our consciousness, at least while we're alive, is ceaselessly at chemistry's mercy. Ironically, at that moment a thumping dizziness brought me to a sudden halt, and I reached out and touched a dogwood to keep my balance.

The woozy spell took me back to the labor of Robin's birth, when a flood of old dreams surfaced. Holding the slim trunk of the dogwood, I recalled one of them.

There's a hair in my mouth. With my teeth I try to work it off the surface of my tongue, and then I pick at it with my fingers until I get hold of it, but now it seems I've swallowed the end of it and must pull it back up from my gullet. As I pull, it begins to cut into the tender tissue of my throat, but I have to get it out! As more of it comes up, I notice other hairs matted around it. It is in fact a hank of hair, and it extends not just into my stomach, but on down to my intestines where it's hopelessly enmeshed with the fetid, smegma-like matter that sticks to my hands as I pull. The pain and revulsion begin to bring on nausea, but I have no choice but to continue; I've already pulled out yards and yards of the stuff. It's too late to swallow it back, and I realize it's not only inside my intestines, but has become a part of their very fiber! I have no choice but to pull out my own guts, up through my mouth. I notice that this hair is the color of Candace's hair, the exact shade of pale honey.

I let go of the dogwood and was just checking my balance, which seemed to have returned, when I saw a man in silver poplin, no coat, approaching from the next fairway. Maintenance people from the country club would shoo people off the course some-times, even when no golfers were out. I moved away from the per-son, whoever it was, and hurried to get back to public property.

Winter alters my brain chemistry: that's what I set out here to say. For years I thought, naively, that my behavior wasn't affected, that I was able to hide the depression and anxiety. To some extent, that was true, though Faye always could tell when I was 'cold,' as she put it. 'Cold' is right. Not that I abhor winter; it has its own beauty, plainly pronounced here in the mountains, and strong liv-ing things survive it.

By the time I reached the street, I was considering my own survival, and Robin's. I could murder him, I was thinking, and fill the resulting emptiness with Faye. I could do that if I wanted to. I had the power. Couldn't work up the desire to do it, though. I had already killed all my other characters, except to the almost meaningless extent that they existed as words written on paper. I did not yearn to destroy my best work, a character who skipped right over the process of writing and emerged in three dimensions. I *could* destroy Robin, yes. But as I hurried back to the house, chilled, a headache coming on, it seemed to me that Robin was the best friend I had.

December 6: Boxelder Street

We're in for snow. It's not sticking, but falling in small, dry flakes, noiselessly batting up against the windowpane and melting there, sublimating, that is, back into vapor that disappears into the darkness outside. Some weeks have passed since my last journal entry. In fact, I'd forgotten I was keeping track of things.

"Seek purity in your paranoia," Zane Green once told me. He was doing a very decent Richard Burton while we were drinking at Cecil's, a now-defunct actors' hangout, smoky and dirty, far at the western fringe of the Broadway district of New York City.

New York City seems so far away now, and Zane, I've discovered, is starring in a new crime drama on network TV this season.

"The paranoid's thoughts outshine those of the genius," Zane said, "burning so true and so hot and with such light that they... uh... blind... uh..."

Zane and I were celebrating our last night in New York before heading up to New Hampshire for rehearsals of my play. I asked him what the line about paranoia was from. It was from nothing, he was just spouting stuff extempore, though he admitted he'd been reading some Camus. We were drunk. I was scribbling his profound-sound words onto napkins. At least I pretended I was; I remember taking his tone and intent and play-writing it into words of my own. He stood up, leaned over the table, his palms down on its surface for support, his huge slobbery face hanging there in front of me. "Final, irrevocable, existentially meaningful acts are committed through desperation, not intellect," Zane inflected, affecting a sort of Learean theatricality. It was a beautiful moment, boozy, his voice slow and low: "And though all through life the mind has chosen this pathway or that, it is at the hour of desperation that the road to final peace shows itself, obscene and frightening, enticing, liquefying."

The cut on my forehead opened back up two days after it happened. Faye and I were having dinner together, Mexican chili and avocados on corn tortillas, strawberry smashes on crushed ice. To have a simple but festive meal somehow appealed to us, and I wondered if, to Faye, that amounted to a tacit agreement that my 'affair' would not happen, or end if it had already begun to happen.

"Hector! Your forehead is bleeding!" She dissembled as much alarm as she could, chewing away.

I put my fingers to my forehead without thinking. Touching the small accumulation of blood started a little rivulet into my right eyebrow.

"Shit," I muttered, and got up from the table. In the bathroom I washed off the blood, dabbed toilet paper at the wound until it showed signs of coagulating, then put a Band-Aid over it and returned to the table.

Faye had finished eating. I heard her in the kitchen cleaning up. I hurriedly stuffed the remaining diced avocado into my mouth and washed it down with the rest of my smash. My appetite was gone. I carried my dishes to the kitchen. To my surprise, I saw Faye quietly crying as she washed a plate.

I stood in the doorway watching her. I could think of nothing to say.

She looked at me once, continued to cry for a minute or so, then set about drying her tears and controlling herself. She got one ice cube from the freezer and put it into a juice glass, then added water from the faucet. This she drank slowly, and when she'd finished, she was also finished crying, though her eyes were still puffy and red.

"What's the matter, Faye?" she said on my behalf.

"Love is sad," I replied, possibly on her behalf. I didn't mean to cut the whole thing short like that, but I had done so. We didn't speak again that evening. I spent my time in my office, occasionally checking the window lights of the house. The bedroom light went off at about eleven, Faye's usual time to retire.

I yearned for Robin. Several times I walked into the garage, once going so far as to open the car door, but I knew that driving off late at night would be a blatant admission that I was seeing someone.

Evidently it was the very next day that Faye engaged a friend of hers, an adventurous young man she'd met at the boutique when he'd come in to apply for a job, to follow me around like a private eye during the day. She certainly didn't have to wait long for results, since I was driving to the apartment every day after Faye left the house.

Yet I received the first reaction not from Faye, but from Mr. Stone, in whom she must have confided in some oblique way. He caught me in the morning on my way from the back door to the garage. He was laying for me near the fence, as close as he could get to our house without stepping on our property.

"Good morning, Mr. Owen," he called, his voice barely loud enough to capture my attention.

Annoyed at the delay, I nevertheless walked to where he was leaning on his leaf rake, and like cartoon neighbors we began a conversation over the fence.

"Out for a drive?" he said, none too brightly.

Already I was looking down at my shoes, counting the drops of dew they'd collected from the grass. "To the convenience store," I said guiltily. "Can I pick anything up for you?"

"Thank you, no," he said, his voice gaining gravity with every word.

"How are you feeling today?"

"Chipper," he said.

"And Mrs. Stone?" I looked at him now.

"Still asleep, I'm afraid. She's taken to sleeping very late in the last few years."

I was, as always, trying to act normal. That meant I needed to chat for a few minutes so as not to seem preoccupied and hurried. "And Lilace. What do you hear from her?"

"Ach! Hardly anything. She hasn't called except when she got back to Dallas to let us know she'd arrived safely."

"Our generation, you know. We're busy, always busy." I hadn't said goodbye to Lilace. In my heart, I said it now. Goodbye forever, Lilace. When you left, you took with you all that remained of a little world where I could still fall in love, a little world I'd kept like a souvenir in my pocket. Lost, now, dissipated like jet exhaust on the wind at Dallas/Ft. Worth airport.

"Well," Mr. Stone said, "if you're busy don't let me keep you."

"Not me," I said, much too adamantly. "I'm retired, you know. Retired and on the bum. Life is beautiful."

"Is it?" He stared at me now; my eyes went back to the dewy shoes in their nests of damp grass. "As long as I have Mrs. Stone, I suppose my life will be nothing but beautiful too. I'll confide in you, she is six years older than me."

"No, really?"

"You'd never know it, would you? We're like children in love. Teenagers." Now he whispered hoarsely, "I pray every day that I will die before she does. Not that I'm in any hurry."

I shifted, leaning now on the fencepost, but angling toward the garage as though that would facilitate my escape. I felt the conversation growing irrevocably deeper, longer.

"You need to go," he said, "I can tell."

"No," I said, but left it tentative.

"I spoke with your wife yesterday," he said, watching for my reaction. There was little, since I knew nothing. "She is to be cherished, your Faye."

"Yes," I said, nodding, chewing the inside of my lip.

"She takes care of you."

"...in important ways," I added.

"When life is safe, people maybe don't attach so strongly." He eyed me, a query as to whether I cared what he was saying.

I said, "The adversity in life helps to form a bond..."

He smiled with half his mouth. "The danger, the fear Mrs. Stone and I felt in our flight from the Nazis, this allowed us to understand how precious is the bond between us."

"I can see that," I said.

"But the bond is precious anyway," he instructed me, and he was so close I could smell his cheesy breath. "The danger, the hardship we faced, even when we came to this country, these things only serve to make us understand. The bond between us, that is the most precious thing we have, whether we are lucky enough to understand it or not." He smiled at me, apparently satisfied that he'd told me what I needed to know. "Well," he snapped, sniffed, turned to look at his yard, "I know you have things to do. I'll walk around and see how many althea blossoms have rolled into cigars and dropped to the ground over the night."

"See you later," I said, watching him amble away across his lawn, waving me on with a single finger barely lifted. I suspected

I'd been given a hard lecture, and I wondered what Faye knew, what she suspected, and when she would confront me.

"She doesn't know anything," Robin said, touching up his eyelashes. He wore makeup all the time now, and although he hadn't worn a dress again, his wardrobe was decidedly feminine.

"She may not know anything, but she knows *something*." I was sipping the coffee Robin had waiting for me when I got there. "If you'd heard Mr. Stone, with all this stuff about bonding with his wife..."

"He's thinking about dying, that's all. He was just spouting things in general, from what it sounds like."

"He was *couching* it in general terms, but he started out with all this crap about Faye taking care of me."

"How do I look?" He turned away from his little makeup mirror and pouted at me.

I choked back the rush of appreciation I felt. He was by now a beautiful, tiny woman, as far as his looks and his voice were concerned. He had figured out how to dress well, and had somehow accumulated a very cute wardrobe.

"Frankly, you look like a little woman," I finally managed. This pleased him immensely. He bounced across the room and sat beside me on the love seat, essentially snuggling up to me.

"Don't snuggle up to me," I said.

"Why not?" he said, and he lingered there in the silence for some time before acquiescing, moving only an inch away from me then. I looked down at his shaved legs protruding from the loose shorts he wore. His thighs had filled out, his knees were narrow, and his calves were shapely and proportionately lengthy. Seeing me looking, he said, "Nice, huh?"

The rest of the morning continued in this manner: he flirted, I cautiously let my guard down in small increments. After we had a pleasant, not to say giggly lunch of potato soup and crackers, he spent half an hour in the bathroom and emerged in a short black cocktail dress, high heels, hair swept away from one side and protruding in a wedge on the other. Full makeup and fake (I hope) diamond jewelry... he was stunning. I didn't even laugh.

"How tall are you now, in the heels?" I asked.

"Four feet seven," he said, "and growing all the time."

We spent our remaining hours that afternoon sitting across the room from each other, conversing like adults, discussing in shallow terms everything we could think of—national health care reform, war and famine in Africa, Asheville's water shortage, anything that came to mind. And we let our eyes explore each other. I found pleasure in noting the way Robin's outfit accentuated his narrow waist and plump, round buttocks. He was no longer awkward and showy, but with some aplomb managed to display his small, pert bust line so that I might appreciate it discreetly.

I left as usual at 4:30. He followed me to the door and we stood facing each other, even though I was so much taller that it seemed unnatural.

"I need a stool to stand on just to say goodbye," Robin said. He gave me a sly smile and watched the implication register. I could feel myself blush.

"I'll see you tomorrow," I said, and turned quickly to leave.

I heard the phone ringing as soon as I got out of the car. There's no phone in my office, so I hurried into the house. It turned out to be my mother.

"Where've you been all day?" she asked me brightly.

"Oh, different places," I said. She waited for the details. "The convenience store," I said.

"I've been calling you all day long," she said. "This was going to be my last try."

"Glad you caught me this time," I said. By now, I'd thought of a few other places I could say I'd gone, but she didn't pursue it.

"How's everything?" she said, not suspiciously but a little forcefully, I thought.

"Pretty good," I said.

"Not according to my mothers' intuition," she said. "I think something's wrong. What's the matter?"

"Why do you think something's wrong?"

"I'm your mother."

"Right...?"

"Hec, I want you to come up and see me."

"Oh, well, I'll see if I can get a trip arranged."

"No, I mean right away. When you say you'll get a trip arranged, that means it won't happen."

"Well, we're on a budget, you know."

"I'll send you the money."

"You don't have the money, Mother. Besides, I wouldn't take your money. I can work something out."

"You won't do it. I can tell. I'm coming down there. It's time I did anyway."

"Oh, well..." I said, but she had my mind reeling. She sounded like she really meant it.

"I'll be there tomorrow. Or if I can't get there tomorrow, in a couple of days. As soon as I can."

"Is everything okay with you?" I asked her. She had me worried; she'd never acted as though she would really come to visit.

"It's you I'm worried about," she said.

"But why?"

"I'll tell you why. Because Faye called me yesterday."

"She did? Well, she didn't even mention it to me." As far as I know, Faye had never called my mother before. I wasn't convinced she had done so this time, either. "So, what did Faye have to say?"

"She said you're acting strange."

"Really?" This sounded completely absurd. Even if Faye had called Mother, even if she thought I was acting strange, even if she thought Mother could be of help, I didn't believe Faye would tell Mother that I was acting strange. "What do you mean, Mother? What did she say? She said I was acting strange? Is that the word she used?"

"Yes, she said your behavior was strange. She seemed to think I should come and help out with you."

"Well, I don't know what she's talking about. I guess because I've gotten a little accident-prone lately. But anyway, come on down to see us, Mother. I'm excited. Call and let me know when you'll be arriving. I'll pick you up at the airport." There was a silence here. "You're flying down, right?"

"I'll let you know. I might take a bus. Is there a train into Asheville?"

"No, but I'm sure you could get a bus. Yes, there's a bus station, I remember seeing it. You just let me know your arrival time."

"Yes," she said, but I barely heard her, as though she'd held the phone away from her mouth. Then I heard her plainly again. "What's the matter, Hector? Is everything okay?"

Owen: Is everything okay? she asked me. Is everything okay? I smiled and felt emotion swell in my chest. I couldn't answer her, because I would have cried. This was my mother, asking me if everything was okay. Is everything okay? I came out of the universe, slipped into a wet, slimy, glove of a human body, and wore it into the world of conscious life, my mother's vagina the doorway between the universe and life.

Todaro: Yes, there are many such doorways, many mothers—one for each of us—and while a part of us always yearns to go back through that door, back into the universe, untrapped inside flesh, that very flesh also exerts such a force on us, blindly urging us to remain in it. While we may see the shortcut back, the doorway we call suicide, we frantically avoid that and try to go back through the vagina.

Owen: What a laugh!

Todaro: What's funny about that?

Owen: Only one small part of us will fit into the vagina! We'll never get back that way. It's a trick; it's the flesh making way for more of us to find the doorway out of the universe, into the trap we call bodies.

Todaro: Like so many sophomoric observations, that one is hard to argue.

"Hector, you're not answering me."

"Yes, Mother. I'm okay. Everything's okay. You come on down to see us when you can. I'm looking forward to seeing you."

I told her Faye would be home any second now. Would she like to talk with her? No, the rates were high this time of day. She would talk with Faye later.

"Yes, you'll have plenty of time to visit when you come," I said.

After we hung up, I stood next to the phone, looking through the kitchen to the back porch, and beyond to the backyard which I could see through the screens. It seemed I could feel the yearning—very tangible, well defined—to return to the universe. Suicide? Out of the question. I liked being alive, was hopelessly attracted to consciousness. But the yearning was real, and it occurred to me that everyone must feel it, because it always wins. Always.

That evening Faye and I ate our dinner silently. The silence wasn't particularly unusual and didn't alarm me. We did the dishes together, and after some puttering around the house, we settled in the living room. I felt like watching some television.

I had barely noticed Faye holding what appeared to be a bill from a credit card company or department store. I was looking at the TV listings when she got out of her chair and came to me, tossed the bill onto my lap, returned to her chair and sat down.

"I was going to let it take its course. Wasn't going to say anything and hope it would eventually go away." She didn't look at me as she spoke.

The bill was from J. C. Penney's. There were many items of clothing listed. 'Petite shop' appeared several times. Finally it occurred to me to look at the address. Robin Owen. Our house address. Not the apartment. How could he have been so stupid, I wondered, to have had the bill sent to this address. But he probably opened this account before I'd found the apartment. I remembered him looking through catalogs, and it seemed now that he had once asked me for a ball point pen while he was browsing.

My mind raced. With a pang, I realized that in my haste to get over to the apartment, I'd forgotten to check the mail for several days in a row.

Faye sighed deeply before she spoke. "Let me lay it all out. Might as well put all our cards on the table. I know about the apartment on Boxelder Street. I haven't been over there and don't intend to go in that neighborhood. Just make sure she doesn't ever come here, okay? And as for this bill..." she let a snorting laugh escape, "she must have some nerve, but anyway, as for this bill, you better not... you had *better* not pay it out of our bank account. Now, if you have some secret income you can use, that's fine."

"Faye, I didn't know about..."

"Let me finish, will you? I'm laying my cards on the table if that's all right with you, and then you can lay... you can do whatever you want."

I waited for her to finish laying her cards on the table, but she just sat there. I gave her time to collect her thoughts, but it became clear after a while that her thoughts were not collectible.

"Faye, this is not what you think. It's going to be hard to explain, but I've been through some emotional upheaval in the past few months..."

"Get out," she whispered.

"How do you know about the apartment?" I asked, holding my ground at least for the moment. "Cards on the table."

"A friend of mine followed you over there," she said, then looked at me straight on. "I asked him to because I suspected."

"But he didn't see a woman, did he?"

"She's a short, cute, dishwater blonde, you asshole."

"No, that's not..." I stopped short, felt ridiculous. I'd been about to correct Faye on the point of Robin's hair color.

She stared me down before she continued. "You have a place to stay, obviously. I don't know if you've been paying for that, or if she has. I don't care. It's your home now. Hope you enjoy it. A garage apartment in a poor black neighborhood. Hope you like it, Hec. Get out. Get out, now."

"Faye, I want to put my cards on the table and I want you to see them," I said, determined not to raise my voice.

"Get out!" she screamed.

She sat like a stone, allowing me to gather some of my things before leaving by the back door. I guessed I would be able to talk to her when she'd had a day or two to calm down. But already I began to wonder just what I would tell her, and what I'd let her go on believing.

I've been here at the apartment since that night, though I've returned to the house several times to gather more of my things. Faye has refused to communicate except to say, on one of the several occasions I called her from the pay phone at the convenience store, that she intends to divorce me. She's contacted a lawyer, but so far, I've seen no papers nor heard anything official. I do have the impression she's serious, though her parents, devoutly anti-divorce and skillfully manipulative, will have a palliative effect. I also get the distinct impression that the man she hired to spy on me is still in the picture, though I really don't care, and frankly I hope he's of some comfort to Faye.

I did manage to ask her if she had really called my mother. She seemed confused, said she had never called my mother. I believe this to be true. I also know that Mother will not find her way to Asheville, though she will undoubtedly try from time to time to contact me by phone or mail.

Several days after Faye threw me out, I returned at night to the house for the first time. I walked all the way from the apartment, a long walk, about an hour, I'd say. I didn't know whether to walk into the house, or knock first, or sneak in. Annoyingly, I didn't have a watch, wasn't sure how late it was. I slowed as I walked past the Stones' house, still unsure. To avoid stopping still,

I turned down the driveway, and ended up in our backyard.

My office was dark. I could have gone in, collected some things—ostensibly the reason I was there. Then I knew that wasn't the real reason; I needed to talk with Faye. I hadn't wanted Robin to know—told him I was going for a walk, didn't take the car because he might have suspected I was heading for Faye. I told myself I needed some things from my office. Now that I was there, the office was irrelevant.

I stood in the darkness at the side of the garage—the spot I liked to sit in the Adirondack chair on warm days. The back of the house was dark, but I could see light reflecting on the shrubbery outside the bedroom window. I thrust my hands deep in my trousers pockets and walked slowly, quietly, to the corner of the house and on around until I was standing on the spot where Lilace and I had lain. From there, I could see that the bedroom light was on, but could not see in. After a minute or so, I decided to get a better angle and see if I could spy on Faye.

To gain a sightline, I had to climb up into the row of bushes which offers privacy from the neighbors across the wide lot next to us. The blinds in the window were down, but the slats were turned open so that I could see a good image of the room.

The absurdity of my position didn't escape me. Spying on my own wife through the bedroom window, like a voyeur but with no sexual impulse involved.

And she was in there, in a strange position on the bed, sitting in the middle of it, profile to me, holding her feet far apart with her hands, her head bent way down. She was at it again! Examining her genitals! Though her butt was sunk into the softness of the mattress, still I could see that she was naked—except for a white brassiere.

What would I do? Go knock on the door? Yikes!

I decided to watch her. I was safe from detection where I stood. I wanted to squat down, relax, watch the show, but I had to remain standing in order to see.

Faye didn't move. She breathed, but only at long intervals, as though she stopped for a while but then had to take a deep breath to make up for it. Other than that slight hunching of the shoulders and expansion of the ribcage, she was motionless. Her head hung so low that I wondered if she had fallen asleep in that position, but she couldn't have; she would have rolled over or something.

Many minutes passed, and I watched, and she stared at her vulva. I muttered into the leaves near my face, "What the hell are you looking for in there?"

Fifteen minutes may have passed, maybe twenty. I was getting angry at her for staying in that position, and at myself for staying in the one I was in. Several times I started to walk on around to the front door and knock on it, but it was becoming a challenge to see how long she would keep it up.

Eventually I did brush my way out of the shrubbery and head for the front yard, but instead of going to the door, I walked on down the sidewalk and turned the corner, vaguely thinking I would take a circuitous route to the convenience store. It occurred to me that I might strike up a conversation there with the night clerk.

I didn't go to the convenience store—just walked around the neighborhood, edging away from Faye until I finally reached an unfamiliar street. Anger was simmering in my gut, and I tried to let it be, let it bubble and burst if it would, though I couldn't identify its source. Some of the anger turned to paranoia as I walked down the strange street, a residential one with bungalows very close together, no barking dogs (strange indeed!), all the cars parked on the street for lack of garages. But when I came out of this street onto Edgewood Road, suddenly I knew exactly where I was, and

I felt a rush of relief.

"Of course," I said. And then I thought that what I've been wanting is to take the choice away from myself, so I wouldn't have to *choose* Robin, wouldn't have to know in the corner of my mind that Robin is there only because I choose him to be, or because I'm cracked. But that's nonsense. I don't have to take the choice away, or deal with choice at all. Robin is there, and that's good enough. For crying out loud, what am I worried about?

"Morality," I said to Edgewood Road, and I laughed just a little bit. *Choice.* A Western idea, no doubt. Instead of choosing, I could go with what *is*—so much more honest. Who the hell invented right and wrong? Answer: all our great diggers of metal, makers of armies, imposers of will. Fighting for the chosen "right" became the moral imperative. Lost, already, was the natural order, the world as it actually *is*. Honor was to be found in killing for the sake of ideas. Just free me of honor and strife, thanks. Let me do the best I can for myself with nobody's right and wrong, and like the Pygmy, I'll leave the earth to heal if it can.

Feeling my spirit uplifted, clarified, I sucked in the moist night air and headed straight back to the bushes outside Faye's window.

I'd have been disappointed if I hadn't seen her—now the better part of an hour later—still sitting on the bed in that same position, her head bowed at that sharp angle toward her inscrutable pussy. I watched for only a minute or two. Nothing was going to happen for a while, plainly. Feeling wonderfully centered, completely in touch with my emptiness and need, I walked back to the Boxelder Street apartment where love could be found.

I've stayed here through the final crisping days of autumn, and watched the tulip poplar outside the back window turn yellow and shivery, the leaves finally falling, flattening on the bare ground, turning grey with the onset of cold weather. Last week the land-lady, Mrs. Zaks, discovered without emotion or concern that I'm living here. She'd assumed early on that I was keeping someone.

Dawn is beginning to break as I write this now. I want to hurry and finish this entry before Robin awakens and we begin our day, a new day, a new beginning for us. I'll refer to Robin in the feminine gender—it would be absurd to do otherwise. She stopped growing about a week ago, topping out at just an inch under five feet in her stocking feet.

We've struggled financially as the weeks have passed while I've been here, but we've been happy. By the time I was thrown out of my house, I'd already accepted Robin's femininity, so that was not a problem. We've spent whole days together inside the single room of the apartment, just talking, piddling around in the kitchenette, getting to know each other better. Robin has revealed some of her clever ways of acquiring clothes, both legally and il-legally. I've revealed much about my past, much about the terrible loneliness I've felt even while in the arms of the several women I've lived with in my lifetime. I brought the bottle of Jim Beam from my office and have carefully sipped it. There's still a little left. I only drink enough to feel the slight uplifting, and I only do it because it flattens the colors of the landscape around Robin while sharpening her image.

Last night, the beginning of the darkness that now is fading into light, Robin sat reading one of my early plays, a manuscript I'd hauled over to the apartment in a box with other papers.

"This character Joycelyn. She's Candace, isn't she?"

I had to think for a moment to remember. "Yes. I guess you'd say she's based on Candace."

"You describe her in your list of characters as 'willowy, delicate.'"

"Did I? That was a hell of a long time ago."

"Maybe I'm too short. Too round, too."

"You mean you don't look like a fashion model out of one of those magazines Faye reads?"

"I have hips."

"Perfect hips, yes. You're proportioned perfectly. Your tummy is flat, your butt is high enough to stack dishes on."

"*Mademoiselle* won't come knockin'."

"I'll tell you, Robin, I haven't seen a fashion photo in years that struck me as sexy. I can't figure who it is that's supposed to think an anorexic figure is a turn on. And now they're sticking these gigantic factory-made boobs onto the poor girls."

She put the script down and came over to me, plopped down beside me and let her hand rest on my knee, bowing her head down low so that her long auburn hair fell across her face and hid it from me. "My bust line is not too bad, do you think?"

It was then that she looked up at me, a smile and a challenge on her face, her hand suddenly gaining strength where it held my knee. I felt my heart contract, and involuntarily I looked at her mouth and it opened slightly and revealed the white perfection of her front teeth. Her lips seemed to tremble just once, just slightly, and I looked at her eyes and saw that she was looking, droopy lidded, at my mouth, and I realized my mouth was slightly open, like hers.

I stood up abruptly just to interrupt the scene, which seemed to be moving much too fast. I said, for no reason but to be jabbering, "You know, Dr. Todaro and I discussed what was motivating you that time we..."

"Oh, Dr. Todaro," she said. "Your imagination."

"As real as..."

"Hush! You've never even met Dr. Todaro. What does he look like? Mm? Blues eyes or brown? Tall or short? See? You have no idea. Skinny or fat? One lump or two? Old or young?"

She had me laughing now. "I was just going to point out..."

"Camel or dromedary?" she said, and we both laughed.

"Stop it!" I laughed. "You're killing me!"

"Which is better? Sex or death?"

"I don't know. Which is better? Sex or death?"

"Sex! Because you can remember it later!" She smiled at me but I failed to see the humor this time.

"No," I said, sobering a little, "I was just going to point out..."

"Point out your heinie back on this couch, why don't you?"

I could feel her warmth from where I stood. Suddenly I wondered why I was resisting her at all. I sat back down. I took her hand and placed it back on my knee, but her grip, her strength, didn't return, and now she turned away coyly.

"Don't you think I'm as cute as Candace was?"

"Well, as cute, yes, physically..."

"I didn't say I had as cute a personality. I know she was clever. She made baby talk that got you hard."

"I was seventeen, Robin. Everything got me hard. The weather got me hard."

"I'm not talking baby talk, and..."

"No," I interjected. "No, you're not, and..."

"And I'm not talking about the weather, either," she said, turning to me with piercing fire in her eyes.

"What do you want me to say?" My pulse was clearly audible in my subdued voice.

She let her hand slide up my thigh and rest on the denim covering my growing sex. "I want you to say I'm not only as cute as she was physically, but also I have just as cute a personality. If that's true. Only if it's true."

"It is true," I said.

She let her eyes close, smiling with satisfaction. She moved away from me just giving herself room to pull down the teal blue jersey shorts she wore. She kicked them off, letting them tug her slippers off as they fell to the floor. She wore lavender bikini panties of silk, and although she held her thighs together, I saw between them the smooth inward curve of a woman. She pulled the light knitted sweater over her head, leaving bare her narrow, white trunk, revealing the sheer lavender bra she wore.

She leaned into me, encircling my neck with her slender arms, and kissed my lips, then forced open my mouth with her tongue. She lingered only a moment, and pulled away, leaving me in an agony of desire.

"Now you," she said. She helped me with my clothes. To facilitate, I stood up and took off my trousers and shorts myself. Naked, with a blindly yearning hard-on, I sat down. Robin leaned over and kissed the head of my penis.

"My god, I'll come all over the place," I said.

"Me too," she said, and she undid the little bra and let it slide off her breasts and fall to the floor. They were perfect breasts, small, round, with large pink areolas, and nipples like pencil erasers. She cupped them in her hands, pushing them up and leaning toward me. I took one in my mouth, then took the other one, needed them both, needed, needed her, needed her, her doorway into the universe.

Once more she pulled gently away from me, again giving herself just enough room. She pulled her panties down to her knees, then worked her legs back and forth until the panties fell off her feet to the floor.

"I want you to know," she whispered. "I don't want you to have any doubts." She lay back on the love seat away from me, lifted one leg up and onto my shoulder, where her ankle came to rest, letting the other leg drape over the edge of the loveseat. This opened her to my view completely. Her labia were mostly concealed in the brown nest, but I could see the tiny button of flesh at the top, and this I leaned down and touched with my tongue. She gasped and suddenly grabbed the hair on the back of my head, not so much pulling me toward her as holding me there.

I nibbled at first, but soon feasted on her, squashing my tongue into her virgin spaces. She gasped each time I licked, and she choked back small utterances when my tongue entered her.

"Oh god," she said, and she screamed and locked her legs around my head. I thought she might injure me in her passion, but in a moment, she relaxed and rolled away onto the floor.

I watched her until her breathing slowed to normal. She lifted her head, looked at me, smiled.

"That's *one*," she said.

She climbed onto me, pushing me down on my back, and she mounted me. Her vagina was tight but wet, and I was completely inside after the course of three or four gentle easings. She rubbed her breasts over the hair on my chest, kissed me gently, rocking her hips slowly all the while. I had to thrust, but didn't want to come. I wanted it to last forever.

I grasped her around the waist and picked her up, swinging my legs off the loveseat and sitting up. We copulated in that position for a few moments before I stood up with her and carried her to the bed. My penis slipped out momentarily as we found our position on the bed, but then it was back in.

As Robin climaxed again, and then, a quarter hour later, for a third time, I kept on thrusting, in sexual ecstasy, as the hour passed, the night deepened, and my energy replenished itself with some insane and inexhaustible supply of adrenalin. I pumped and pumped into her velvety vagina, panting and moaning, sometimes crying out with each incredible thrust, but I would not come, would never come, would only go on and on in ever-increasing ecstasy.

In the end, I was too exhausted to continue, yet my erection stood firm. Trouble reaching an orgasm; I'd heard of that; not a serious problem. Robin curled up against me, licked at my armpit a little bit, like a kitten at a morsel, then fell asleep with a smile on her lips.

I smiled too, but I didn't fall asleep. After a while, my erection subsided, but I continued to relish the soft warmth of Robin's body against mine. Beyond her prettiness, she has a particular look I like, nicely proportioned, small, rounded in a way that suggests warmth and fertility. The smooth white skin between her bellybutton and her sex wants to swell up, wants to be smelled and kissed, and I did smell it while she slept, and I did kiss her there until she moaned and I was afraid I'd disturbed her sleep. It was still dark outside, but morning was not far away. I found my pajamas and put them on, sat here at the kitchenette table looking across the room at Robin, a beautiful young woman by anyone's standards, but especially mine.

And then I found my journal where I'd left it on our little knickknack shelf. Actually, I ran across it when I was looking for a photograph of Mother which I know is here somewhere. I thought it might be a nice touch to display it in the room. It's a photo from about the time of Ophelia, and although it's not particularly dramatic—just a posed studio shot of her sitting on some satin-draped chair–her expression captures both her youthful exuberance and her deep connection with the mystery of art. But maybe I just like it because it's the only shot of her I've seen in which my resemblance to her is obvious.

Dawn's light is all across the sky now, and maybe, since we were up so very late last night, Robin won't awaken for a while. When she does, I'll make us some toast and eggs and coffee. Then we'll stroll openly along the sidewalks, enjoying the dusting of snow, and the absence of color, which in its autumn abundance somehow injured my retinas, or optic nerve, and prompted me to sip whisky in small amounts, so that now, for the past few weeks, I see mostly in black and white and grey. Though I see all the color in and about Robin, generally in the world around me only the very brightest colors assert themselves strongly enough that I perceive them, and then only as pale shades of themselves.

We'll breakfast, and stroll, and later—exciting prospect— we'll spend our first evening exploring the mall.

February 17

Robin has been away for two weeks and a day. I don't know where she is. I don't know if she intends to come home or not. We had some fun and a close call or two in December and January. We started going to the Asheville Mall almost every day. Then Robin got the bright idea to go out to the Biltmore Mall. It's such a drive out there—a good twenty minutes—that I didn't really want to make the trip, but Robin insisted and we did go. She made a beeline for an expensive boutique, the kind of place Faye has dreamed of putting in.

I was happy to hang back and watch Robin scrutinizing the dresses, shoes, accessories. She gets such a cute little look of concentration on her face when she's shopping, I could watch her forever. She started showing me some bra and panty sets that tickled her fancy, holding them up and raising her eyebrows at me to query for my approval. I always approve. I never see any article of clothing that I don't think I would like if Robin wore it.

I began to notice that Robin was taking unusually long in this store. We try not to linger very long anywhere because we never buy anything, having virtually no budget for clothes. I glanced around the shop just in time to see a young woman approaching me without a smile. I met her eyes and she glanced quickly away, but continued approaching me. She had striking hair; it was blonde, streaked with silver, and looked as though the wind had been blowing through it when it was suddenly frozen in position, stiff and unmoving. For a moment I thought she was going to walk past me. She had a tiny waist but very wide hips, which gave her a sort of unstoppable bearing.

"Can I help you?" she said. What could I say? Robin had ducked to the other side of the lingerie rack and was out of sight. I considered leaving immediately, but hated to abandon Robin, who no doubt would have taken her own sweet time. I would have had to wait outside for her.

"I'm looking for something for my wife," I muttered.

"Mmm hmm," the woman said, and shot me a glance that seemed to challenge.

"What's her size?" she said, indicating the brassiere display I was facing.

"Well, that's the problem," I said. "I'm not sure."

The woman sucked air in audibly — it was as close to a sniff as it could be without being blatantly offensive. "Probably the best thing is to ask her," she said, and she stood aside, opening the pathway toward the front of the shop.

I was being asked to leave, and it rankled, very seriously. In fact I was trembling with anger, and hoping it didn't show. I wanted to curtly dismiss the woman with a "thank you" and a view of my back, but I knew I would sound guilty. Guilty of what? Nothing! But guilty nevertheless.

I walked as slowly as I could manage toward the front of the shop. The woman followed a few paces behind me, making little shuffling noises with her ugly navy flats on the wooden flooring to make sure I knew she was ushering me out, out, out.

I stood in front of the athletic shoe store next door until Robin finally came out of the boutique. She didn't even look around for me, but headed away toward the department store anchoring one end of the mall. I hurried to catch up with her, ready to spout venom about the store clerk, but decided instead to put it out of my mind and enjoy the department store. I ended up buying Robin a scarf that she wanted to use as a sari.

Robin and I had wonderful sex every night for a few weeks, but by Christmas it had tapered off to a few events a week. The night after I bought her the scarf, we had settled back for an evening at home and I didn't have sex on my mind. I think I was still a little upset, disgruntled with that rude store clerk, though I wasn't consciously brooding about it. About nine o'clock Robin disappeared into the bathroom and stayed there for quite a while—not unusual in our little home. When she emerged, I looked up from the magazine I was reading and I literally lost my breath for a second. Robin had, as she'd planned, used the scarf for a sari, but she had done it in such an exquisite way, over her otherwise completely nude body, and with well-planned backlighting from the bathroom, that she presented a vision of feminine sexuality unlike anything I'd ever experienced.

She was pleased with my dumbfounded reaction. Smiling, she walked toward me, ever so slowly, leaned toward me, sucked my lips gently with her own, took my hand in hers and placed it on her breast. I was delirious with desire, and she, apparently, was too.

Straddling my lap, wrapping her arms around my neck, she whispered wetly into my ear, "You were good this afternoon. You handled that bitch perfectly. You were strong, Hec. Strong. Hold me." She was already pulling at my shirt, and when my chest was bare, and I felt the soft warmth of her breasts pressing through the sheer fabric against my belly, I lost all but the most ecstatic of consciousness, and once again entered the universe through my woman's doorway. Love was never better than that time. It was not our last, but it was the pinnacle.

I had a difficult phone conversation with Mother on Christmas day. She began by telling me she was coming to see me. I tried to laugh out loud—she'll never come to see me. But the laugh I wanted just wasn't there. I managed a sigh, but even that was not loud enough to travel over the phone line.

"Let's let the holiday rush die down," she said, "and I'll take the bus down. First week of January."

"Sounds good," I said.

"Second week of January," she corrected herself. "Would that be good?"

"That'll be perfect," I said.

Robin was eavesdropping, pretending to look for something in our kitchen cabinet, under which our phone is connected.

She soon dropped the pretense and started purposely bumping my elbow and trying to distract me.

"I might as well tell you Faye called me again yesterday," Mother said.

"What's on her mind?" I said. "Does her story match mine?"

"It does and it doesn't," she said. I had simply called Mother as soon as I had a phone installed in the apartment, and told her that I had moved out after Faye and I argued.

"What doesn't jibe?" I said.

"She's under the impression you have a girlfriend."

Suddenly I realized I was cornered. I didn't want to admit my affair to Mother, but I was sure Robin would be infuriated if I denied her existence, and she was standing there listening to my end of the conversation.

"That's not the case," I said.

But Robin said right out loud, "What's not the case?"

Mother didn't drop it. "Well, there's some guy she was talking about, a guy who isn't a detective but she hired him to spy on you and he told her you have a girlfriend and you already had that garage apartment a long time before you moved out and there was a woman living there."

"She said all that?"

Robin was now right in my face, and said "Who said all what?"

I turned away from Robin, hunkered over the phone up against the window over the sink. Robin tried to squeeze in front of me.

Mother was pressing on. "She called me, you know. I didn't call her. She's upset. But she says you've had problems for a long time."

"Really? How long?"

"Well, it sounded like from way long back in New York."

"You know, Mother, when you come visit, we can talk about all these things." She met this remark with silence. I hadn't intended to be so obvious about cutting her off.

Then she said, "Is there somebody there with you, Hec?"

"No," I said. Again, she gave me some dead air to indicate she knew I was lying.

"Why don't you call me when it's more convenient," she said.

Rather than try to mitigate the obvious wrong I was doing her, I simply said, "Okay, that sounds like a good idea."

"Oh Lord," Mother sighed. "I hope she's half as good for you as Faye has been."

It was the kindest thing she had ever said about Faye, and this time I did laugh. "Looking forward to your visit, Mother," I said. She hung up without another word.

"You haven't told her about me, have you?" Robin said.

"It hasn't come up," I lied. "She's coming for a visit in January, though, so you can have a shot at her then." There was nothing

Robin could say to that, really, and we both knew it. I could tell, though, that Robin was thinking about it for the next few days. I never told her how doubtful it was that Mother's planned visit would materialize. By the end of January we'd both relaxed into the idea that Mother wasn't going to show, although we never talked about it specifically.

While the Mother cloud was dissipating, however, another was forming. Robin was peeved that I'd let her worry about Mother's coming. She told me at breakfast one morning that I'd known all along that Mother wouldn't come.

"You've been enjoying watching me squirm," she told me.

"Not true," I said, and freshened her coffee with a smile.

"Yes," she said, "you enjoyed thinking about what it would be like if your mother did knock on the door. You were thinking about what I would have to do. Hide. Hide in the bathroom. No, that wouldn't work. I'd have to go out the window and hide in the bamboo bushes, wouldn't I? Like a sitcom. Discovered with your girlfriend! Hide in the closet! Oh my god, it's Mom!"

"Calm down, Robin. I wasn't thinking that."

"Because you know I would hide, don't you? You'd make me, wouldn't you? Wouldn't you?"

I sat there dumbfounded because although yes, I had been thinking in terms very much like that, until now I hadn't thought I was actually controlling what Robin did. Yet she was right. The implication was that until I admitted her existence to other people, I had not committed to her.

"You won't commit to me," she said.

"You know, this really is sounding like a sitcom now."

"You can't admit to your mama that I'm your girlfriend."

"But she wouldn't be able... I mean..."

"To see me? So what? Just tell her I'm here. Somewhere. I'm

out doing some shopping. Or I'm away visiting. Just admit it, Hec."

"Relax into it?"

"That's it."

The prospect of bringing Robin into the open was so frightening that I felt lightheaded. I took a sip of coffee, tried to find my voice. "But that would just be a game," I said.

"Only if you made it into one," she said. She took a bite of toast, assessing my state of mind, apparently gratified that I was in terror. "You could just say I was in the bathroom."

"Oh, but no..." was all I could utter.

"And then, when the time was right, I could come out and you could speak to me."

"Admit my insanity."

"Commit to me."

The terror lodged in my gut; I began to feel ill.

"See, Hector, that's the whole problem," she said offhandedly. "You think a lot about things, and use your mind in amazing ways, but you don't actually do anything."

"I got this apartment, didn't I?"

"Yeah, but you didn't divorce Faye. And you wouldn't let me kill her."

"Kill her! My god, Robin, Faye doesn't deserve to die."

"You're being unfaithful to me if you don't get rid of her. In some real way, not just in your head."

"You have no idea what you're talking about. For one thing, Faye is divorcing me."

"And once again, you are not the do-er but the do-ee."

"I don't need to divorce Faye to be faithful to you. And she doesn't deserve to be harmed."

"Pooh," Robin said, and got up from the table. "Faye deserves anything she gets. But that's not what we're talking about, Hec. You wouldn't go after Lainie Wishnick, either. You just don't *do* anything."

"I don't *want* Lainie Wishnick." I was almost shouting. Robin was searching for something in the chest of drawers.

"Yeah, and you don't want Lilace flat-chested bitch, either, I guess."

"No, I want *you*," I shouted, and kicked back my chair, thinking I would grab Robin and force her to make love to me, and then never let her talk like this again. But I stood there at the table without moving, just watching Robin as she rummaged through some of her clothing.

"Where's my yellow sweater?" she said to herself. She found it, went to the mirror next to the bed and watched herself put on the dainty cardigan as she said, "You can't even see what's going on right in front of your face with that guy Faye's dating."

"Dating? Faye's not dating anybody."

"Right. Because if she's not dating the guy, then you don't have to *do* anything about it, *do* you?" She headed for the door.

I lunged toward her and took her by the wrist as she reached for the doorknob. She spun toward me and gave me a look that was full of defiance and challenge, all wrapped in an expectant smile. My stunned feeling of awkwardness gave way to a sort of awe when I met her eyes and suddenly saw a family resemblance. She was of my flesh. I tried to hide my epiphany, but she caught it, did a rather perfect double take.

"What?" she demanded, the smile on her face intensifying.

"Nothing," I said, loosening my grip on her wrist.

"What did you see, Hec? Come on..."

"Nothing," I said, and turned away from her. I managed to take a couple of steps toward the bathroom, but she followed me, stepped around in front of me.

"What did you see?" So coy, so cute. "Was it a family resemblance?"

"No." Why did I even bother to deny it? She gently pressed the palm of her hand on my crotch and moved it up to my belly. I was instantly aroused. I looked her in the eye, her expectant gaze unrelenting. "I saw myself, okay?" I admitted. "Not a family resemblance. Just myself."

She smiled, let her mouth open slightly, revealing her moist pink tongue. I ached for her.

"Uh huh," she said, nodding slightly before she moved away, but just tentatively.

Something, a mystery, was happening. I recognized the old feeling. I was missing something. Something was happening and would catch me by surprise when it was too late to do anything about it.

Robin put her knee on the couch and both her hands on the back rest, arched her back so that her delicious little butt jutted toward me. "You don't really want me, Hec," she said. Then she turned to look at me. "Because if you did, you'd do the necessary to get me and keep me."

"I do want you..." I said weakly. I wanted her so badly that I was near tears, but I felt nothing so much as confusion and being lost.

"I'm not going to do it for you, Hec," she said. "Those days are over. If you want me, you can have me. You just have to make room for me. And I don't mean a pissy little garage apartment."

She was not smiling, but gave me a cute wink, which left me more stunned than ever. She walked to the door, giving my crotch one more passing little stroke on the way.

"Where are you going?"

Robin didn't answer. She walked straight out the door and was halfway down the stairs by the time I got out to the landing. "Where are you going?" I said again, this time trying to sound more composed. She didn't even hesitate, but hurried right down the steps and up the alley. I followed quickly but she was already to the street by the time I caught up with her. I touched her arm and she stopped abuptly and turned to me.

"What?" she said, much too loudly.

"I just want to know where you're going," I said, glancing around to see if anyone was in sight.

"What are you whispering for?" she said, very loudly.

"Robin, please..."

"Robin, *nuthin'*," she said smartly. She glared at me and once again I glanced up the street. "You're standing here acting crazy, talking to thin air. Aren't you afraid somebody will call the cops?"

"Come back home," I said quietly. "We'll talk about this."

"Stop whispering," she said in a normal tone. "Stop trying to act like you're just out for a breath of fresh air."

Apparently my awkward attempt to comply with her request was insufficient. "Don't follow me," she said, looking me right in the eyes. She turned and walked on down the street, an agony of beauty disappearing. When I finally stopped staring after her and turned back toward the alley, I noticed a young woman, child at the hem of her skirt, watching me from behind a screen door across a porch cluttered with broken indoor furniture.

She was back home that afternoon with stories of people she'd met in the neighborhood, friends she'd made. I never saw any of Robin's friends. They certainly never came around here.

One afternoon she left the apartment, saying she was going

to venture down the block just because she was bored; she didn't come home until about eleven-thirty that night. She had walked all the way downtown and talked with some people she called "college students," though to me they sounded more like street people. I worried myself into a dazed state while she was gone. It was warm for January but she had gone out in a sweater that in my opinion was too light. When she came back she was also wearing a tattered bluejean jacket, a loan from one of her new friends. That jacket inspired an intense pang of jealousy in me. When I tried to question her about this new adventure, she took advantage of my weakness by seducing me, making rollicking love, wearing me down, expertly not letting me come for a long time, so that when I did finally climax, I fell immediately to sleep.

She went out again the next night. I tried to stop her, but she just turned to me, touching up her lipstick, and said, "Hector, you don't ever take dramatic action." And she went to the door.

I said "Dramatic action is hardly ever called for in real life. That's for plays." She gave me a smile I can only describe as wicked, and it made her look delicious, and I could hardly stand the thought of her being with these other "friends" of hers. Especially the kid who had given her the bluejean jacket. I was burning with jealousy, dizzy with it.

And again the next night she went out. I was exhausted from worrying about her, unable to sleep. I was barely awake when she got home around midnight Saturday. Finally, on Sunday, I slept until past noon, and when I woke up, she was already out again. She came home around ten-thirty Sunday night and I tried to talk with her, demanding to know at least some details about where she'd been going. "Friends," she mumbled, and then she ignored me. She was exhausted and fell asleep even as I harangued her.

When she didn't come back at all, I began castigating myself, right out loud in the apartment, for not being more forceful with her and demanding that she stay home or at least take me with her. After a week, I realized that there was nothing I could have done. My control over her was nil, and had been nil, or practically nil, since the very beginning.

It occurred to me three days ago that I should get out of bed, clean myself up, and write in my journal. I've done it now. Now I wait for a while. I don't know. I don't know anything. I wait.

February 21

I received a letter from Robin. There was no return address, but the envelope has a postmark from the downtown Asheville station. I guess that means she's still in town, but there's no evidence that she intends to come home.

No point in copying the whole letter into this journal. It's written, front and back, on a sheet of lined notebook paper, the sort used by school children. She wrote it, apparently, in two sittings. In the first part, using a green ballpoint, she tells me in very chatty terms that she's fine and has been with some "friends," and not to worry about her. She tells me she enjoyed her time with me but finds me "transparent" now.

I'll have to think about that.

Then she starts again, using a pencil. *I might know something about that guy Faye's seeing,* she writes. *He's dangerous. I wouldn't say he intends to kill her, but I wouldn't rule it out, either. Just thought you ought to know, and I don't have any proof or anything, but believe me I think I'm right even though I'm not free to tell you how I found out. His name is Michael something foreign-sounding and he once applied for a job from Faye and she hired him to tail you instead of selling underwear!!! Now they are involved and I'm not saying you should do anything about it but I thought you should be alerted.*

She goes on for a few more sentences awkwardly trying to say nice things about me and her together, without actually apologizing for leaving. She cites only the most superficial aspects of our relationship—how nice I was to buy her things she wanted, etc. The really touching thing about this letter was the way she signed it. She simply wrote *Robin* and superimposed a kiss with her lips, using the lipstick she well knew was my favorite color on her.

She's gone. I don't expect to see her again. So. Does that mean I'm sane?

February 24

Twice I've gone to Faye's house to check on her. Spy on her, that is. After receiving the letter from Robin, I couldn't stop worrying about Faye and the Michael something foreign-sounding. I walked over there and stationed myself in the bushes in the side yard. It was only about six o'clock but dark already. Faye wasn't home. I waited until my feet were so cold they were numb, maybe an hour. I walked back home, didn't check the time but it was probably around eight. Then last night I drove to within a block of the house, again stationed myself in the bushes. She was home, I'm sure. It was around eight. I didn't see her—could only see into the bedroom but she wasn't in there. I believe she was in the living room, which would make sense. The light was on in there, and she always did read in there.

It was very cold last night. Today's paper says it went down to 25 degrees, although it wouldn't have been quite that bad when I was out.

No evidence of Michael something foreign-sounding having been at the house, although how would I know? I'm not a detective. About the only way I'll know is if he's there while I'm spying, and then only if I actually see him through the window. Plan now is to stake out the house every evening after dark for a while. Maybe Robin was just playing with my mind. Maybe she made all that up, but since I know Faye really did engage this guy to tail me, at least his existence is not in question.

February 27

Faye knows what I've been doing. Mrs. Stone apparently saw me in the bushes or something. The police have been by to see me.

There were two of them. Officer Bullock was a blonde young woman, quite a looker, although her waistline was no-nonsense. She mostly hung back and let Officer Ferebee do the talking. He was thirty or so, athletic and dark. They stood on the landing at the front door—I didn't invite them in. Once they were satisfied I was me, they told me that my wife had informed them of our estrangement and that I had been seen on the premises acting suspiciously. Like a window peeper, they said. No, there was no law against my looking into my own house, but in view of the estrangement and Faye's complaint, they advised me not to be snooping around in the dark. They seemed to be interested in seeing my reaction to this advice. I said "I understand," then gave them my best 'Anything else?' look, and apparently there wasn't.

In a way I don't care one bit about that incident, but something else has come up so that it behooves me to keep out of trouble. I'm still worried about Faye's safety, but while I was out spying on her two nights ago, Robin evidently came by the apartment. I have no way of knowing if she intended to see me or would have simply left the note without knocking on the door.

Before she started going out and staying out late, Robin had gained my total confidence, or pretty near anyway. I had let her read any of my old plays that she wanted to. Now I find a note on the door telling me that her friends downtown have formed a troupe doing "street theatre" and want to see some of my work, that she has told them about the two or three plays she looked at. They generally "hang" in the center of town, near the fountain and the reflecting pool. They want me to do a reading for them there on the square.

My first reaction to the idea was that it's ridiculous, and it is. However, I realized that if I go, I'll see Robin. It'll be a chance—however slim—to get back on the old terms with her.

Owen: So, Robin, good to see you. Listen, I know you're hanging with your new friends, but hey, come on over and have lunch with me tomorrow...

Something like that. It might work. Everything is swirling around me, sucking the wind out of me so that I'm struggling to catch my breath. It's the anticipation, just at the chance to see her, talk to her. There's no denying that I love her. I love her very much. I've been miserable without her. I'll do anything I can to get her back. Anything.

CRS37725 BUNCOMBE COUNTY

State of North Carolina vs. Hector Owen

EXHIBIT 9

DESCRIPTION: Handwritten notes on paper napkin with restaurant logo "Cecil's." Discovered tucked into journal surrendered voluntarily to Detective James Horne by defendant upon his arrest. TRANSCRIPTION ATTACHED.

Final, irrevocable, existentially meaningful acts are committed through desperation, not intellect, and though all through life the mind has chosen this pathway or that, it is at the hour of desperation that the road to final peace shows itself, obscene and frightening, enticing, liquefying.

Like his protagonist, Jerry Stubblefield is a sixties survivor—experienced in hallucinations of various kinds, and able to walk comfortably, skillfully and with good humor next to realities unshared with the neighbors. The playwright-turned-author is a graduate of the drama school at the University of Texas at Austin and recipient of the Samuel French Award. Throughout the 1970s and 1980s he lived and wrote drama in New York City, where a number of his plays were produced. He is a member of the Ensemble Studio Theatre, and through the Dramatists Guild's seminars, he studied under renowned playwrights Arthur Miller, David Henry Hwang, Wendy Wasserstein and others. He has a long history of teaching creative writing classes, workshops and seminars at all levels, including university and adult.

Currently he lives with his wife of thirty years in Asheville, North Carolina. Their children, Nick and Phoebe, are both college students.